Dedicated to my Georgian friends and family, this story comes from a huge love of and respect for this beautiful, ancient country in the South Caucasus. It is a country of tradition, friendship and wild nature - one that I have called home for so long. May you grow ever stronger, ever happier, and ever more peaceful. Angels are watching over you.

"The enemy within is more dangerous than

the enemy without." – Hinten Bergen

The Ten Commandments:

1. "I am the Lord God, thou shalt not have any strange Gods before Me."

2. Thou shalt not take the name of the Lord God in vain.

3. Remember to keep holy the Sabbath day.

4. Honour thy father and mother.

5. Thou shalt not kill.

6. Thou shalt not commit adultery.

7. Thou shalt not steal.

8. Thou shalt not bear false witness against thy neighbour.

9. Thou shalt not covet thy neighbour's wife.

10. Thou shalt not covet thy neighbour's goods.

Contents

CHAPTER 1

I dreamed I was dead.

Dead and free.

I was flying over England, looking down, my body feather-light but powerful as it soured. I don't know if I had wings but I felt the cool damp air on my skin: fresh and clean. Sometimes the cloud blocked my vision of the land but for the most part it was clear; beautifully clear.

I know where I got the image from. I remember flying on Turkish Airlines- flying home to London for my grandad's funeral, just three months before I lost my nan. Ten minutes into the descent into Heathrow, the cabin crew switched on a bird's-eye camera on the belly of the plane so we could watch the myriad of greens and browns and chalky yellows of the fields below: a patchwork of hand-cut farmland carved out centuries ago and expanded or divided since; the grey and red tiled roofs of the workers' cottages, the grand country estates surrounded by vast expanses of well-kept green lawn and the grey-blue twisting snake of the River Thames winding through the landscape.

Like a spirit set free, I flew over it all.

Smiling, I looked to my right and saw a boy flying beside me. He did have wings- huge, white, soft feather wings spread as wide as his arms.

He grinned at me and I laughed and reached for him and we linked fingers and looked once more down at my country.

No. Not my country. My mother's country.

My country was Georgia. His, too, I thought, this boy-angel beside me.

Ilia.

Ilia from Svaneti.

He'd been with me for as long as I could remember: never changing, while I grew from child to teenager. When I was little, my parents and teachers had been amused by my imaginary friend, indulging me with smiles when I told them I was "playing with Ilia." Then, when I didn't grow out of him, they started taking me to head doctors. I was doing well at school, making normal friends, but they'd occasionally catch me talking to him or laughing at a joke he told me. "You're too old to have an imaginary friend," they admonished.

I remember sitting in one psychiatrist's office describing what I saw in the shadow pictures the doctor kept holding up.

"Hairy mushroom," Ilia whispered in my ear. I giggled and repeated what he'd said.

"This guy before he lost all his hair," he whispered about the next one- clearly supposed to be a clown.

I burst out laughing, then repeated the description.

The doctor frowned and my mother gasped.

"Ilia said it, not me," I told the doctor, trying to hold back the laughter.

"Ilia does not exist!" my mother said through gritted teeth.

They put me on medication for a while- drugs that made me sleepy. They talked about electro-therapy but my father drew the line at that.

"They don't want me to be with you anymore," Ilia told me sadly as he sat by my bed one lunchtime on another day of missed school, holding my hand.

"You won't leave me, will you?" I asked him, my eyes wide, the fast beating of my heart fighting back the drowsiness.

"*Ara*- no," he said with a reassuring smile. "I'll be with you as long as you need me."

Then he kissed my forehead.

We spent the rest of the day talking about how to hide him from my parents. It took a few weeks of practice but he learned not to comment when there were people around, not to do anything to distract me when I was in class. And I learned not to look at him too much, or to answer him without first checking we were alone. He started leaving the classroom when I was studying, and fading out of sight- even invisible to me- during family dinners or parties. I missed him, but I knew he was only trying to protect me. And when the doctor asked me about Ilia, I lied and said he was imaginary and had gone away. I even told my parents I wanted to do after-school dance classes just to show them I was busy and 'normal.'

They never knew I practised dancing with Ilia late at night. It turned out he'd been the best in his village when he was alive.

We were happy in our secret world: I loved him and he loved me.

But everything changed between us the year I turned 16.

CHAPTER 2

"Still trying to get a tan?" my best friend asked as she rubbed the black, volcanic sand over her bronzed, wet legs.

"No," I replied. "I'm catching freckles. I gave up on tanning last year. Mikey got the Georgian genes, remember?"

"You got the dark hair, he got the skin. It's a fair trade."

"Wish I could have both!" I complained, adjusting the beach umbrella so its shadow covered my body.

"Like him, you mean?" Nina asked, glancing past me.

I followed her eye-line. Three towels away from us were a boy and two girls- clearly siblings, just drying themselves off from a swim. Saba, Nina's cousin, was with them, chatting, but it was too noisy to hear what they were saying.

The boy looked over at me and I smiled shyly, then turned to Nina and talked about something inconsequential.

"You're blushing!" she said.

"Nii! Shut *up*!"

"He's still looking at you," she said through gritted teeth as she pretended to laugh at a joke I hadn't told.

I glanced his way again, my cheeks aflame, and this time he returned my smile. Then his eyes shifted focus over my shoulder and the smile turned into a frown.

Frowning myself, I turned to see what had bothered him, but there was nothing there except other sunbathers...and Ilia's shadow, and I knew there was no way he could see that.

"Hi, I'm Toma."

I jumped and looked up at him, my cheeks reddening further in embarrassment.

"Eliso," I said, standing and shaking his hand- warm and soft, but strong.

"You're not from around here, are you?" he asked, glancing towards Nina where she now stood chatting with Saba, though I knew her ears were burning. "But I heard you talking in Georgian."

"My father's Georgian," I told him.

"And your mum's English, right?"

"Is my accent that obvious?" I laughed.

"I've done a lot of travelling- I'm good with accents," he said, smiling.

"Where are you from?"

"Everywhere," he said mysteriously.

"And now you're in Georgia on holiday?"

"Oh, we might be staying a while," he answered, flicking his eyes towards Ilia again. I decided to ignore the temptation to look at my angel. I knew he'd be glowering at me. He was never good with my flirting.

"Are those your sisters?"

"They're triplets!" Nina said, bouncing over and holding out her hand with a grin. "Aren't you going to introduce us, Ela?"

I rolled my eyes at her energy.

"Nina, this is Toma."

"Nice to meet you. Saba's cousin, right?"

She nodded.

"Are you really triplets?" I wondered. I'd never met any triplets before.

He nodded. "Arabella and Emily are the rest of the set."

We looked over towards them- the one dressed in a pink bathing suit with curly black hair and ice-blue eyes was rubbing sun lotion into her sister's shoulders. The second one was dressed in a skimpy dark blue bikini and had long, straight hair and eyes as green as her brother's.

I quickly checked out their brother and smiled, liking what I saw. Toma was black-haired, his eyes a marbled green- the kind that changes shade with the weather. Right now, they were olive, set off by his tanned skin and a shadow of beard.

Then a mark on his stomach caught my eye and I laughed shortly.

He looked back at me with a frown. "What?" he asked, puzzled.

I pulled down the edge of my bikini bottoms a centimetre and showed him.

"We have the same scar," I said.

For a moment his expression darkened, but then a smile broke through. "Appendix?" he asked.

I covered my scar and nodded. "Yep. I don't actually remember, thank God."

"She's a real scaredy-cat, our Eliso," Nina said, nudging me.

"I'm just not good with pain," I replied, blushing.

"I was a new-born when I had mine out," Toma said.

"Really? I was four..."

"Why don't you guys come sit over here?" Saba asked, handing Toma a Coke from our cooler.

"Thanks. I'll go ask the girls."

We watched him go and speak to his sisters. They glanced our way and I noticed the girl in blue narrow her eyes at me, then turn an assessing look on Saba, who smiled hungrily at her.

I rolled my eyes and laid down on my stomach, cradling my head on my arms, pretending I didn't care that this gorgeous boy was about to make my day even hotter.

"Sooo," Nina said with a wicked grin. "What did you think of him?"

"Who?" I asked, falsely casual, flicking a look towards the sofa where a dark shape shimmered. I could feel the disapproval rolling off him and saw his arms were crossed and his chin down.

"You *know* who!" she said, hitting my arm lightly. "The new boy- Toma!"

I shrugged. "He's ok."

"Ok? Just ok?! He's an angel, El! Sent from heaven to brighten up our dull little mortal lives!"

I laughed and shook my head, seeing the shape on the sofa shift in anger, but keeping the smile on my face for Nina's benefit.

What was his problem, anyway? I wondered.

"Where do you think he's from?" Nina asked. "He looks kind of Spanish to me."

"Well, he's not Georgian," I answered. "But I don't think he's Spanish. His accent was different..." I said.

"So, what did you find out?"

"Like you weren't listening in!" I teased.

"Come on! I left you two alone for a whole ten minutes!"

"What am I supposed to find out in ten minutes?! Especially seeing as we were both chewing on corn cobs!"

She crossed her arms, waiting.

"Fine!" I said, going to the fridge and pulling out a Borjomi bottle. It hissed as I turned the cap.

"He's 17, he's a vegetarian and his dad is some hotshot lawyer."

"That's it?!"

"The basics, yeah," I said.

"Well, vegetarian means he's definitely not Georgian- Saba and his friends are pure carnivores. And it means you have something in com-mon..." she teased, stretching out the word.

"We have something else in common," I said, perching on the arm of the sofa next to Ilia. "His dad's working on a contract with mine. They're nearly done, but..."

"Seriously?!"she asked. "What kind of contract?"

"Don't know, don't care," I said with a shrug.

My dad was in the cigarette business and after the fact that I hated smoking was the fact we barely ever spoke. Ever since mum disappeared, he'd kept himself to himself- in most cases at the office. It upset Mikey more than me. And it didn't mean he left us to our own devices- Levan drove us everywhere and the cook and housekeeper kept us in order at home. This beach holiday was a welcome exception, though Nina's dad had his own minions on hand watching over us.

"Well, he's definitely a mystery we need to unravel," she said.

"Toma's *dad*?!" I asked in mock-surprise.

"You know who I mean!"

"Why are you so interested, anyway?" I asked her. "You have a boyfriend, remember?"

"While the cat's away, the mice will play," she teased.

"Well your cat's serving in Afghanistan, so you should show some respect."

"Don't be such a spoil-sport!" she complained.

I relaxed my frown and smiled.

"Have you heard from him?"

"We Skyped before I came. Dad nearly caught me at it but I convinced him I was watching a movie."

"Wish my dad was as caring as yours."

"Being an only child helps!"

"Yes, Princess Nina," I teased. "And you can have my brother anytime you want!"

"I might take you up on that," she joked.

"What?!" I asked incredulously.

"Well, he is a cutie..."

"He's *twelve*!"

She laughed. "Speaking of siblings, what do you think of the other two? Toma's sisters?"

"Arabella and Emily Morgan. Hmm... hard to say. They stuck together so it was hard to judge. But, I don't know. There was something about them that looked like trouble."

Nina shrugged, unconcerned. "We'll see. Which do you think is the oldest? I think Toma."

"They're triplets. It's probably only a few minutes' difference!" I said with a laugh. "So, what are the plans tonight?"

"Oh, I forgot! Dad's on his way over from Kutaisi. We have a dinner date in Batumi. You don't mind being alone, do you? I can call Saba to come over..."

I narrowed my eyes at her. "That crush was sooo last year," I told her airily.

She laughed.

"Actually, I've got that history homework to do."

"You're on HOLIDAY!" Nina reminded me.

"Fine. I'll watch a movie and leave my homework till the day before we go back to school- just like you do!" I said with a sweet smile.

She stuck out her tongue. "Maybe you should go for a walk, see if you can bump into Toma..."

"Stop it!" I warned her with a grin, grabbing a cushion and making to throw it at her.

She skipped back, holding her hands up in surrender. "Your loss," she said. "But I bet he's a bad boy in bed..."

This time I did throw the cushion and it hit the bathroom door as she shut it.

I got up once I heard the hot water running and went to my own room to shower.

"So, what's your problem?" I asked as soon as the bedroom door was closed.

At first, Ilia remained in my shadow, shimmering in pulsing angry waves.

"Fine, don't tell me," I said petulantly, throwing my beach towel over the back of the chair and flopping down on the bed in my still-damp bikini. I got out my iPhone to message my other best friend, Mariam, who was home in Tbilisi with her parents packing house to move to her dad's next diplomatic posting.

"He's no good for you," he said after a moment.

I kept my eyes on the screen, scrolling down the Facebook page.

"Toma, you mean?"

"Hmm."

The phone beeped in my hand and I glanced at it.

'Found him on fb. Wanna friend him?'

A small smile lifted my lips but, seeing Ilia's expression, I put the phone down, Nina's message unanswered.

"You should stay away from him."

"I barely know anything about him," I pointed out.

"Exactly."

"If he's interested in anyone, it'll be Nina," I predicted.

Blond, beautiful, and smart, too, Nina was every schoolboy's dream. Only I knew that none of them stood a chance. It didn't stop them lining up to give it a try, though.

"If he senses me, he'll get interested in you," Ilia predicted.

"Why would he?" I asked. "No-one can see you but me."

He shrugged.

"Well, stop hanging around me all day and he won't," I said, sitting back against the pillows and bringing my feet up to cross my legs.

"I'm here to protect you," he reminded me.

I had my eyes back on the screen as I typed: *'Let's do it.'*

"You'll regret it," he warned.

My thumb hesitated over the send box and I looked up at him. My angel; my real angel.

"Tell me why and I'll take your advice."

He sighed and shook his head.

My thumb hit send and I smiled up at him.

"Then I'll just have to trust my own instincts, won't I?" I said.

Lips pursed in disapproval, Ilia faded into shadow again and then disappeared.

NINA: He says he likes rock music.

ME: You're chatting to him, too? What about your dad?

NINA: He's talking on the phone- business. And I don't wanna give you the monopoly!

ME: Cow!

TOMA: You're the British girl, right?

ME: Half-Brit, half-Georgian. You never said where you're from...

TOMA: I did. Everywhere.

ME: Gypsy?

TOMA: Something like that.

ME: Coming to the beach tmrw?

TOMA: If you are.

I felt butterflies kick up in my stomach and a warm trickling sensation in my chest. I glanced up at the mirrored wardrobe and saw I was wearing a silly grin.

ME: He says he'll come to the beach if I will.

NINA: Now who's the cow?

ME: Young, free and single. Read it & weep!

NINA: Haha

I posted a selfie on Instagram and then went to fix myself a sandwich. When I next looked at my phone, I saw Toma had liked the picture.

To celebrate, I put music on extra loud and danced around the living-room. Then I went online and found the best romantic comedy I could and settled down to watch it, the grin still on my face, deliberately ignoring Ilia.

CHAPTER 3

"Blue," he said, lighting a cigarette.

"Lucky guess. Ok. My worst school subject?"

"Er…" he looked out to sea thoughtfully. Then: "Maths!"

"No way! Ok…this one you'll never get." I grinned wickedly. "What's my favourite food?"

Toma stopped, thinking, and let out a mouthful of smoke with a smile: "Those little mushrooms with cheese in."

I stared at him open-mouthed. "That's impossible! Can you read minds?"

"Something like that," Toma told me with a grin.

"I heard twins had a bond- didn't realise that extended to telepathy…" I spotted the phone in his hand, held the other side of his thigh, and narrowed my eyes. "Nina's been helping you, hasn't she?!" I accused.

I heard laughter behind me and Nina plumped down on my lounger, phone in one hand, Coke bottle in the other.

I nudged her with my shoulder. "You two really had me going!"

Toma laughed. "Well, I promise everything is memorised for future reference," he said, making my insides light up.

"I'll test you!" I promised back.

He didn't react and I saw his eyes were on Nina, his expression cool.

I turned in time to see her lob her bottle hard at a mangy street dog begging us for scraps nearby. I'd been planning to give it the leftovers from Saba's sausage roll. The bottle hit it hard on the head and it cried out and limped away, whimpering, its tail between its legs. The bottle rolled to settle next to a washed-up tree branch but Nina made no move to go and get it.

I looked back at Toma and felt an icy stab of inexplicable fear at the way he was looking at her.

"Are you ok?" I asked him, touching a gentle hand to his knee. For a moment, he didn't respond. Nina was bent over her mobile, obviously in the middle of a chat, her fingers flying across the screen. Then he gave me a small smile and looked out to sea, frowning.

"You should throw that in the bin," I told my friend quietly, nodding towards the bottle.

"Yeah. In a mo.," she said, not taking her eyes off her phone. She clearly had no remorse for hurting the dog; nor did she plan to pick up her rubbish.

I saw Toma narrow his eyes and glance at his sister, Arabella, laying on a lounger on his right. She took her glasses off and looked at Nina, then turned her eyes to our friends splashing around in the sea.

"Arabella, come swim," Saba called. It was clear who this year's summer fling was going to be.

She gave her brother a twisted grin and went to join the boys in the water.

"Chatting to Giorgi?" I asked Nina, casually getting to my feet and picking up her discarded bottle.

Toma watched his sister out in the water, ignoring my move to pacify his anger.

Nina nodded in reply and Toma suddenly smiled and stood.

"Coming for a swim, girls?"

I frowned and was about to decline the invite when Nina jumped up and dropped her phone in her bag.

"Love to! Let's go, El!"

I hung back as she ran towards our group and Toma followed.

"What was that all about?" I wondered.

"An animal lover?" Ilia guessed.

I glanced at him and over at Toma swimming alongside Nina.

"Yeah, maybe."

"Stay away from him, El," my angel warned.

I kicked off my flip-flops and dove into the water.

"Nina- wait up!" I called. My friend kept swimming. "Ni!" I called again, switching to the butterfly to try and catch up with her. I heard the lifeguard calling us back- we were in the boat-lane and even if it wasn't used by much more than the occasional banana-boat or pedalo, the risk of an inattentive jet-skier or speedboat driver made what my friend was doing dangerous.

"Ela- go back!" Ilia's voice told me.

"Something's wrong!" I told him.

"Ni-naaa!" I called. She was five metres away, no more.

She hesitated, looking back at me, then frowned, turned, and kept going, but slower, clearly getting tired.

At last, just as the lifeguard on a jet-ski caught up to us, spewing a load of warnings in fast and angry Georgian, I was able to grab my friend. We were both panting.

"Feeling energetic today, are you?" I asked. "I could hardly catch you!"

She looked at me with a frown, treading water. "Yeah, I...got the urge to just keep going."

"Ready to head back?" I asked, ignoring the grumbling lifeguard, a too-tanned forty-something man with wiry muscles and reflective sunglasses.

She nodded and we began a slow breast-stroke towards the beach.

Half-way back, me ahead of her by a few metres, my friend suddenly disappeared.

"Nina?!"

I looked around, then down. She was struggling just below the surface, her eyes wide in panic, her cheeks blown out as she fought not to breathe.

"No!" I said, taking a breath and ducking under. I reached out for her but her fingers slipped out of my hands as something tugged her further down, even though she was kicking furiously upwards. I went forwards into the cool darkness but, again, she was inexplicably tugged just out of reach.

I could hear Ilia above calling for me, could hear splashing as others swam towards us, the water-dulled hum of the jet-ski coming back.

Nina's kicking grew weaker and I could see the panic in her eyes dulling as she realised that she was fighting the inevitable.

'Hold on. Don't breathe!' I wanted to tell her, but my mind had gone blank. I didn't know what to do: every time I reached for her she was pulled further down into the water.

Then hands grabbed my waist and pulled and at the same time Nina was released, and both she and I shot up and out of the dark, me gasping and spitting up salt water, her barely breathing. My throat and eyes burned. Toma held me from behind while the lifeguard pulled Nina onto his jet-ski and zoomed off toward the beach with her.

"Is she ok?" I gasped. "Is she...?"

"She's going to be fine," Toma said.

I leaned my head briefly back against his shoulder, looking gratefully up at the blue sky, letting the air fill my lungs.

About four or five other swimmers had come to my aid and were bombarding me with questions. I nodded that I was alright and looked to the beach where Toma's sisters were meeting the lifeguard. They were joined by our other friends and a small crowd of onlookers. But, to my relief, Nina walked off the jet-ski herself.

I closed my eyes and swallowed.

"You ok to swim?" Toma asked.

I nodded and he let me go.

"What happened?" Ilia asked me quietly.

"Something crazy," I said.

I asked Nina the same question some twenty minutes later when all the fuss had died down. She was laying on the lounger; pale, wrapped in towels, still shivering in shock. And for some reason throwing distrustful looks towards the triplets as they sat talking TV shows with Saba and Mate.

"It was Arabella," she told me in a whisper.

I frowned and looked over to where Arabella lay on her blanket, handing the sun-oil to Saba to rub into her back while he chatted to Toma.

"She was already on the beach when the lifeguard brought you back," I told Nina. "I saw her here with Emily."

"I swear to you it was her!" she insisted. "I heard her- she told me to keep swimming. Then she dragged me under once I turned back."

"Ni, sorry, but there's no way she could've got back so fast. You must've imagined it."

My friend looked like she wanted to argue. Instead, she looked at the triplets again.

"Are you sure?" I asked, unaccustomed to seeing her so serious and determined.

"Sure," she said.

But it couldn't be...

As if hearing us, Arabella turned and smiled. It wasn't friendly.

"I think maybe you shouldn't hurt street dogs anymore," I told Nina.

CHAPTER 4

"Volleyball, anyone?" Nina asked after lunch, stretching her arms high above her head, showing off her toned, tanned body. I glanced at Toma and was glad to see him looking up the beach.

"Nothing like a near-death experience to get the competitive spirit going, eh?" I asked. She grinned and I shrugged and stood. "I'm in."

"Girls versus boys?" Arabella suggested, flicking her luscious wave of black hair over her shoulder.

Saba immediately stood up, like an eager puppy.

"Me, Mate, Lasha and...Toma? You in?"

Toma shook off his distraction, crushed out his cigarette, and stood with a nod.

"Winner gets...?" Nina asked.

"To throw the losers in the sea," Mate suggested.

"Like we could pick you up!" I said.

"Well, you're the ones who're going to get wet, so you don't need to worry about your backs," Lasha answered with a confident grin.

I scowled at him and got into position.

"We can drag them to the sea one-by-one," Arabella suggested in a low voice and we laughed evilly.

Forty-five minutes later and Saba was running with Arabella over his shoulder into the waves.

Lasha grabbed Emily, and Mate Nina, leaving me and Toma eyeing each other with the net between us.

He tilted his head and beckoned me over.

I stayed put and smiled. I wasn't going to make this easy for him.

He bit his lip and shook his head in mock admonishment, then darted to the right.

I squealed and ran away from him, laughing, pounding up the beach, with him bare metres behind, dodging the sunbathers, blankets and flip-flops. Laughing, I tripped and collapsed to the sand, rolling onto my back as his shadow fell over me. I covered my eyes, trying to block out the sun burning behind him and making him a dark silhouette.

"Give up," he said, holding a hand out to me.

"I don't give up," I told him with a grin, then rolled quickly to the left, scrambling to get to my feet, the sand slipping away from me.

I felt the shock of his hands on my waist for the second time that day and he pulled me up and put me over his shoulder, walking with me into the waves while my friends cheered and clapped.

"Always playing hard-to-get, Ela," Saba said with a grin as I came up for air and pushed my hair back.

I splashed him. "You had your chance!" I reminded him.

I glanced at Toma and saw him looking up the beach, distracted again. Emily also saw his look and put a hand on his arm. He spoke to her quietly and she looked up the beach, too, frowning. I couldn't hear what he said over the sound of Arabella trying to dunk Saba.

"Everything ok?" I asked them.

Toma looked at me and for a moment I remembered that cold look he'd given Nina before she'd nearly drowned herself. Then he smiled.

"Sure."

CHAPTER 5

"Let's have a beach barbecue tonight," Nina suggested as we walked back up the sand between the last few families and umbrellas. "It's our last night – we should celebrate!"

"Is that allowed?" Mate asked. "A fire on the beach?"

"It is if the local police chief is your father's cousin's brother-in-law," I told him with a grin.

"Riiight," he said. "You gotta love Georgia."

"Will you come?" I asked Toma.

"Beach fire? Just my kind of thing," he said.

"Great!" Nina said. "Ela, you and Lasha are on salad, bread and crisps; the Morgans are on meat. I'll bring the skewers and drinks..."

"The Morgans, like me, are vegetarian!" I reminded her, throwing a quick smile at Toma.

"We'll get the meat," Saba said, back-handing Mate, who nodded in agreement.

"And we'll be on wood duty," Emily offered sweetly, tucking her hand into the crook of her brother's arm and steering a gap between us.

"Please be careful tonight," Ilia said, drying my hair with a towel, then beginning to brush it. The motion was soothing, comforting. Normally, I would have been focused on his fingers as they worked out the knots... but tonight my head was filled with Toma.

"Why are you so worried? Are you jealous?" I asked, grinning at him in the mirror.

Something in his face changed, he frowned, then gave a small smile back.

"No, of course not. But these Morgans are bad news."

"They seem ok to me, though they seem very close for brother and sisters," I shook the thought away. "Let's give them a chance, ok?"

"You're not worried by Nina's accusation?"

I laughed. "Of course not. I saw Arabella on the beach. Nina was probably just hallucinating after the swim."

Ilia looked at if he wanted to say something, but seemed to think better of it and shook his head. "Just watch your back."

I'll be watching Toma, I told myself, smiling at my reflection.

Most of the sunbathers had left by the time we got back to the long stretch of black sand, heading back to their hotels and cabins to eat and get ready for a night of drinking and fairground rides. The burning orange sun slipped into the sea just as we got the fire going.

An hour later and we were full of roasted corn, salad and bread, and the boys were trying to decide who should get the last piece of pork off the skewer.

I was sitting next to Toma. We didn't talk much but we kept smiling at each other- which, I saw, seemed to really annoy his sisters.

"A toast to us!" Nina said.

"To new friendships!" Saba said, with a meaningful look at Arabella beside him, who smiled demurely back.

"To us!" I said, blushing as I chinked Toma's plastic cup.

"It's so quiet!" Emily said with a sigh, looking out to sea. "I wish we could stay like this forever."

"It's too quiet!" Mate observed. "We need some music!"

The others cheered his idea.

"I wish we'd met at the beginning of our holiday," I told Toma shyly so no-one else could hear.

"Me, too," he told me back in a whisper, his words sending my heart thumping hard against my chest as he leaned in close.

"El- do us a favour and bring Ni's speaker," Saba begged, clearly not wanting to leave Arabella's side.

I tore my eyes from Toma and growled at Saba, but stood and brushed the sand off my bum.

"Where is it?" I asked Nina.

"In my room- on the desk..."

"Er- maybe we should move this party elsewhere, anyway," Arabella said.

"What? Why?" Saba asked, hurt. I could only imagine the late-night sand-and-sea activities he'd had in mind for the two of them.

"Look," Toma said, pointing skywards.

It was then we noticed the breeze picking up, bringing with it the heavy scent of salt and rain. Chasing the moon, then quickly swallowing it, was a huge bank of black clouds moving from Batumi northwards towards us.

"Then how about we head up to dad's hotel, light the fire-pit and warm up in the Jacuzzi?" Nina suggested.

My eyebrows shot up and I swallowed a giggle.

Before anyone could answer, the clouds, now above us, broke. We were soaked in an instant. We leapt up, shouting and scream-ing as the torrent of cold water ran down our necks while we tried to grab up the rubbish and leftovers.

"Leave it!" Nina shouted, dropping her plastic bag carelessly to the sand, letting the bottles, tins and plastic containers spill out. "Let's go!"

I saw the triplets exchange a look and Toma said something in Emily's ear and she nodded.

Everyone started running after Nina, laughing. Before I could fol-low, Toma took my hand and tugged me in the opposite direction.

"Come with me," he said, grinning.

I looked back at Nina and the others disappearing into the alley-way between the beach houses and smiled. "Ok."

I ran with him, leaping crazily over puddles until we arrived at a metal gate facing onto the boulevard. Behind it was an old bungalow- an original, made of wooden boards, with a veranda decorated at the top corners with intricate woodwork, and a corrugated metal roof. We ran through the bare garden and onto the deck, where we stopped, looking back out at the grey beach through the curtains of rain, panting and laughing.

I realised I was still holding his hand and let go, blushing, my heart suddenly starting to beat faster and hotter, even as I shivered from the wet. He noticed the change in mood and looked at me, smiling; studying my face as I studied his.

He reached up and tucked a strand of dripping hair behind my ear.

I was totally caught up in his eyes...then he leaned forwards and I got caught up in his lips.

"You're cold, let's go in," he said, pulling away a minute later.

The door was unlocked and we walked into a simple 1960s kitchen-diner; red-painted wooden floorboards creaking underfoot, walls of faded floral print, circles of brown damp on the grubby cream ceiling, a table, four chairs, sink, humming Russian fridge, and a black wood burner.

Toma bent down and shoved some ready-cut log quarters into the stove, added some kindling and then put his hand, palm out, into it and closed his eyes.

The kindling smoked, burst into flame, and he withdrew his hand and shut the door.

"Did you just...?" I asked as he stood. I was going to ask, "Light that without a lighter?" but realised it would sound stupid and stopped myself, not believing what I'd just seen.

"You need to take off those wet clothes or you'll get ill," he said, standing and shoving his hands in the pockets of his sleeveless black hoodie.

I blushed.

"Don't be shy with me, Ela," he said. "I won't hurt you."

At those words, I felt Ilia, who'd been a lurking, grumpy, dark shadow all evening, shimmer and fade away, confirming that I must be safe. He'd told me once that he could sense a person's intent from their aura. And when he was sure I was safe, he was pulled back into nothingness until I needed him again.

"So, you just disappear- you don't even see or think?" I'd asked him, aged 10, when I'd nearly slipped down the stairs at school, only to be grabbed at the last second by my angel suddenly materialising beside me.

"I can come back if I want, but I have to fight the force pulling me away, and that zaps my energy. Otherwise, if you're safe, I become purposeless."

"It sounds sad when you put it that way," I'd said.

He'd shrugged and smiled. "That's just the way it is."

And now Toma had said those magic words that meant we were truly alone.

"Wait here, I'll get you something of the girls'."

He walked off into the back room and I heard him open a wardrobe.

I stood in front of the stove, hugging myself, my stomach doing somersaults in nervousness. The smoke drifted through a crack in the thin metal door. It smelled sweet- herbal, almost like church incense. I breathed deep, wondering what kindling he'd used. An idea drifted into my head and I smiled. Toma was right. I needed to get out of these clothes.

"I got you a dress or..." Toma turned and stopped, his mouth dropping open.

I stood in the doorway in my underwear, smiling at him, blushing, with a nervous laugh stuck in my throat.

The corner of his lips lifted in a half smile and he came to me and kissed me, his hands in my hair; my hands on his shoulders, feeling his hard muscles beneath his damp top.

His lips moved down to my neck but I stopped him.

"We should get you out of these wet clothes..." I said breathlessly, the smell of that warm incense all around us.

He laughed and complied.

CHAPTER 6

"What happened to Ela and Toma?" Nina wondered, looking at the group raiding her father's generously stocked fridge and drinks cabinet.

"Do you need to ask?" Saba threw at her, holding out a beer to Lasha.

When he didn't move to take it, Saba looked at him, frowning. Lasha's eyes were fixed on the centre of the room, where Arabella stood in front of them all, her bikini hanging limp in her hand, her golden-brown body revealed in full.

"Did someone mention a Jacuzzi?" she asked.

Nina laughed in surprise, shrugged, and then slipped off her own clothes. Emily did the same.

"Follow me," Nina said, winking over her shoulder at her cousin and his friends, who were standing looking after them, wide-eyed and open-mouthed. The boys glanced at each other, came to silent agreement and, grinning, got naked and went after the girls onto the covered roof terrace.

Emily, lagging behind, went to the window and closed her eyes, her lips moving in silent words.

I looked down at our entwined fingers and legs. My skin was glowing white compared to his tan.

"Snow white," he said softly, as if he'd read my mind.

"Beauty and the beast," I joked.

He pulled away and I felt the atmosphere cooling.

"What's the matter?" I asked.

"Nothing," he said, getting up, unashamedly naked, and throwing another log into the stove.

"Did I say something wrong?" I wondered.

"No," he shook his head and smiled, though I could see something unsaid in his eyes.

My phone beeped on the table. Toma passed it to me without looking at it.

"It's Nina," I told him. "Asking where I am."

"Do you want to go?"

"If you come, too," I said.

"Jacuzzis aren't really my style," he said, sitting back down next to me on the rug.

"Have you ever tried it?" I teased.

"I've tried a lot of things," he said. "And sharing a Jacuzzi with our friends is not top of my current bucket list." He leaned over and kissed me.

"Then let's just go and party. It's our last night tonight," I said.

"'*And I had the time of my life…*'" he sang softly against my lips, quoting one of my favourite old films, Dirty Dancing.

"Don't, you'll make me cry," I said, pouting, only half joking.

"So attached, so soon?" he whispered, kissing my cheek, my neck; down, making my body tremble.

"Mmm-hmm," I affirmed.

"Tell Nina we'll be there in 30," he said.

CHAPTER 7

Toma pressed me back against the wall beside the hotel door, a hand on my shoulder, another on the back of my neck, his mouth on mine.

The scent of pine and salt water filled the night-damp air.

"Erm, Eliso?" a nervous voice asked.

I looked up, smiling, as I gently pushed Toma away.

"Giorgi?!" I asked, astounded.

The young soldier in the khaki uniform smiled back. He was tanned and looked older than I remembered, his eyes haunted by everything he'd seen. I gave him a hug, feeling Toma tense beside me.

"Toma, this is Giorgi, Nina's boyfriend." They shook hands. "When did you get home? Does Nina know?" I asked in Georgian.

"No," he said, grinning. "I wasn't going to come till the morning, but something told me now would be the perfect time for a surprise!"

It will be if that Jacuzzi's still on, I thought, as Toma went to the lift and pressed the button.

"Miss Eliso," the concierge greeted me. "Are these your guests?"

"Er, yes," I said. "Mine and Nina's."

"Very good," he said, making a note in his book. His smile was tight, though, and I could feel disapproval rolling off him. I was sure Nina's dad would be getting a report of this.

"Please call Nina and tell her some special guests are on the way up," I told him.

"Of course," he said, reaching for the phone while trying to keep his face neutral.

34

"The VIP kind," I added, smiling and linking my arm through Giorgi's, hoping that Nina would answer.

"So, did she miss me?" Giorgi asked.

I nodded. "You know she did!"

As the lift came down, I got out my phone and sent a text to Nina:

ME: Get dressed NOW. Bringing VIP!

I prayed she'd get it in time- I knew she was attached to her phone but I doubted she'd have it near the Jacuzzi.

We went into the apartment and I called Nina's name. We could hear screaming and laughter from the terrace, along with splashing and the motorized bubbling of the Jacuzzi. I shot a worried look at Nina's boyfriend.

Then her bedroom doors opened and she walked out, fully dressed and towel-drying her hair. I threw a relieved smile in Toma's direction and saw him frowning, looking disappointed.

When Nina saw Giorgi, she squealed and ran at him, jumping into his arms. He dropped his holdall and squeezed her tight. She looked at me over his shoulder: 'Thank you!' she mouthed.

"Come on," I said, smiling and inviting Toma into the living area.

"Sounds like we have some catching up to do," Toma said as more laughter erupted outside. He grabbed a vodka bottle off the kitchen bar and took a swig. "Want some?" he asked, offering it to me.

I took it and sipped, cringing at the sharp taste.

"I need a Redbull with this," I said, heading to the fridge.

"Nii," I called. "Where's the Redbull?"

"None left. Just Boom, top cupboard," her disembodied voice answered me from the depths of her bedroom.

Boom was the local Georgian version. It would do.

"Did something wear you out today that you need an energy drink?" Toma asked innocently as I poured.

I laughed. "Near-death and mind-blowing sex can do that, yeah!"

Emily padded in, a white towel tucked around her, looking around. She pursed her lips when she saw me.

35

"Is everything ok with Nina?" she asked.

"Very," I said with a smile. "Her boyfriend's back in town."

"Yep," Toma agreed, though his tone was heavy. "Luckily she got a call warning her Giorgi was coming before he saw her in the jacuzzi."

I saw a look of exasperation flash across his sister's face.

"Sorry," she told him.

"Better luck next time," he said, then turned his back on her to get a glass for his vodka.

"What was that about?" I asked as Emily went back outside.

"Nothing," he said. Then he pulled off his t-shirt. "Ready for a dip?"

"Are you serious?!" I asked.

"Deadly," he replied, pulling me against him.

CHAPTER 8

"So...what happened?" Nina asked teasingly when I finally dragged myself out of the shower the next morning.

"None of your business," I replied with pretend haughtiness.

She threw a pillow at me and I ducked out of the way.

"It so IS my business!"

I laughed and threw my wet towel at her and turned to the wardrobe to get dressed, hiding my blush from her perceptive gaze.

"We kissed," I said, taking out a black and blue print summer dress.

"For nearly two *hours*?! I was going to send out the security guards looking for you!"

I looked at her, horrified, the image of being discovered by her dad's lackeys sending shocks of revulsion through me.

She laughed. "Fine, I wouldn't do that. But I was worried."

"Well, thank you for being worried and thank you for not over-reacting."

She waited while I did up my bikini bra and pulled my dress on.

I looked at her. She was sitting with her arms crossed, frowning at me. I laughed and fell onto the bed next to her. She laid down next to me, our heads touching like when we were little and wanted to whisper secrets to each other.

"Did you go all the way with him?" she asked quietly.

I bit back a laugh and nodded.

"Now THAT is not like you."

"I know. It just felt...right."

"He didn't drug you, did he?" she asked, sitting up and looking down at me.

"No!" I said. But then I remembered that strange burning incense and flicked a look at Ilia. He was standing at the window looking out to sea.

"And was he good?"

I nodded, aware of my angel listening. But I couldn't hold in the laugh this time.

She laughed with me and when our giggling had subsided, I sighed.

"But it's just a summer romance, right? We're going home tonight and he'll be going wherever his parents take him."

"Emily said they might be staying in Georgia for a while."

"Yeah, Toma said the same. But that doesn't mean I'll ever see him again."

"It's a small country..." Nina said optimistically. "Anyway, we've got a whole 12 hours left to enjoy so let's get up and get busy!"

"Busy at the beach?!" I said with a smile.

"With boys on our hands, life is always busy!" she informed me matter-of-factly.

"Nice to have Giorgi back?"

"Yeah. He's on leave for a week- then he's at camp. He'll fly out again soon, though."

"But you get a whole week!"

"I do!" she said with a grin.

"Are you finally going to...you know...lose it to him?" I asked her.

She gave a small smile, her cheeks colouring lightly. "I told you- not 'til after we get married."

Not for the first time, I thought she was too young to be so seriously into a guy. Especially an older one who might get blown up by terrorists. But she was stubborn like that and I loved her for it regardless.

"So..." she said, glancing at the door. "There's more that can be done other than...*it*...so if you could, you know..." she tilted her head.

"Right. Hint taken. I'll meet you at the beach, then," I said with a grin.

CHAPTER 9

Everyone was there but Toma and his sisters.

"Still in bed?" I sent him with a cheeky grin. He didn't reply.

Disappointed, but trying not to show it, I swam, joked and played ball with the others until lunchtime. Saba suggested pizza at the hotel but I had no appetite and told them I'd catch up with them later in the afternoon.

Bag across my shoulder, I walked along the sandy boulevard to the house the triplets were renting.

I knew there was something wrong the moment I saw it.

The gate was rustier than I remembered, and padlocked. In fact, it looked like it hadn't been opened in a long time, though I knew it wasn't possible.

I looked at the buildings to either side of the house, one a three-floor hotel and the other a small modernised guest house, just like yesterday, so this was definitely the right place.

A cat appeared through a hole in the wire fence and, without looking around to see if I was being watched, I threw my bag over and pulled the fence up and ducked in.

"Ela, what are you doing?" a voice asked.

I jumped.

"Ilia!" I complained.

The porch where I'd kissed Toma not 15 hours ago was just as it had been- white wood, the paint flaking off. I tried the door. It was open.

"Hello?" I asked, letting it swing back until it bumped gently against the wall.

No answer- and a layer of dust that I didn't remember coating all the furniture.

"This is crazy!" I whispered.

"There's no-one here," my angel told me.

I walked across the red floor with its threadbare rugs circa 1960 and touched a hand to the stove.

"It's still warm."

"But no-one's been in this house for a while," Ilia pointed out.

"You know I was here just last night, right? I mean, you saw me and Toma here?"

"I saw," he said, looking pointedly at the rug, making me blush.

I went into the bedroom- only one bed had sheets on it, though I remembered the four beds there had been made up. The wardrobe doors squeaked in protest when I opened them- empty, except for cobwebs.

I swore, feeling scared, then went back to the kitchen and touched the stove again. I opened it- the grey and white ashes were still warm; some glowed red when the air hit them and I caught a whiff of that heady incense again and felt my heart hammering in sudden inexplicable desire. I looked at the rug where Toma and I had laid together, then took out my phone. This time the call didn't even connect.

"Where the hell...?" I wondered, feeling angry now. "How dare he sleep with me and leave without even saying goodbye!"

"Best forget him," Ilia advised, following me as I shut the stove and left the house as I'd found it.

I strode angrily back to the beach and swam hard and fast, thinking of all the things I'd say and do to Toma if I ever saw him again- and swallowing back unbidden salty tears of hurt. I'd fallen deeper for him than I thought. I swam until the lifeguard shouted me back in. The swim had burned off some of my anger but not helped the broken heart.

"What's up with you?" Nina asked, seeing my dark look as I

dumped my beach bag on the living-room floor. She was snuggled up with Giorgi, drinking coffee.

"The triplets left."

"What?" she asked, putting her mug on the coffee table with a 'thunk'.

"Yep. Gone. No goodbye, no note, nothing."

"Did you try calling?"

"Of course," I said.

"Got an address?" Giorgi asked. "I'm happy to go shoot the bastard."

I shook my head, trying on a smile, but it felt tight and out of line with my heavy heart.

"I'm going to go and pack," I said.

The last thing I wanted was to play gooseberry to Nina and Giorgi's happy-coupleness.

I shut the door and Ilia immediately materialised beside me.

"Sorry," he said quietly, pulling me into a hug.

I tried and failed to swallow back tears.

"You did warn me," I reminded him.

"I did," he agreed.

CHAPTER 10

"I'm going to miss you!" I told Mariam, squeezing her tight.

When she pulled back, we both had tears in our eyes. We wiped at them self-consciously, aware of the buzz of the departures hall around us.

"You write to me, ok?"

"Every day," I promised solemnly.

"I wish dad would leave me and mum here," she said for the hundredth time. "Stupid posting…"

"Well, it's his first time as Deputy Ambassador, he needs you guys with him."

"It's more his stupid fascination with Zoroastrianism than wanting to serve his country," she reminded me. "If the Ministry knew…"

"Passengers for Qatar Airways flight 0254 to Tehran are asked to proceed to Gate 1. We are now inviting those passengers with small children, and any passengers requiring special assistance, to begin boarding…"

"Come on, sweetie, we have to go," Mariam's mother told her, a gentle hand on her daughter's shoulder and a sympathetic look towards me. She reached forward and squeezed my hand as Mariam bent to pick up her rucksack.

"It's been great knowing you, Eliso," she said. "Come and visit us any time!"

"Mum!" Mariam complained. "Why would she bother coming to a desert?"

"Tehran is not a desert!" her mum answered, exasperated, clearly voicing an argument they'd had before.

"As good as..." her daughter pouted.

"Don't spoil our goodbye by being grumpy," I scolded.

She grinned and pulled me into another hug.

"I don't want to leave," she whispered in my ear.

"I know," I whispered back.

"Girls, let each other go!" her dad said warmly, coming over to us, wheeling his black business-like suitcase behind him.

"Goodbye, Mr Walker," I said, holding out my hand. He pulled me into a hug instead and smiled down at me fondly.

"Stay in touch," he said.

I nodded, and they turned and got on the escalator heading up to passport control and security.

Sometimes going to an international school sucked. Tonight was one of those times.

I wiped my tears with the back of my hand and settled back into the leather upholstery of Levan's car, looking gloomily out of the window at the dark night as my best friend of four years got ready to fly out of my life.

This was going to be the worst school year ever.

CHAPTER 11

Two days till the start of school. I sat at my desk, my homework spread out across it in front of me, paper and pen ready to write. But I was blind to all words but the one I'd scrawled in the top right corner: Toma.

"Why can't you forget him?" Ilia asked from the rocking chair.

I shrugged and circled the name with a heart, then added my own name.

"He was no good for you."

I drew a crack down the centre, dividing our names.

"He dumped you in the worst possible way."

I stuck an arrow through the heart; a vain attempt to hold the two halves together.

"And he's out of your life."

"I know," I said. I sighed and dropped the pen, pushing away from the desk and throwing myself face-down on the bed.

"Distract me," I told my angel, my voice muffled by the pillow.

"How?"

I turned onto my back as he came and sat on the bed beside me, his back against the headboard.

"Hmm...Tell me about your village," I said.

"I've told you about it a million times," he complained.

"Not for ages, though," I said. "There must be something you missed."

He thought about it. "I can tell you about the time the harvest failed," he suggested.

I nodded and settled back into the pillow, my head on my arm, looking up at him.

"We spent weeks preparing the fields," he began. "The whole village- men, women, children. Children under two stayed in the village with our *bebia*- our grandmother. Once they were three, they came with us up the mountains. The ways were stony and steep so we used cattle to pull our carts- wheels wouldn't work. The little ones picked nettles for *bebia* to make soup..."

"Didn't that hurt?" I asked.

"We got used to it," he said with a smile. "The grown-ups beat at the ground, turning the earth, softening it. Then we planted the wheat and waited for the rain."

"Did it come?"

He nodded. "The weather's unpredictable in the mountains. And when it rains, it can get heavy fast."

"Which is bad for the crops," I prompted when he fell into a thoughtful silence, remembering.

"The crop was good that year- one of the best we'd ever had. We were half way through harvesting it- *bebia* even came up to help tie the bundles before the cart brought them down. We laid them out in the village square and all of us women and children walked round and round on it.

"Why?"

"Separating the wheat from the chaff," he explained. "It was great fun- we'd sing as we walked, the whole community together... Then one day we were sitting eating breakfast near the fire- the little ones outside playing and the old men setting up the backgammon board - and the ground started shaking. It was terrifying. Everyone was screaming. I was seventeen- already a man- so the first thing I did was to make sure the horses were tied well. My sister Elene took care of the little ones. When the shaking stopped, there was total silence. Not even the birds were singing."

I closed my eyes, picturing it all too clearly. I reached for his hand and, solidifying, he took it, entwining his fingers between mine, playing with them as he talked.

"Then we heard crying and shouting," he said. "My aunt Mtvare was running up the street with her husband Iakob hobbling along behind her. She was flapping her apron, still floury from baking the morning *shoti* bread. She was crying and shouting."

"What was she saying?"

"'The fields have gone! The fields!'" he said, frowning at the memory.

"We all ran then- from *bebiebi* to tiny tots- running up to the harvest...It was gone- buried. The earthquake had broken off the side of the mountain and it'd come sliding down onto our crops. All the women stood at the edge of the field, crying and rocking and hugging themselves. Some of them scratched at their faces."

"Why so dramatic?" I wondered.

"It was our food for the winter," Ilia reminded me patiently. "We had enough for maybe one or two months of bread, but the winters are long in the mountains and we had just a month left until the pass closed up in snow."

"Meaning?"

"Meaning total isolation. No one in, no one out- no trade, no supplies. Trapped."

"So, you starved?"

"No. The men left the village."

"Left?"

"Yes. Every able-bodied man."

"Including you?"

"Including me. The whole village got together to dance, sing and wish us well. We prayed and danced together in a circle- matching each other step-for-step: one community. Then those staying walked with us down to the edge of our land, to the wooden bridge, and said goodbye as we crossed the river."

"Wasn't it dangerous leaving them? What about raiders? If all the men left, who'd protect them?"

"It was safe enough. There was only one route in and the men left behind, even if old or lame, were still able to shoot a gun. Even our mama- our priest- was good with a hunting knife. No. We were the ones at risk," he said heavily.

"Where did you go?"

"To the forest, to cut wood and sell it down-river so we could buy winter supplies for our families. We'd chop the trees down, pull them to the river and tie them into giant rafts. We'd make long wooden oars and then we'd float the rafts down in teams of two or three to the nearest mill. It was dangerous work. People didn't always survive..."

"When did you go home again?" I asked in a whisper, squeezing his hand. He squeezed back.

"I never did. At least, not alive."

I shivered, suddenly putting it together- the age, his voice, his words. He'd never told me how he died, though his face always darkened at the mention of it, his lips twisting at some bitter memory.

"You were only seventeen," I said.

"Yes."

I felt my throat tighten.

"What happened? Did you drown?"

"No. We'd got the wood sold way ahead of schedule- when we left the village, we thought we might have to spend all winter down in Zugdidi, but we seemed to have luck on our side. Then on the way home, it started to snow heavily. Some of us got separated. I lost my way in the wood. Then I fell down a crevasse."

He said it so quickly, so bluntly, that it took me a moment to absorb it.

A tear fell and he scooped it up with his finger.

"It's ok, El," he said. "It was a long time ago."

"Did they come for you?"

"I don't know. I died in the fall."

"Doesn't that make you sad? Or angry?"

"It did," he told me softly. "But now I'm here with you. I'm over it."

"What happened after you died?" I asked.

"Nothing," he said. "Nothing I remember, anyway. Not until I was told to look after you."

"Who told you?"

"God."

"You met him?"

"Not exactly..."

"Ela, din-ner!" Geta called.

"I'm study-ing!" I called, irritated, sitting up.

"It's ok," Ilia told me softly. "Go eat."

"I want to hear more..." I complained, looking at him.

"About my death?" he asked with a sad, gentle smile.

"About you."

His blue eyes widened and he reached out and stroked my cheek. Then he leaned forwards. For a crazy, delicious, confusing moment I thought he was going to kiss me on the lips- I wanted him to. But he hesitated, reading me, his breath on my cheek, and then pulled back and stood up.

"Another time," he promised, then disappeared.

But he didn't reappear after dinner, though I called him.

Alone, I stood looking down at my desk. I traced my finger around the heart that circled Toma's name, frowning. Then I screwed up the page and threw it across the room.

CHAPTER 12

Nina dragged me, complaining, into the red-carpeted library, which was warm and would've been cosy if not for the wind whistling in at the windows. The school, built on a hill just outside the city, got battered by the wind so often it'd become more of a pain than an excitement now, though the primary kids on the first floor could always be heard screaming with delight or fear as the wind beat at their classrooms.

"Levan's going to be here to pick me up soon!" I pointed out as she flung her bag into the corner and pulled me down onto one of the beanbags.

"Your driver's always late and one of these days your dad's going to sack him for it!" she pointed out, tossing her long blond hair over her shoulder.

"If my mum was around, maybe. But you know dad doesn't have time to care," I reminded her.

My mum was British and a stickler for timing, but my dad was Georgian so we tended to function on GMT (Georgian Maybe Time), which dad got away with because he was the director of his company but which had caused my mum no end of stress. Not that mum was around anymore to argue with us about it- she'd disappeared on us nearly ten years ago, her lasting legacy a note saying 'I can't do this anymore. Take care of the kids. I love you.'

"So...Why do you think they're here?" she asked.

"Who?" I asked indifferently, grabbing one of my favourite books off the book shelf – Blood Omen, it was called – and flicking through it with unseeing eyes.

"The Morgan triplets, of course! Your summer romance!"

It'd been a total shock to see them walking the corridor with the Headmaster, even more when Emily was brought to our class in the first period after lunch and introduced as a new student. She'd looked amazing in the shirt-and-skirt combo she had on, though I predicted the teacher would have something to say about the hem-length by the end of the day as the boys around me shifted awkwardly in their seats.

She'd smiled and chosen an empty desk near the back. Feeling eyes on me, I'd looked back at the door and seen Toma watching me with a smile from under the hood of his sweater. I scowled at him and his smile widened. Then Arabella touched him on the shoulder and they were gone.

The teacher had resumed her lesson and it wasn't until now we'd had a chance to talk about it. But I didn't want to admit how I'd felt when I saw Toma. Didn't want to feel it.

"The same reason all of us are here," I answered Nina. "It's the top school in the city and our parents work in the embassies or big companies and can afford to send us here. Or the students are so fantastically intelligent they got scholarships!" I said with a smile.

Nina laughed, her teeth so white she could've been in a toothpaste ad.

"And you don't think it's a coincidence you and Toma had a thing this summer and now he's here?" she teased.

"It was a two-day romance and he didn't get back to me after. I wouldn't even call it a 'thing,'" I said, trying not to let the hurt back in.

"But still, of all the schools..." She sighed and gave me a wicked grin. "Want me to kill him for you?"

I grinned back. "No. But thanks for the offer. He's clearly not interested in me so I'm just going to ignore him."

"Easier said than done- he's gorgeous."

"Been there, done it," I said, flicking my hair over my shoulder, Pantene style.

Nina clapped her hands in delight. "Good for you!"

"So, changing the subject slightly, why'd Emily end up in our class and the other two in 12th grade? Aren't they the same age?"

Nina shrugged. "Maybe she missed out on a year- that's what happened to you, right?"

I nodded, wondering if Emily had also had an "invisible" friend. But I'd caught up with my lessons- why hadn't she?

"I guess we'll find out. So, Mrs Parsons set us another thrilling history project," I said, my voice dripping with sarcasm. "Who are you going to profile?"

My phone beeped before she could answer.

"It's Levan," I told her. "Gotta go. Speak later?"

"Sure," she said, getting to her feet with me. "I've got to go and get my physics book- Ms Nozadze's testing me tonight."

Ms Nozadze was Nina's private physics tutor.

"Why are you still studying with that old bat?" I asked her.

"Daddy insists," she said with a smile. "But I swear she's going to drop dead at my desk any day now."

"You can only hope!" I said with a sigh.

We giggled.

"Mikey- time to go!" I called out across the room.

My little brother climbed out of the beanbag where he'd been sitting with his geeky best friend Simon, both hunched over their mobiles. He picked up his rucksack, said goodbye and joined us.

"Hi, Nina," he said shyly.

Nina kissed his cheek. "Hi Mikey!" Then she blew me a kiss and walked away, a light bounce in her step.

I caught my brother eyeing her long legs and behind and thumped him on the arm.

"Don't even think about it!" I warned him under my breath.

"As if!" he said with a scowl, blushing.

"So, what did you do today?" I asked as we headed downstairs, the shadow of Ilia trailing behind us.

He shrugged.

I knew this was the only moment I could reach him before he shut himself away in his room with the computer. Mum's leaving had hurt him more than me- I guess he had a childish hero image of her. I'd never felt that way- she hadn't let me get close enough to. And Dad, when he did manage to get home on time to eat with us, just didn't know how to relate to us.

"Come on!" I encouraged.

He threw his thumb reluctantly over his shoulder and mumbled, "We did the digestive system."

I looked back at the notice board at the top of the stairs and saw that the life-size cut-out people, which his group had been adding to over the past few weeks, now had a full set of guts, coloured and labelled in detail.

"Nice!" I said with a grin.

He grinned back. "Come on. Mrs B told me she's doing burgers tonight."

"Your favourite, not mine!" I reminded him.

"Aren't you bored of being vegetarian yet?" he teased. "Beans, salad, apples, corn..."

"Definitely not!" I said. "Eating dead animals is disgusting."

"Whatever," he said. "More for me!"

CHAPTER 13

ME: You remember the triplets from Ureki?

MARIAM: Yeah.

ME: They joined our school.

MARIAM: No way! Do you want me to come back and cut something off The Bastard?

The Bastard was Mariam's name for Toma.

ME: No. I'll handle it.

MARIAM: You have an evil plan?

'Let's just see how it goes,' I typed.

MARIAM: You still have a crush on him, don't u? Seriously, El, he's not worth it!

I sat back and thought about it. Ilia was sitting on my bed, reading a book. *Can't help it*, I typed. *He's too cute.*

On the outside, maybe, she returned. *But inside, I guarantee the Morgans are all twisted. You remember how Toma looked when Nina hurt the dog. Then she nearly drowned!*

ME: But there was no way Arabella was involved in Nina's crazy swim. She wasn't anywhere near!

MARIAM: Just be careful.

...Yes, mum, I replied.

Then we talked about her new school and life. Luckily, she wasn't the only newbie- the daughter of the Italian Ambassador had also just joined, so she had some company until she got absorbed into one of the cliques- the coolest one, no doubt. I missed her and I wanted to talk to her more about Toma, but she, like Ilia, was so disapproving, I didn't dare.

CHAPTER 14

"God, I hate these places," I mumbled.

The earth-shaking voice of the Georgian singer, standing, grinning, microphone securely in hand in front of his laptop, drowned my words. We were in a plain over-crowded banquet hall, the kind that line the roads by the dozen near Dighomi. White walls, disco lights and long tables accommodating ten to twenty people each- the people on them feasting on the standard Georgian fare and toasting loudly with local wine (the men getting to their feet for toasts to the dead, the Church, and to women). The crowd was a real mix- our table of 16-17 year olds, college boys at the back celebrating an engagement, a large family with a baby toasting a Christening, and next to them a group of pensioners celebrating a 70th birthday... it was all about drinking, eating and dancing...and besides the shouted conversations and the too-loud speakers, the place stank of cigarettes.

"WHAT DID YOU SAY?" Nina shouted.

"I said I HATE-"

The music stopped, everyone clapped and the singing was replaced by a quieter tune while the singer rested his tonsils with another cigarette.

I breathed a sigh of relief.

"I was going to say I hate these kinds of places!"

"I know. I mean, why did she choose to have her birthday *here*?!" Nina complained, looking over at Susan as she sat giggling with Lasha. "Especially the first party of the season."

"You know her family aren't well-off," I whispered. "I suppose it's better this than a bash at her flat."

"Don't be stuck up," my friend scolded me. "I've had brilliant parties at home."

"You live in a mansion," I pointed out.

She smiled demurely and then I saw her eyes fix on something over my shoulder and her pink lips drop into an 'o' of surprise, her eyes growing soft from pleasure.

I looked and saw a familiar figure walking through the door- our new boy, dressed in a black shirt and black jeans, his hair gelled. His sisters followed behind him holding hands- Arabella dressed in dark blue with severely straight hair and Emily with curls in a dress of multi-shades of pink.

Their entrance, or rather Toma's, caught the attention of the table next to ours- a group of giggling 13-year-old girls, their parents sitting just two tables away as one of them, a wavy-haired elfin girl called Natalia, celebrated her birthday.

"What's *he* doing here?" Nina breathed.

I shook my head and glanced around to see if Ilia had also turned up. There was no sign of him.

I took a gulp of cherry liquor and pulled Nina to her feet.

"Let's dance," I suggested as a folk song- Adjaruli- came on.

Anything to stop her staring.

I felt his eyes on me and couldn't help feeling a flare of flirtatious-ness warm my insides. Those Georgian dance classes of the past ten years had me dancing like a pro. Nina and I swirled around the circle, our long hair flowing with our moves, as our classmates clapped. Adjaruli was my favourite dance, the most energetic for girls; my arms held out to the sides, my shoulders rocking with the beat, my hands turning delicately at the wrist, twisting my hips and occasionally spinning on the spot, up on my toes. One of the boys from the college table jumped into our circle, his feet moving fast and his arms held stiffly up, a big grin on his face- the picture of power and grace as he leapt around Nina and played the chasing game. I wriggled my eyebrows at her and she laughed. Then he dropped to one knee and clapped her as she circled him.

The music stopped and we all applauded.

Then the DJ started the wedding dance, my next favourite, and it was Nina's turn to flick her eyebrows up at me. But I couldn't do it alone- a boy had to start it by 'inviting' me to dance. And it involved some fancy footwork so I doubted any of my classmates would be up for it. I gave a good-natured shrug at my best friend and turned from the dancefloor, planning to head back to our table. But Nina grabbed my arm to stop me.

"No way!" she breathed.

"What?" I turned back.

I swallowed, feeling heat in the pit of my stomach as I saw Toma, one arm outstretched, the other bent at the elbow, his fist closed near his chest; his feet moving fast, delicately, perfectly – towards me.

He hesitated in front of me, gave a small smile in response to my surprised expression and then backed away and made a wide circle- body gliding, shoulders strong.

"Go on," Nina dared me, giving me a nudge as Toma closed in again.

I scowled at her and fixed a smile on my face and raised my arms slightly, fingers in position, waiting for him to arrive.

Our classmates had remade the circle, joined by the college table- all curious to see the 'foreign girl' and the dark-haired mystery boy pair up.

They clapped to the beat, and Toma arrived in front of me, both hands held up and open, arms wide- then he stepped down.

It was my cue. I took a breath and began to move. Toma followed immediately behind, matching me step-for-step, becoming my shadow, not touching but close enough that if I stopped...

I thought of Ilia's warning but pushed it from my mind.

The trick of the dance is to lead the boy- to make him chase you and flirt with you by showing off his dancing skills and strength.

I tilted my head back as I glided- catching his eye. Then I stopped, allowing him to dance around me, in front of me. I raised my hand in front of my cheek- pretending innocence and shyness, backing away. In front of me now, he again matched me step for fast foot-step. My breath caught as his eyes, lit with heat, held mine. And then, teasing as the dance dictates, he backed away to the far side of the circle, leaving me in coolness without his proximity, giving me time to turn slowly and delicately in place- in the spotlight for everyone to see. I winked at Nina and we laughed.

Then he came back, heels down, pointing his toes, strong legs, right arm locked bent, the other thrown wide. Again, he stopped and I led him forwards on the chase, another slow turn and we divided, taking our own paths around the circle to meet face-to-face the other side.

Now it was my final show- small steps, body steady, only my wrists turning delicately on outstretched arms as he watched me turn and move gracefully towards him.

His look was hungry.

I heard a wolf-whistle and appreciative shouts- knew that one was most likely Nina, the other almost certainly Saba. *And if Ilia were here?* I wondered.

I saw Toma narrow his eyes, as if he'd caught the thought, and then it was my turn to do a little chasing, both of us moving back and forth- towards each other, away; teasing. My cheeks flushed every time he got close, cooling when he circled away. And then the final spin and the music stopped.

Breathless, I smiled and curtseyed.

He bowed.

We hadn't touched once.

And as he turned away, I found myself hoping that the DJ would switch on something romantic so that he would perhaps turn back, tempted to tease me more. But no, the DJ chose dance music and all my classmates began jumping around wildly, calling out in relief to be released from the traditional folk dances passed down the ages from grandparents to parents to children- an accepted part of childhood obligation, equally loved and considered a waste of time, and a must-know for all dinners and weddings.

Toma went over to chat with Saba while his sisters made small talk with Susan. A few minutes later, having not even looked at me again, Toma headed outside with Saba- no doubt going to smoke. I saw his two sisters head out almost immediately after, throwing a look my way before they did, their expressions unreadable.

"You were staring at his ass," Nina pointed out crudely in my ear.

I jumped and looked guiltily away.

"I was *not*!" I insisted, turning quickly to our table, trying to hide my blush, hoping that Ilia was far, far away tonight.

No such luck. As soon as I hit the bathroom some ten minutes later, he was there.

"You danced beautifully out there," he said from the other side of the cubicle door.

I ignored him, very aware that no-one else could hear him and that there were two girls at the washbasins touching up their make-up.

"It's a shame you chose such a partner."

"What was I supposed to do, ignore him?" I snapped as the hand-drier burst into life, knowing that he'd hear me over the noise.

"Yes."

I came out of the cubicle and frowned at him, before turning my attention to the mirror as I washed my hands.

The girls left, gossiping about some photo someone had posted online.

"What's the problem?" I demanded, looking at him now, trying to ignore his golden...well...creaminess. "It was just a dance."

"You can't lie to me," he reminded me. "You're still attracted to him."

"Seriously?!" I demanded. Though I wasn't sure what I meant-seriously that he thought I was attracted to him or seriously that I actually was.

"You have to stay away from him."

I touched up my lipstick, then glanced at my angel.

"*He* came up to *me*."

"Ela," he started with a heavy tone, in no mood for word games.

"Fine, fine!" I held up my hands.

He narrowed his eyes and, lips pursed, I scowled at him as I walked out, zipping up my bag.

And bumped straight into Toma.

"Sorry," I said, a blush heating my cheeks.

"Who were you talking to?" he asked, curious, glancing into the empty bathroom as the door swung shut behind me.

"Myself," I said quickly.

"You look upset," he observed.

"I'm fine," I said, wanting to change the subject. "I didn't know you knew Georgian dance."

"There's a lot about me you don't know," he pointed out.

"I know you must've lived here longer than you let on this summer," I said.

"Maybe I'm a fast learner," he suggested.

"More likely you're a liar."

"Still angry with me?" he asked with a smile.

"I have to go back in," I said stiffly, trying to step around him. He shifted, blocking my path, a hand on the wall.

"You *are* still angry."

I remained still, looking at his strong fingers pressed against the grey wallpaper, unwilling to meet his eyes.

He brought his other hand up and tucked a loose strand of hair back and out of my face. He was so close, if I'd turned my head I could have kissed him.

Remembering Ilia's warning, I moved my head away from his gentle fingers and turned to glare at him.

"I thought we had something good. You dumped me. Yes, I'm angry!" I said tightly.

"I didn't think we'd ever see each other again," he explained.

"And that's a reason not to reply to any of my messages?"

He shrugged. "I..."

"Toma?" Emily sang out, appearing behind him. She looked at me with suspicion, reading everything in a glance. Arabella appeared next to her, glaring daggers.

"We have to go," she told him.

Toma hesitated, his eyes fixed on me with that burning heat that made my stomach bubble. Then he dropped his arm and turned to his sisters, dismissing me. I walked away, head held high, Ilia by my side, feeling the triplets watching me in silence.

I shivered as the banquet hall door shut and I re-joined humanity.

"Wassup?" Nina asked when I plonked down at the table and poured myself some liquor.

"Nothing," I said, downing it and turning to watch the dancers.

"We're going to Night Office after this, want to come?" the college boy Nina had danced with asked, leaning over us, his hand on Nina's shoulder, his breath smelling of beer.

Nina looked my way, leaving the decision to me.

I shook my head. Clubbing with strangers was not what I was in the mood for right then.

"Another time," Nina told him.

He launched into a list of reasons why we had to do it tonight and I tuned him out.

The song 'Hallelujah' came on, sung beautifully by one of the college girls. I'd never had a good singing voice, sadly, and as I listened to her, I felt my mood dip even lower.

Toma, Toma...why do you play hot and cold? Part of me wanted him to just leave me alone, another feared him doing just that, even if his sisters hated me for it...

"Can I have this dance?"

I looked up and my jaw dropped.

It was Ilia, dressed in smart jeans and a pale blue shirt. I got the same thrill as I always did to see him in the flesh. He was as shockingly beautiful as ever- tall, lightly tanned, medium golden-blond hair, sky-blue eyes, dark lashes and a body of hard muscles from years of mountaineering and horse-riding...

I looked quickly around and saw that everyone could see him-Nina's eyes were showing the whites in shock. She nudged me with her foot without dropping her gaze, and I could almost hear her saying, "Do NOT miss the chance to dance with something so beautiful."

With a shy smile, I took my angel's hand and he led me to the dancefloor.

"What are you doing? You'll burn up your energy!" I reminded him quietly.

"You looked sad," he said.

I rested my head on his shoulder, choosing not to reply. I suddenly felt I like I'd cry- as much at his love and consideration as Toma's rejection.

I was glad when Ilia chose not to push the issue, though I was pretty certain we'd be having a talk about the triplets at some point that night. It was nice right then just to feel his arms around me.

"Hallelujah...hallelujah..." he sang softly against my hair as we turned slowly to the beat.

I looked up at him and smiled. "Did you ask for this song?"

"Totally by chance," he said with a wink.

I went up on tiptoes and kissed his cheek and he blushed.

When the dance finished, the other dancers clapped but for a moment he and I were in a bubble, smiling at each other- I could feel happiness radiating from him, and something else... I frowned, and then, before I could say anything, he gave a slight bow and turned away.

"Wait, where are you going?" I reached out and grabbed his hand.

"I can't go up in smoke in front of your friends, can I?" he said with a grin.

"Oh, right."

"I'll be back," he said. And for a second, he touched a hand to my cheek, stroking his thumb down my cheekbone, then turned.

I went back to our table as Susan's birthday cake was brought out, candles burning. While the others sang, Nina dragged me down onto my seat, her eyes now burning with curiosity.

"Please tell me you didn't blow off that specimen of heaven because of Toma," she begged.

I choked on the sip of water I'd taken and looked at her with a grin.

"Of course not. He just wanted one dance, that's all."

I glanced towards the door and saw Ilia coming back towards our table, now only for my eyes.

"So, where'd he go?" she asked.

"I guess heaven couldn't be without him," I said, smiling at him as he leaned against the column near us to watch the dancers as the music started up again.

"Did you get his number at least?"

"Nii," I complained.

"Come on," she said. "You're 16 and boyfriendless. It can't go on and it can't be The Bastard."

"Hey- you're the one that pushed me to dance with him!" I pointed out.

She shrugged. "A dance is a dance. And he may be hot but he hurt you, and if Mr Right from Heaven had just spun me round the dance floor...I'd be singing Hallelujah and running after *him*."

Ilia glanced at me and wriggled his eyebrows. I laughed.

"Well, you look tons better than before he whisked you away, so there's that," Nina allowed.

"I feel better," I admitted. "How about we go clubbing?"

"With the college idiots over there?" she asked, surprised, glancing at the raucous table of boys singing and clapping each other on the back.

"Why not?" I shrugged. "It's your uncle's club. We'll be fine."

CHAPTER 15

Even though it was a Thursday, Night Office was packed wall to wall, a cloud of cigarette smoke hovering above the dancers' heads, cut now and then by various coloured laser-lights. The music vibrated through me and I grinned at Nina. It was a European DJ tonight, and though the Georgian DJs were often just as good, I always preferred European style.

We headed to the bar to grab a soft drink. Our group stuck together and the college boys, finding easier female prey, soon disappeared.

"Vodka-Redbull?" an amused voice offered next to my ear.

I turned to see Toma beside me at the bar. "If you're offering," I said with a reluctant smile.

He ordered and paid.

"So, what did you get up to the rest of the summer?" he asked.

Pining after you, I thought. "Nothing much," I said. "You?"

"Family stuff."

"And how did you end up at our school?"

"You," he said with a smile.

"Yeah, right," I scoffed.

"EL!" Nina shouted. "Stop propping up the bar and come daaaance!"

She pulled me after her, laughing, and we climbed onto the stage and began moving to the music.

I saw Emily at the bar scowling, arms crossed, as Toma tried to placate her. I wondered where Arabella was, then saw her pushing towards us through the crowd, looking determined.

"Uh-oh. The sea-snake's after us..." I warned in Nina's ear. She laughed and turned her back to the crowd, shaking her bum in Arabella's direction.

I saw Arabella's look sour, but then she turned her eyes to me and smiled coldly. Her lips moved and I frowned, trying to understand. Then she held up her hand and beckoned me forward.

"Woah!" Nina said, grabbing my arm. "You trying to break your neck?"

I shook my head and looked down- I'd been about to step off the stage. Not a dangerous fall, but it would've hurt. I glanced around and saw Arabella at the bar talking to her sister.

"I was sure I saw her here..."

"Hey, are you ok?" Nina asked.

"Yeah. Too much liquor," I said with a forced grin, feeling dizzy. "I'm just going to the loo. I'll be back."

She nodded and I took the steps down and went to the bathroom. There was a queue and while I was waiting, I realised I hadn't seen Ilia for a while.

"What do you want with our brother?" a cold voice asked and I turned to see Emily behind me, her sky-blue eyes lined with kohl, her pink lips a tight, unhappy line.

"What's it to you?" I asked.

"Everything. He's too good for you."

I flicked my eyebrows and turned my back on her.

"Hey!" She grabbed me. Her touch was like a shock of cold water on my arm and fire in my stomach. I froze, feeling the chill of inexplicable dread- and she must have felt it, too, because she let go and looked at me strangely: for a moment uncertain, then with hardening resolve. I noticed no-one else around us even looked our way. "Stay away from him, alright?!" I could smell her perfume: tangy, wild. Her eyes up close were like ice- unnaturally clear, but beautiful; hypnotic.

"He's a big boy," I reminded her with a voice that came out stronger than I felt, and turned away again.

"You think you were the only girl he slept with this summer?" she hissed, smiling to see the flash of hurt in my eyes when I looked back.

"You think he was the only boy *I* slept with?" I lied, as soon as it was out realising how bad it made me look. She shook her head, looking disgusted.

"Just stay away from him."

She turned and the sound rushed back at full volume, as if someone had turned it down for the benefit of our conversation.

I watched her disappear into the crowd. I was starting to think Ilia was right to warn me about the Morgans.

CHAPTER 16

"I can't believe she's doing this!" I said, watching Susan snogging the third boy of the night.

"It's her birthday," Nina pointed out, handing me an orange juice which Saba had bought. "Let her have some fun."

"While her boyfriend's in bed sick?"

"Lasha's only sick because he drank too much at the restaurant. And you saw them arguing before we left. Come on, just ignore her."

I tried to get back into the music but kept looking over at Susan. Her attitude really bothered me. Bothered me more than it would normally, though I couldn't explain why. It was like a scratching, niggling sensation that kept drawing my eyes back to her again and again, and the frustration at her flirting, at her betraying Lasha so blatantly, kept growing.

She went to the bar to get another drink, stopping to chat with Toma as she paid. They laughed.

Get away from him! I thought at her.

When Susan turned to talk to his sisters, Toma frowned, looking towards the stairs as if hearing something.

I followed his eye-line but couldn't see anything there that might have captured his attention. He looked back at Arabella, said something, and then started away towards the exit.

Susan watched him go hungrily and I scowled at her.

Don't you dare!

I caught Emily looking at me and turned my eyes away. When I looked back, her attention was on Susan. She whispered something in her ear and Susan, face suddenly alight with more than hunger: desire, nodded like an eager puppy and started off up the stairs.

I instinctively knew she was going after Toma.

Emily looked at me and winked, actually winked, before turning her back on me.

I knew she was setting me up, but the thought of Toma and Susan...*no. It was NOT happening.*

Without a glance back at Nina, I began pushing through the crowd towards the stairs.

CHAPTER 17

I went out onto the street and listened, though my ears were ringing from the music.

And it wasn't so much that I heard them, but sensed them.

They were half way up the steps to Baratishvili Bridge. I hid at the corner, watching them, ignoring the strange looks as new arrivals passed me and went in the glass entrance.

Toma was standing with his hands by his sides, his hood up. Susan was all over him, pushing herself on him.

He laughed at the attention, put one hand on her shoulder and leaned down towards her. The jealousy boiled like lava in my stomach.

No, no, no!

Toma stopped and looked up and I whipped back, a hand over my mouth.

Had I spoken aloud? I didn't think so.

I peeked back and saw Toma whispering in Susan's ear. She giggled and tilted her head up, her hands on his chest.

Suddenly, overwhelming, the jealousy burst out of me and I felt the venom, hate and envy leave me. Weakened without the strength of my anger, I collapsed to the ground.

CHAPTER 18

"Hey- up you get. Slowly..."

I struggled to focus my eyes as my mind crawled out of a black tunnel of darkness.

"Wha-?" I let Toma help me to my feet and self-consciously straightened my clothes. "What happened?" I asked. One minute I'd been dancing with my friends, the next I was outside on the pavement, slumped against the wall. I smoothed my hair back, my hands shaking.

"I was going to ask you the same thing," he said. Something in his face was off: suspicious, shocked...I couldn't place it. I noticed behind him, off to the side, there were three strange boys- one blond, one a red-head with a ponytail and another with dark skin and a shaved head. They were staring at me and talking amongst themselves.

I blushed and shook my head in answer to Toma's question, swallowing. My clothes were saturated with the smell of smoke and my voice was raw.

"You don't remember?" he pushed.

"I guess I blacked out," I said. "I don't remember coming up here... was I with you?"

He shook his head.

"I think I need to go home," I mumbled, shivering and wrapping my arms around myself.

"Let's get a taxi," he said, turning to the road.

"Wait...I...I need my coat. And bag. They're in the club."

"Give me the tag- I'll go get them for you."

He was looking at me, concerned now, but still a small smile curled his lips when I pulled the cloakroom tag out of my bra. He told me to stay put and I nodded agreement, absently rubbing my temples as he walked away, trying to remember and getting nothing.

I realised my right side was aching, as if I'd been sick and stretched the muscles there, though I couldn't taste any tell-tale bitterness in my mouth. My hand rubbed over a sensitive spot and I winced. When I lifted my shirt, I saw a dark bruise forming in the area of my scar. *Must've bumped myself when I fell,* I thought.

Then I remembered Nina. *I can't leave without telling her.* I glanced over and saw Toma at the entrance, speaking familiarly to the three boys. Then Toma shifted and I saw Arabella was with them. Suddenly, as if sensing me watching, they all stopped and looked my way. The blond said something and Toma frowned and replied, Arabella argued and Toma shook his head and then went in the door and down.

Arabella and the boys stopped speaking as I approached, looking me up and down, assessing, curious. The blond, in particular, looked almost too fascinated.

"You know her?" I heard one of the boys ask in Russian as I passed.

"She's in my sister's class at school," Arabella answered.

I couldn't stop: didn't want to. My head was pounding and I felt sick. I just wanted to go home, but first I had to tell Nina.

Toma didn't see me as I passed the cloakroom and went down into the club proper, stuck as he was in the crowd clamouring for jackets and bags.

I found Nina at the bar chatting to Emily. Toma's youngest sister threw me a haughty look, pushed away from the bar and nudged past me.

"Where were you?" Nina asked me. "God, you look like hell."

"I'm done for the night," I told her.

"Want me to come with?" she asked, a longing glance at the stage giving her away.

71

I shook my head. "Toma's going to grab me a taxi," I told her.

"The Bastard, Toma?"

I nodded and rubbed my right temple.

"Well, don't do anything stupid. And text me later, K?"

I nodded and gave her a hug and she wove her way back into the crowd.

I turned and bumped into someone's chest. Head down, I apologised, but he blocked my path when I tried to move around him.

"Look who we have here," he said in accented English, and I looked up to see the blond boy from upstairs. He was tall, half his head shaved, the other half flopping over into his eyes and damp with sweat, eyes a bright blue which caught the laser lights as the DJ worked his set. He had a tattoo on his neck- a scorpion. I instinctively knew he was bad news.

"Do I know you?" I asked, glancing around for Ilia. I hadn't seen him since the restaurant.

"Not yet. But you will...So, who is it? *Empusa? Hantu?*"

"I've no idea what you're talking about," I said, feeling my stomach twist.

"You just underage-killed someone and you don't know what I'm talking about?!" he asked mockingly.

I looked up at him sharply and saw him nod. "I saw you do it."

Of course, I knew I'd done nothing wrong. Killed? Who? No... This was just some sicko who could see I'd had one too much to drink and was trying to mess with me.

Disgusted, I shook my head and started to turn, but he held me in place.

"Get off me! I don't know what you're talking about!" I said, snatching my arm away, part scared, part angry.

"You wanna tell me you really don't remember what you did?" he asked in disbelief.

I shook my head, trying but failing again to remember. Nothing but a blank, and I was starting to panic.

"Ilia!" I breathed.

"Run!" A voice whispered back.

Was that Ilia? No way to find out without looking crazy in front of the blond, who was still looking at me, assessing, judging, as if weighing up his options. He seemed to come to a decision.

"Don't go anywhere," he warned. "I want you to meet my friend..."

He turned and beckoned to the tall red-head who was standing by the bar watching us.

"I'm here, but I'm stuck, Ela," Ilia's voice whispered near my ear.

I looked around me.

"I can't materialise," he explained. "Our dance earlier. You have to get out of here."

My heart was hammering. I had no idea who these boys were or what they wanted with me.

"Do you know them?" I asked quietly as the red-head approached.

"No, but I know they're trouble. Go! Now!"

As if his words were a start gun, I turned, bumping into people as I pushed through them to get to the stairs. Glancing behind me, I saw the blond and red-head following me but get caught in the middle of the writhing crowd. They passed Nina, dancing with her hands up and her hair flicking side-to-side. I hesitated.

"Leave her," Ilia said, reading my mind. "They aren't interested in her."

"What do they want with *me*?" I whined.

He didn't reply.

Finding energy through fear, I turned and bolted up the stairs, pushing roughly past the people coming in.

"What the-?"

"Hey!"

I ignored them.

Toma was nowhere to be seen and I didn't have time to look, so I ran the last few steps to the street and through the carpark- away from the club, away from my friends, away from Toma. It was stupid, but my feet had already taken me before my brain could process the risks. And the boys were chasing- I'd heard pounding feet on the club stairs and the angry cries of indignation as they pushed the other clubbers out of their way.

"Get a taxi," my angel advised, but although the area is usually busy with buses, minibuses, taxis and tourists traveling to and from Avlabari, the time of night meant there was barely any traffic. The one taxi that passed already had passengers in.

"Keep moving!" Ilia said.

"There she is!" I heard a voice shout.

I ran for it between the Antishkhati church and the Ambassadori hotel which was well-lit, warm, inviting, but empty, and past the dark and equally empty Gabriadze Cafe. A glance back showed the two- no, three- boys were crossing the street behind me.

"He said I killed someone," I panted at Ilia as I passed Hangar Bar and entered the narrow, cobbled street running towards the Patriarchy. As I passed it, I pushed on the door and found it locked shut: no refuge to be found with the Church.

"And did you?"

"I don't remember."

"I leave you alone for ten minutes..." Ilia lamented. I smiled but it turned into a grimace as I heard the boys gaining on me. I was a fast runner, and luckily, I'd chosen boots not heels, but I had a burning stitch by the time I reached Erekle 2nd Square.

"I...can't...run...anymore..." I panted, panicking, as I got to the road. I debated making a go for Apkhazi Street, thinking there might be other people around- the area was renowned for its bars and clubs: tourist central. But first I had to make it uphill through the residential streets and that would slow me down.

"Ilia?" I asked. Silence.

I decided to turn left, to run back along the riverbank road, get a car to stop and help. Maybe even go back to the club...

"Ilia?" I asked again, grabbing at my side and pushing myself forward as I heard the boys calling one of their number back where he'd started straight across the road to the square- I hadn't managed to hide on time and they'd seen me. As I flew round the corner of the Patriarchy wall, I stumbled and fell, crashing down on my knees. I felt the sting of open flesh and the warmth of blood.

I tried to get up, but the sound of feet rounding the corner and skidding to a stop behind me made me freeze.

"Gotcha!" the blond said.

CHAPTER 19

The red-head crouched down and I looked up at him through tears and messed-up hair while the two other boys loomed over me threateningly.

"You ran away before we could be introduced," he said. "I'm Alastor. What's your name?"

"E-Eliso," I said.

He gave a small admonishing frown. "No- I'm interested in your *real* name."

"That *is* my real name," I said.

"Don't play with us, girl. We don't take kindly to killers. You know that..."

"I..."

"Ela?" a voice asked. I turned my head and saw Toma walking towards us. His face changed in a second from confused to angry. Not taking his eyes off the boys, he held out a hand to me and helped me to my feet.

Alastor stood, too, and Toma stepped between us. Trembling with fear, exhaustion and pain, I held onto the back of his shirt, watching the boys warily.

"What are you doing?" he asked them.

"Chasing her," the blond answered in Russian.

"I told you before- she's mine," Toma replied, also in Russian. I'd had no idea he could speak it.

"But you know what she is, right? What she did?" the blond asked him.

"I do. And so does my father," Toma told them.

At that, the three glanced at each other uncertainly, trying and failing to look unfazed.

"She should be locked up," Alastor growled.

"You'd better stop talking now," Toma warned, his voice hard and cold as ice.

"You've got until the solstice to sort it out," the blond said.

"I know," Toma confirmed.

I watched and listened, struggling to stay upright.

"Good. If not..."

"What? *You'll* do it?" Toma suggested with a sneer, his eyes taking in each of them in turn.

The blond squared his shoulders. "If we have to."

"Get out of here," Toma snapped. "And keep your mouths shut. Nobody else needs to know about this. If you blab, I'll find you. And Father will not be happy."

The boys stiffened, their nerves showing through. Then, with a dirty look thrown my way, the three stepped around us and headed back to the club.

CHAPTER 20

"Are you ok?" Toma asked, speaking in English again.

I wiped my wet cheeks with my sleeve and nodded.

"Taxi time," he said, stepping to the curb-side, one hand in his jacket pocket, the other out, ready to wave.

"Friends of yours?" I wondered, leaning on the wall, trying to get my breath back.

"Kind of."

"So, what got them so interested in me?"

"You being half-British," he said, not meeting my eye.

"You're lying."

Now he did look at me. He smiled but didn't answer.

"They wouldn't believe my name was Eliso."

"That's strange," he said, keeping his eyes on the road.

"And what's supposed to be happening on the solstice?"

At this he frowned, but just then a taxi appeared.

He waved it over to us and they negotiated the price in Georgian. Toma opened the door.

"You're not coming?" I asked, unable to stop myself feeling disappointed.

He shook his head. "I live near Marjanishvili," he said.

"Oh, ok."

"Here," he said, digging my mobile out of his pocket. "The jacket and bag are with Arabella- Emily'll bring them to class tomorrow."

"Thanks," I said.

I got in and he shut the door. I pressed the window button and it wound down as the driver put the car in gear.

"Be careful," Toma said, glancing over my shoulder. Then he turned away.

I put up the window and sat back as the taxi pulled out, seeing Ilia now semi-transparent beside me.

"Are you ok?" he asked quietly, taking my hand, though I couldn't feel him as he still didn't have his full strength back.

I nodded and unlocked my phone, feeling far from ok. My thumbs hesitated over the screen. Then I took a breath and typed the question I'd really wanted to ask Toma:

ME: What did u mean when u told those boys I'm "yours"?

He replied in seconds.

TOMA: Aren't you?

CHAPTER 21

"Oww, my head…" I groaned.

Emily walked past and dropped my bag and coat on the desk with a bang. I winced. My scowl only got a sweet smile from her.

"Sorry. Too loud?"

Nina stuck a finger up at her on my behalf and Emily gave her a cold glare.

"Susan's not here," I pointed out quietly as the teacher began the lesson.

"Not surprised. Did you see the way she was eating that guy's face?!" Nina asked.

"Yeah. So much for having a boyfriend," I said, frowning, trying to grab hold of a memory that skipped, wisp-like, away from me.

"Speaking of which, did you see Lasha come?"

She shook her head. "Hang on, I'll text Saba."

The answer that came back was 'no'.

"Maybe he's feeling the way you look," she whispered with a grin.

I swore at her and buried my head in my arms, praying the aspirin would kick in soon.

"Who has a birthday on a school night?!" I complained.

"Who drinks so much on a school night?" Ilia commented helpfully from where he stood leaning against the window.

I checked no one was looking and stuck my tongue out at him. He laughed, then glanced behind me and disappeared.

I looked back to see Emily staring transfixed at the exact spot where he'd been. I remembered what my angel said about the Morgans being able to sense him.

But how could they? I wondered.

When I looked again, Emily's head was back in her book.

At lunchtime, we called Susan. She didn't answer. She hadn't even logged in to read our morning messages on Facebook and she was a social media nut. We even phoned Lasha but he hadn't heard from her either.

"Maybe we should go round to her house and check after school?" I wondered.

"I'll go. She's just up the road from me."

"Ok. And let me know."

"Er...it looks like The Bastard wants to talk to you," she hissed.

I glanced over to the doorway and saw Toma beckoning me.

I turned to Nina and grimaced, then set my face neutral and, hoisting my rucksack on my shoulder, put my tray on the shelf and left the canteen. The corridor outside was empty but for us. As I brushed past him, he caught hold of my hand and squeezed gently.

"How are you feeling?" he asked, his voice filled with quiet concern.

I frowned down at our joined hands and pulled away.

"Hungover, but fine. Why?" I replied coldly.

His eyes widened in surprise. A group of sixth years burst out behind me, squabbling and laughing, and he waited till they'd passed before speaking again.

"You don't remember?"

"Last night? I remember your sisters threatening me. I remember hearing about the numerous girls you slept with after you dumped me in Ureki, I remember dancing with my friends and those crazy boyfriends of yours chasing me for no obvious reason..."

And I remember your text, I thought, but didn't say.

"Ari and Emi threatened you?"

I nodded and crossed my arms so he couldn't take my hand again, even though 70 percent of me wanted him to. The other 30 percent was fuming that he hadn't denied my accusation about the beds he'd shared this summer.

"And you've got no memory of anything else?" he asked, frowning, looking confused.

"No. I got drunk, didn't I."

My head throbbed and I pressed two fingers to my right temple, wincing.

"If you don't mind, I need to go and get another aspirin."

I turned to leave but he grabbed my arm. His body was so close, I could feel the heat of him. His face was inches from mine. My breath caught as I looked up at him.

"You really don't remember?" he asked, his voice intense but still quiet.

I frowned, trying to push my memory through the thick fog that coated it, but nothing budged, so I shrugged and shook my head. For a delicious moment, his eyes searched mine. I wanted him to lean down and kiss me; to light me up like he had in Ureki. I wasn't sure what I'd do if he did- push him away or give in to it. He didn't give me the choice, though: his expression cooled and he let me go and stepped back.

"I'll talk to my sisters- tell them to lay off."

"Don't bother," I said dryly. "I'll be keeping my distance, as requested."

"Ela..," he started, reaching out. I held both hands up and backed away, shaking my head. Then I turned around and walked quickly up the corridor, head down so no-one would see the tears in my eyes.

CHAPTER 22

NINA: OMGOMG

ME: What?

NINA: Susan.

ME: What about her?

NINA: She's missing. The police are here.

ME: I'm coming.

I pulled on my jacket and ran out to the lift, calling Levan on the way down to take me to Vake. Luckily, he hadn't set off home yet.

"Everything ok?" he asked, seeing my worried expression.

"I don't know," I admitted, then settled back into the leather seat, biting my nails and looking blindly out the window. Missing? How could one of our friends be missing? That kind of thing just didn't happen here. It was the stuff of movies, not Tbilisi.

"Maybe she fell asleep somewhere..." Ilia had suggested as I was putting on my shoes.

"It's been a whole day!" I said.

"Maybe she went off with that boy you mentioned."

"That would be beyond forgivable. She's got a boyfriend for God's sake..."

"Well, I'm sure they'll find her."

"It's not like her to not call or text, though. Hey- do you remember what he looked like?" I didn't trust my alcohol-memory but Ilia might have taken in more than I could see.

He thought about it and wagged his hand side to side in a so-so gesture. "I wasn't so strong last night after our dance...I was coming and going. But maybe it won't matter," he said. "Maybe she'll turn up."

The police cars outside her apartment block on Abashidze, lights painting the street blue and red, told me that she hadn't turned up.

Nina was standing outside with some of our friends and a lot of gossiping neighbours.

"What's the latest?" I asked, hugging her.

"Well it's not been 24 hours yet...but..." her eyes glistened and I took her hand.

"What, Ni?"

"Someone found her coat on the bridge near the club ...but that's the only sign..."

"How'd they know it was hers?" I wondered.

"You know her gran still sews those kiddie name tags into her jackets," a 12th grader friend of ours, Megan, said.

"Have you seen her family?" I asked them.

"Her mum's a real mess. The police are in there now," Megan said, glancing up at the block above us.

"They said we should stick around. They'll need to question us," Nina said.

I rubbed my mouth, feeling my hands shaking.

"Are you ok?" Ilia whispered. "You look white."

I shook my head and he nodded to a concrete flower pot, inviting me to sit. But I couldn't keep still- I paced, waiting for news with the rest of them.

"What do you think happened to her?" I asked them.

"The first suspect is that boy," Nina said with a dark look. "But I don't really remember what he looked like..."

"Me neither."

"Tall, dark haired...a shirt- maybe red."

"I thought it was purple."

I swore and paced some more, trying to remember more from the night. After Emily's warning, I'd gone straight to the bar, ignoring

Toma's smile and the desire to grab him- instead grabbing my drink, downing it, then pushing back into the crowd. I shouldn't have had that vodka on top of the restaurant liquor. But I was feeling annoyed- reminded of that summer rejection; upset about Emily and Arabella's animosity towards me; angry that Toma had clearly used me, and not only me... So, I'd danced as sexily as I could. I got a lot of attention. It was stupid, especially without Ilia to help me, but I'd wanted Toma to see what he was missing, and to show all three Morgans that they couldn't hurt me.

Susan was dancing very intimately with a boy. I remember feeling disgusted, angry, even, that she would do that to Lasha. I remember thinking it would serve her right if he turned out to be a sleazebag. Like Toma. My mood darkened further. While I was dancing with three boys I didn't know, Nina handed me an orange juice. Hot from dancing, I'd downed it gratefully. The bitter taste told me there wasn't only juice in the cup. That second shot of vodka was the last thing I remembered before waking up in the street with no memory and Toma looking down at me with that strange suspicious look in his eyes.

My phone pinged.

A Facebook message from someone called 'Demon'.

There were no words – just a YouTube video.

I wasn't in the mood and turned the screen off.

"Nina Tsereteli and Eliso Machabeli?" a man's voice asked.

I looked up, startled, to see a grey-haired policeman in a dark blue uniform standing at the entrance to the building peering at the crowd. A part of me wanted to shrink back and quietly creep away. It wasn't like I'd done anything, but police always made me feel guilty for some reason.

"Here," Nina said, grabbing my sleeve and pulling me forward. The crowd parted to let us through- voices whispering: some curious, some suspicious, others mourning the fate of our friend.

They asked simple questions, looked disapproving when I explained drunkenness as the reason I couldn't remember, and leaned forward in interest when I tried to describe the last boy I remembered Susan kissing. Half-way through the interview, a female police officer with sizeable hips came in and spoke quietly to grey-hair.

"The videos from the club are in," she whispered.

He nodded then looked at me. "You can go. But give your number to Officer Lena here, in case we need to contact you again."

Shaking, I did as I was told and took her card in return.

Once outside, the small group from our school decided to go to Domino's, feeling too nervous and helpless to wait at home for news.

As we sat waiting for our pizzas, I got out my phone to scroll through Facebook.

The video from 'Demon' popped up again and I played it, frowning more deeply as it went on.

Nina came back from washing her hands and saw my expression. "What's up?"

"I got a video sent to me earlier," I told her. "I didn't have time to look. It's a song."

"Cool. Which one?"

"'My Songs Know What You Did in the Dark'. It's got the lyrics, too. Look."

"Pretty good," Nina said when it got to the chorus.

"Why do you think they sent it to me?"

"First- who's 'they'?"

"No idea. 'Demon'... no other name."

"Check their page."

It was a fake account. The profile picture showed a black square with two watchful red eyes. There were no photos and no contact details. It was as if the account had been set up just to send me that message.

"Should I reply?" I wondered.

Suddenly, the green dot appeared in the message box. 'Demon' was online.

"Who are you?" I demanded.

DEMON: The witness. The watcher. The avenger.

"A comic strip nut," I summarised, making Nina laugh.

Don't message me again, I typed.

DEMON: Then don't kill anyone again.

The green dot blinked out and I dropped the phone, feeling the blood leave my face.

"This is crazy," I said shakily.

"What did he mean?" Nina wondered. I shook my head.

"Susan's gone and this 'Demon' is clearly accusing me of being the..." I shut my mouth as the waiter brought our pizzas, then leaned towards her: "of being the killer!"

"Don't worry," she reassured me. "It's just some nasty piece of who gets off on winding traumatized classmates up. We don't know Susan is...you know. Maybe you should show the police," she suggested, catching the cheese strings dripping off her pizza with her tongue.

"Come with me," I said, getting up and pulling her with me to the bathroom. I checked the cubicles were empty then turned and faced her, my hands gripping the edge of the sink so hard my knuckles went white.

"What's going on, El?" she asked, looking scared.

"Tell me everything you remember about what I did last night at the club," I begged her.

She shrugged. "You got drunk, got angry about Susan getting off with all those boys... but you walked away to cool off," she said quickly, seeing my eyes widening.

"Walked off where?" I asked.

She shrugged. "I guess outside. I was asking Emily if she'd seen you when you turned up looking ill."

"How long was I gone?" I asked.

"Er...not more than ten minutes...I'm not sure, actually..."

Just enough time to kill someone? I wondered, for the first time seriously considering the possibility of it, however crazy unlikely it was. *To kill Susan?*

"Don't you remember what happened?" Nina asked quietly.

I shook my head and told her what happened after I woke up outside.

"Did you tell the police about those boys?" she exclaimed.

I shook my head again.

"Are you *crazy*?! You just told me the blond accused you of killing Susan, then chased you! Now you've got this 'Demon' stalker..."

She took out her phone.

"What are you doing?" I asked.

"Phoning Lena."

"The policewoman?"

She nodded. I reached out and snatched the phone away from her.

"Hey!" she complained.

"Please don't," I begged.

"Come on! You have the key to the case- those boys might know where Susan is!"

"What if I killed her?" I whispered, the horror of it sending a shudder down my spine.

"Of course, you didn't!" Ilia said.

"No way!" Nina exclaimed.

She came close and grabbed the hand not holding her phone.

"Ela- you got drunk and passed out," she insisted.

"But I was angry at her. What if...?"

"No!" my friend stopped me. "But those boys might have."

"They said they saw me do it...if I tell the police on them, they'll turn it back on me," I said weakly. "*And* they're Toma's friends."

"His, not yours. You don't know him. And they can say what they want but you are innocent."

I glanced at Ilia and he raised his eyebrows pointedly.

Nina held out her hand for her phone. I hesitated.

"It's the right thing to do," Ilia reassured me.

I swallowed and gave it to her, my stomach lurching in fear.

CHAPTER 23

"We need to talk," Ilia said after Levan brought me home from the police station that evening. Dad had come with a lawyer, then gone back to work once the formalities were over.

"Pass me my pyjamas," I begged tiredly as I pulled off my tights.

I saw Ilia's hand appear, my thin strappy nightgown hanging on his fingers. I looked up at him and saw him deliberately looking the other way.

Always so polite, I thought. *You'd never guess he grew up a farmer's boy.*

"What is it?"

"Get dressed, then we'll talk."

I stood and stepped into the nightie, pulling it up over my hips, bringing the spaghetti straps over my shoulders. I swear I could feel his eyes on me. Smiling, I swept my hair off my back.

"Could you do the buttons up?" I asked, watching him in the mirror.

He stepped forward and took hold of the lowest button, his fingers twisting it into the hole quickly before moving onto the next, tightening the fabric around my ribs. His fingers brushed the back of my neck as he finished and I shivered uncontrollably, feeling my heart skip a beat. I looked at him in the mirror and he held my gaze. Then he frowned.

"It's about Toma," he said.

"Not that again..." I sighed, starting to turn away.

"And his sisters and those boys the police are looking for."

I frowned and rubbed my fingertips together where they'd inked me, *"just a precaution...and don't leave town,"* Officer Lena had told me.

"They're dangerous, El," Ilia said now.

"Ari and Emily maybe...the boys definitely...but Toma saved me from drowning at the beach," I argued. "And last night he got rid of those boys..."

"His friends," Ilia pointed out.

"...and put me in a taxi," I finished.

"He's still one of them, however much the gentleman he acts."

"For all I know, *I'm* dangerous!" I exclaimed.

"Ela," he said softly, putting a hand on my shoulder, a comforting weight. I looked at him, the tears in my eyes blurring his outline. "You had nothing to do with Susan's disappearance."

"How do you know?" I asked. "Did you see?"

He shook his head. "I told you I was more out than in after dancing. But I know you. And I know what they are."

"What do you...?"

"They're demons, Ela."

"You mean like the one who sent that Facebook message? Is it a gang or something?"

"That one I don't know. But I know the triplets and those boys are the real deal. Actual demons. I didn't want to tell you this way but it's better out than in."

"They say that about wind, not about shocking news of the supernatural variety," I pointed out, my voice shaking.

He gave me a reluctant smile and moved to hold back the sheets for me to get into bed, covering me and coming around to the other side to sit next to me, fading to preserve energy.

"Are you sure?" I asked, feeling cold. "I thought that stuff was just Church propaganda."

"Like angels?" he asked with a wry smile.

"Ha ha. So, what does it mean exactly? Toma goes home, turns red and grows horns and a tail?"

Ilia laughed. "No!"

"So?"

"He's human but inside he's hosting a demon."

"And he knows this, right?"

"Of course. The body is human but what talks and thinks is the demon."

"Jeez..." I said, sitting a moment in shock. "What happened to the real triplets? And how did a demon get in?"

"I don't know exactly," Ilia replied. "But I heard they tear the human souls out of the bodies when they're babies...then the demons take over."

Boom! My mind flashed to another place and time. *A dark room, old fashioned flaming torches. People in long red cloaks, me lying on a cold surface in front of them. Voices chanting. I look around, then blackness fills my vision.*

"Where's daddy?" I ask.

A pain in my side, whispered words... Then Daddy's voice, shouting, screaming in anger... and cold fingers of sensation spreading out from my right hip, up and outwards over my abdomen.

I sat up as if I'd been electrocuted.

"What is it?" Ilia asked, a hand on my back, his eyes alight with worry.

I shook my head, clearing it, and realised I had a hand to my right side, the ghost of a pain there fading fast, though yesterday's bruise had been gone when I woke up.

A knock at the door and Ilia disappeared as my dad stuck his head round. He was dressed in his suit, just back from the office. It was past 3am.

"How're you doing?" he asked.

"Ok," I said with a shrug.

"Petre called about your riding class tomorrow- they're postponing it until Sunday. Some show-jumping competition..."

"I know. He messaged me, too."

He nodded. Then frowned. "Mrs B said you got back late last night. By taxi."

I shrugged.

"It was Susan's birthday. We went to Night Office after dinner."

"Then you got chased by random boys," he said. "I remember the story. Why didn't you call Levan?"

"At 3am? He already did a 12-hour day for me."

"That's his job," dad pointed out.

I sighed.

"Why can't you just let me have even a teensy bit of independence?" I whined.

"You just came under fire in a possible murder investigation, Ela. You're still a child."

"I'm 16!" I argued.

"A 16-year-old who doesn't understand just how cruel this world can be!" he said.

My retort died in my throat and I looked at him, frowning, then glanced at Ilia beside me, wishing he could mind-read, because what I was thinking was: Did he know something?

"What do you mean, dad?"

He gave a deep sigh and rubbed a hand tiredly over his face. When he looked back at me, he looked haggard.

"I'm sorry, Ela. Nothing. It's just been a rough day. We're being audited...the team are tough...it's...well, what with Susan going missing..."

"You know I didn't do it, right?" I said in a small voice.

He nodded, but made no move to come and comfort me. "Of course, sweetie. They caught the boys."

I sat up straighter.

"Really? When?"

"An hour ago. I got a call from a friend. No-one else knows yet."

I swallowed. So, tomorrow the police would be coming for me...

"Did they find Susan, too?" I asked.

"No. And we don't know that she's actually dead - the boys are just being questioned at this stage."

"But..."

"Just be careful, ok?" he said, interrupting me. "I'll let you get some sleep."

He turned to go.

"Dad," I said, stopping him.

He waited.

"I'm sorry I made you worry."

He smiled. "How's Misha?"

"He likes to be called Mikey, dad."

"He's part Georgian. He's Misha to me!"

"Whatever. He's good."

I wanted to say, 'he misses you' but realised this was no time to be sending our dad on a guilt trip.

"See you at breakfast," he promised.

I nodded, knowing better- he'd be gone back to the office well before me and Mikey were up, Saturday or not.

"Goodnight."

"Goodnight, Ela."

He shut the door and Ilia re-materialised next to me. I shifted down under the covers and moved my head so he could lay down and share my pillow.

"What did you see before your dad came in?" my angel asked.

I shrugged. "I don't know. It felt like a memory but..." I shook my head again, remembering the sound of my child's voice asking for my father and the pain in my abdomen.

"Do you think he knows something?" I wondered. "Cruel world, demons…"

"How could he?"

I shrugged again.

"So, Toma and his sisters are demons in human form…" I said, thinking. "What do you think they want at my school?"

"I'm hoping it's not because of you," he said.

"Why would you think that?"

He shrugged. "Because of me."

"Can they see you?" I asked, remembering Emily in school today.

"I'm not sure. But they might be able to sense me."

"What are demons, exactly? And how can you pick them out from regular people?"

"They're spirits who use hosts to keep them existing over the ages. I can see the darkness in them…I can't explain how, but I can."

"Why didn't you tell me before?"

He shrugged. "I never had reason to."

"Protecting me?"

He smiled. "Isn't life exciting enough with an angel around? You want more paranormality?"

It was my turn to smile.

"Werewolves, witches, vampires? Do they exist, too?"

"Now that *is* crazy!" he said.

"Tell me more about demons."

"I don't know much. I know they seem to thrive on hurting people for their own amusement…and the last thing I want is for you to get hurt," he said.

"Toma's never acted like he wants to hurt me."

"Except by breaking your heart," Ilia pointed out. "And I still don't trust him."

"So those boys chasing me were demons, too?" I asked, still struggling to take it in.

He nodded.

"That's a lot of demons for a small city. You know, they seemed kinda worried about Toma's dad...and scared of Toma, actually..." I said, remembering how he'd told them to keep quiet about me. Maybe they wouldn't say anything to the police after all.

"You could understand what they were saying?!" Ilia cut in, surprised.

"Yeah," I said with a confused smile. "It was Russian. I thought even you knew..."

"That was *not* Russian," he said.

"It was!"

He shook his head. "I've no idea what it was but it was definitely *not* Russian."

"So, how come I could understand it? I'm good at languages but..."

Ilia took a deep breath, shaking his head. "I don't like it."

I bit my lip, frowning.

"So, what did they say?" he asked after a moment.

I told him.

"Toma's higher up in the demon ranking than those boys. His dad's regional head," Ilia told me as explanation for their reaction to him.

"Like a president?"

"More or less," Ilia agreed.

"Jeez...but how do you know?"

"I've been listening in, piecing it together."

"Listening to who?"

"The triplets."

"They seemed convinced I did something wrong," I said, frowning down at my phone as I twirled it between my fingers.

"*I'm* convinced they're mistaken. You the 'goodest' person I know," he said.

"You're biased."

"True," he said with a smile.

"Any idea why they were talking about the solstice?"

"Nope."

"You don't have a hotline to God, by any chance?"

"He doesn't have that kind of phone-in service, no," Ilia said with a smile.

I unlocked my phone and typed something. When I saw the result, I frowned, then turned the screen so Ilia could see. He didn't look happy.

"What does it mean?" I asked.

"There are two solstices- December and June..."

"June 21st to be exact- my birthday."

"Yes. That's the summer one. On both days, they say the gates between worlds are wide open. There's a lot of spiritual traffic- that's the day I came to you, on your fourth birthday. Do you remember?" He looked at me curiously.

I shook my head. I couldn't remember anything of my life before Ilia.

"What's the solstice got to do with me, though?" I wondered, switching the phone off and putting it on the bedside table.

"I don't know," Ilia replied.

I snuggled into him, wanting to feel safe, but reeling inside. Demons...Susan...the police...and Toma, Toma, Toma.

The world suddenly felt like a much darker place. I hoped Ilia was enough to protect me from it.

CHAPTER 24

At lunchtime, I walked to Nina's gran's house- a flat on the Mtatsminda plateau with a view up to the Mama Daviti church and a pantheon filled with the graves of Georgian's best writers, philosophers and artists. Beyond it, at the top of the mountain, was the Funicular complex of restaurants topping the 500-meter funicular railway, first built at the beginning of the 20th century and renovated a few years ago. Behind it was Mtatsminda Park and the Bombora theme park. I'd come to meet Nina to go up there with her for a *ponchiki* doughnut and coffee. She'd slept at her gran's house last night- putting off the questions her parents were guaranteed to bombard her with once she got home. Most Georgian grannies were over-protective and paranoid, but Nina's gran, who we all called Tata Bebo, was cool.

A few hundred meters to the right of the funicular building was the iconic red and white TV tower, and my eyes were magnetically drawn up to it as I arrived outside Tata Bebo's old building.

As I went into the rickety, old, shared courtyard, I wondered- not for the first time- why Tata chose to stay here when her son-in-law owned a 5-bedroom house in Tskneti. But she was a stubborn old bat, and she'd grown up in the flat here with her four siblings, so she was kind of set in her ways.

The warm spicy smell of tarragon and boiling beef made my stomach grumble even though I knew I could never eat it. Tata Bebo's Chakapuli was legendary. I ran the last few steps up and walked along the wooden communal balcony into her kitchen. It was a tiny two-room kitchen-diner, separated from the main house and sleeping area in that strange, broken, higgledy-piggeldy way so many Tbilisi houses had adopted in Soviet times.

"Eliso!" Tata Bebo cried when she saw me, enveloping me in an immense hug. I hugged her back, comforted by her familiar smell of cooking and lavender.

"Tata Bebo," I said, kissing her cheek and pulling away.

"Skinny as ever; we need to feed you up!" she said in Georgian.

I laughed. She always complained at my figure- less than half the size of hers.

"If I was the size of a house, you'd still think I was too skinny!" I replied, dumping my bag by the door and hanging up my jacket. "Is Nina around?"

"She just woke up. She's speaking to Giorgi on the computer," she told me, her voice dropping in disapproval of her granddaughter's relationship with an older boy.

"You know he's good for her," I said.

"Hmm," she replied. "But he's so far away."

"She loves him," I said with a shrug.

"You're too young to know what love is," Tata Bebo said fondly, glancing at the black-and-white photo of her late husband that hung on the far wall.

"Are you expecting guests?" I asked as she turned and bustled back into the kitchen, for the first time noticing the table laid out with plates, forks and a variety of salads.

She was a big socialiser was Nina's gran- she always had girl-friends round to chat and play cards, or gentleman friends to play backgammon and chess. Tata Bebo's kitchen was a hub of activity. Today was clearly no exception.

"Saba and his friends are coming," she said. "They asked for my Chakapuli," she added proudly.

"Then I'll grab Nina and we'll get out the way."

"No, you won't!" Tata Bebo insisted, coming out with a plate laden with salty guda and creamy sulguni cheese in one hand and a basket of Georgian shoti bread and cornbread patties in the other. "You stay and eat!"

"If you're sure the boys won't mind," I said with a grin, grabbing a piece of bread and biting off a chunk.

"I insist!" she said, smiling.

I heard the pounding of feet and voices coming up the stairs, deep laughter and a back being slapped.

Then Saba burst into the room, followed by Mate.

"Rogor har, be?" Saba asked, kissing his gran.

"As always," she said, glowing with pleasure.

"Smells great!" Mate said, peering appreciatively over her shoulder at the bubbling pot on the stove.

"Sit!" Tata Bebo commanded.

"Hey, El," Mate said. "Didn't see you there."

I got up and kissed them all on the cheek.

"Heard you were taken in yesterday," Saba said, his expression serious.

I nodded. "They just asked me questions, took my prints...but they caught the boys we think did it last night."

"No kidding! Glad to hear it!" Mate said, giving me a pat on the shoulder.

I smiled. "No Lasha?" I asked, glancing behind them.

"He's...not up for hanging around right now," Saba said. "Hey, Toma, aren't you coming in?" he called out the door.

My stomach clenched. Toma was here?

"Who's Toma?" Tata Bebo asked, bringing in a plate of cheesebread which the boys fell on hungrily.

"New guy," Saba told her. "He's outside smoking."

"You boys are too young to be ruining your lungs with all that," Tata said, tutting.

"Be," Saba said, complaining. "We're nearly 18..."

She shook her head sadly and turned back to the cooking.

"Let me help you," I said, jumping to my feet and following her into the kitchen.

My hands were shaking as I picked up the fresh bunch of spring onions on the draining board and began washing.

"Sit, *shvilo*," Tata scolded, trying to take it from me.

"I'm ok," I told her.

"Then I'll just go and get the compote," she said. "Turn the potatoes when you're done washing, dear," she said, nodding towards the frying pan.

I swallowed and glanced up as she walked out the door, listening as she stopped outside to say a few words to Toma- though I couldn't hear what over the chatter of the boys and the oil in the pan. I kept my back to the dining table as Toma came in, deliberately not looking that way, terrified of how he'd react to me after I'd got his friends arrested.

"The new boy seems nice," Tata Bebo said when she came back a few minutes later with a two-litre jar of peach compote, which she then decanted into a jug. "And his Georgian is quite good."

I shrugged, blushing and avoiding her eyes as I took the jug from her. She frowned, seeing my blush, and I turned before she could question me.

"Good one, El!" Saba said, eyeing the compote thirstily. "I've got a hell of a hangover..." then he put his hand over his mouth and glanced towards the kitchen.

"I'll pretend I didn't hear that," his *bebia* called.

The boys laughed and I handed Saba the jug, deliberately ignoring Toma. But Saba saw it.

"You remember Toma, don't you, Ela?" he asked with a wicked grin.

I scowled at him as Toma moved over, forcing me to have to sit next to him.

Then I switched on a smile. "Of course, I do," I said with false brightness.

"Hi," Toma said with a smile, as if we hadn't had a heated moment not 24 hours ago.

"Hi," I answered, blushing and looking down at the table.

Demon, demon, demon... I had so many questions inside but I felt terrified of the answers, so I sat and said nothing.

Tata Bebo served the chips, promising the Chakapuli would follow soon, and the boys helped themselves, throwing jokes and comments across the table noisily. Nina came in the same time the main dish was served, looking pristine in a shirt and jeans.

"Move over," she told me, forcing me and Toma to shuffle up.

I was very aware of Toma's thigh pressed against mine.

He's a demon, he's a demon! I thought at myself. But I still felt more hot than scared. Even the anger I'd felt yesterday seemed to have evaporated with my hangover.

"So, El, tell us about those boys who-" Saba started, quickly stopping when he got a sharp kick from Mate, who shot a meaningful look in Toma's direction. I looked, too, but Toma was deliberately focused on serving himself salad.

"So, where are we going?" Mate asked Nina's cousin around a mouthful of beef, changing the subject.

"I was thinking about Borjomi," Saba answered from his place at the head of the table.

"What about Borjomi?" Nina asked.

"We're going camping next weekend while the weather's still good."

"Camping? You be careful of wolves," Tata Bebo said, topping up the compote.

"Of course, *be,*" Saba answered carelessly, reaching for more bread to dip in his soup.

"Why don't we invite Ela and Nina?" Toma suggested in English, not looking at me.

"I'll have to ask mum and dad, but I'm sure they'll be ok with it," Nina said when I shrugged.

I knew my dad probably wouldn't even notice I was gone. Or he'd be away on another business trip, leaving me in the care of Geta, our housekeeper, and Mrs Beridze. Camping, even with a demon, was better than being stuck at home eating Mrs B's borsch.

"We'd need an extra tent," Mate pointed out.

"I've got one," Toma said.

"You should bring your sisters along," Saba told him with gleam in his eye, clearly still not over his summer fling with Arabella.

I threw a worried look at Nina behind Toma's back and she shrugged helplessly.

"Sure," Toma said.

Make that three *demons,* I thought, gulping my compote nervously.

"Saba's the biggest wolf there is- you watch your sisters!" Nina warned him with a laugh, punching Saba lightly on the arm.

"I'm sure they can handle themselves," Toma told her, glancing at me.

I felt my cheeks grow hot.

"You're the only guy I know who actually enjoys hanging with his little sisters," I said.

"There's only a few minutes between us," he replied, filling up my glass and then his.

Meaning he tore the soul out of a baby first? I wondered grimly.

"The more girls the merrier," Saba said.

Nina rolled her eyes. "Yes. We can keep *Ana* company," she said pointedly in Georgian.

Ana was Saba's latest hot item.

"I think Saba will be keeping her company enough," Toma said, and everyone laughed.

"Shut up!" Saba warned, glancing out the window to where Tata Bebo stood chatting with her elderly neighbour, Tsira. Their gran definitely didn't approve of Saba's over-active love life. Luckily, this time she was out of ear-shot.

CHAPTER 25

The week passed quickly, though it didn't start well, with my horse- Enguri- throwing me twice. I'd been riding since I was eight, with Ilia helping me when the teacher was busy with other kids. He used to ride bare-back in his village and won all the riding competitions during the festivals- so it was thanks to him I was so good at it. But this Sunday, Enguri- usually quite docile- had been skittish and uncomfortable with me.

"He was fine with Beka before me," I'd grumbled to Petre after my second hard fall, dabbing at the cut on my forehead. Beka was the yard-help and always fed, groomed and warmed Enguri up before I arrived.

"I know. I really don't get what's got into him," my teacher had replied, watching as Enguri shied away from my hand, whinnying in uncertainty.

"Yeah, it's like he doesn't even recognise me."

Then, at school, our teachers started drilling us about the mid-terms we had to study for, and doubling our homework. Stress, worry, Susan still missing... but all me and Nina could talk about was the up-coming camping trip; what to wear, what to take, what might happen...

Nina invited me to Tbilisi Mall on Thursday and I maxed the card dad had given me: sleeping bag, thick socks, hiking boots, a few new vests, a jacket, a new hoodie and skinny jeans. I bought everything with Toma in mind, though I'd only seen him twice- on both occasions in passing in the corridor. I just couldn't get him out of my head and though I tried to act indifferent, I'd catch myself staring at his last message to me, my thumb hovering over the reply button but not daring to do it. Ilia was not happy with my obsessing but whenever we were alone, he now deliberately kept off the subject of the Morgans.

"What do you think?" Nina asked, coming out of the changing room wearing an emerald dress. I was about to tell her how wrong it was for a trip to the wilds of Borjomi when she held up her phone. It was a white Putin Khuilo vest. I grinned. I already had two.

"That's what took you so long in there, online shopping?"

She grinned. "I was inspired."

"Can they deliver tomorrow?"

"Hey- did you hear about Susan?" Megan asked, appearing beside us, looking excited.

"No, what?" we both asked at the same time.

"They're saying someone pushed her off the bridge!"

"What?!"

"No way!"

"They're saying they found a video of it. Those boys were there."

"They pushed her?"

She shook her head. "Apparently, they weren't anywhere near her. But someone was."

"Who?"

She shrugged.

"They're not saying. I heard the video is glitchy and they're still trying to clean it up."

"Are you sure she didn't just...jump?" I wondered.

"But she was so happy," Nina said, frowning.

"She was drunk," I reminded her, feeling my face flush and my heart speed up as a mix of guilt and worry washed through me.

"Have they found her body?" my friend asked Megan.

"No," she replied. "They're dredging the river as far as Abano-tubani tomorrow. But my guess is she'd be in Azerbaijan already."

We remembered the story of the penguin which survived the 2015 flood that killed 20 people and half the zoo animals- he'd been found near the Azeri border some days later, alive.

"Do you think she could've survived?" I wondered hopefully.

Megan shook her head and we shared a moment of quiet reflection.

"Anyway, gotta go." Megan kissed our cheeks. "Have a good camping trip."

The next day Nina wasn't at school. And she wasn't answering my calls or messages, either. Saba's entire group was on study leave so I had no idea what was happening and I was more than a little freaked considering Susan was still missing. I got the school receptionist to call her mum, who confirmed she was home safe, and then sent my friend a pile of angry messages for making me worry for nothing.

Finally, that evening, she replied.

NINA: Bad news, gran got flu. Can't come.

I groaned as I looked at the phone screen, sinking down onto the bed next to my rucksack and sleeping bag. It was Friday night and I was getting ready for the weekend adventure but my best friend had just killed my mood. I started typing, my thumbs moving fast across the screen.

ME: Ur bailing on me? Can't ur mum look after her?

NINA: Mum on double shift this wknd, remember? Dad useless. All on me. Feel like I'm coming dwn w it 2.

ME: Come on, please? U were fine yesterday!

NINA: Sorry. Night of the living dead over here. No choice. U go, have fun.

ME: No u, no fun.

NINA: No me, lotsa Toma= fun + more!

ME: grrr.

NINA: Haha.

ME: I thought u didn't like him.

NINA: He was ur knight in shining armour twice already. He redeemed himself in my book.

ME: Fickle.

NINA: Enjoy.

ME: What about his sisters?

NINA: Just b careful. Don't go anywhere alone w them.

ME: I'll try. But I still wish u were coming.

CHAPTER 26

We met the hired minibus in front of the giant bike sculpture on Rose Revolution Square at 10 the next morning. The driver was typically grumpy at having to wait for late-comers: Saba's girlfriend and her friend Sarah, who turned up 20 minutes late only to ask us to wait while they went to Smart to buy coffee. Emily and Arabella tagged along with them but Toma stayed, lighting up a cigarette and leaning against the stone balustrade overlooking the city on the other side of the River Mtkvari, blowing out the smoke into the cool semi-autumn air. It was the perfect time to ask him about Night Office. I approached cautiously, feeling the words sticking in my throat. *Was he really a demon in disguise? Why had his friends chased me? Why had he told them I was his and that his dad knew about me?*

He caught me studying him and raised an eyebrow in question.

"Isn't smoking bad for your health?" I blurted out, feeling like an idiot as soon as I said it.

"True, but it's also good for the environment," he said with smile.

"How do you work that out?" I said with a dry laugh.

He crushed it out and stuck the stub into the empty cigarette packet he'd been using as an ashtray, just as he had on holiday at the beach- though I'd expected him to flick it over the edge.

"Because it kills humans," he answered.

Humans, not people. Was he hinting that he wasn't one of us? Did he know I knew?

I glanced at Ilia and he shook his head in warning.

"Guys! Let's go!" Saba called- the girls were back and we all piled into the minibus. I sat behind the driver, Sarah beside me. She was in Saba's class and I didn't know her well, but I soon found out our fathers had worked together on a project a few months back- he was a marketing manager and his team had designed the latest ad for dad's new cigarette contract. We talked a bit about Susan, though there was nothing new to add to Megan's version of the story and the fact Toma's friends had been questioned and released. They must have kept quiet about me because I hadn't heard anything back from Officer Lena, though the fear of what they'd find on that video had kept me awake nearly all night.

"So, are you and Toma going together?" she asked me quietly as we sped past the Tserovani IDP settlement, glancing back at the eldest triplet where he sat, legs out in the aisle, laughing at some joke Saba had made.

"No! Why? You fancy him? I thought you had a boyfriend."

"I do," she said. "But we're not married," she said, with a knowing smile, and when she saw me frown: "It's an *open* relationship."

"Oh, ok. Sure. Right. Well, I'm not dating Toma," I said, feeling my heart give a small protest as I said it. I wasn't sure how I'd handle it if I had to watch Toma and Sarah at it all weekend.

Dark depression tugged at the edges of my mood and I looked out the window, trying to swallow it down.

"You ok, Ela?" Mate asked, popping up from behind us to offer something pretending to be a snack that stank of fake bacon. I shook my head at the crisps but told him I was fine.

Sarah moved to sit with Arabella, and Emily came up front to smoke and flick her ash out the passenger window.

She glanced at me, at her brother chatting to Sarah, and back at me with a smug smile.

I glared at her and turned to the passing Georgian countryside again, letting the music wash over me as I looked thoughtfully out the window at the passing Shida Kartli landscape: the October fields of dried or cut corn, hay in stacks under tarp, those trees left with leaves still showing the bright variety of golds, oranges and yellows, a small lake reflecting the autumn blue sky, a villager in a cart drawn by a grey donkey taking the latest bountiful cabbage harvest to the local roadside market stalls and those stalls, laden with mandarins, potatoes, persimmon, late corn and apples of every colour. I opened the window and took a breath, trying to let the dark thoughts out, trying to hold onto the feeling of peace and beauty the landscape gave me.

"It won't work you know," Emily said, plumping, uninvited, down beside me.

I looked at her, waiting.

"Pretending you don't care that my brother and Sarah are getting it on."

"You talk as if you wish it were me instead," I said snarkily.

"Hardly," she sneered. "But it'll be fun to watch you hurting this weekend."

"Leave me alone," I told her.

"Alone is the word," she agreed. "Enjoy it."

She got up and I watched her go to the back and sit with Ana and Saba.

"Don't let her get to you," Ilia said softly, appearing in the empty seat next to me.

I narrowed my eyes. "I won't." I handed the driver my USB stick and got him to put on a song I knew everyone loved.

"Good one!" Saba called out as the beats pounded hard out of the rear speakers.

I laughed and pulled Mate to his feet to dance with me, throwing a smile Emily's way, to which her lips pursed and her look soured.

This weekend will be fun, with or without Toma, I thought, ignoring my heart which told me that without would make it the worst weekend ever.

CHAPTER 27

"Sarah?" I asked, looking around me.

She'd gone.

"Sarah?"

Silence. And darkness.

I heard a crack- someone stepping on a stick. I nearly screamed. Nearly. *You're not a screamy girl!* I reminded myself as my heart sped up. I turned in a circle, peering into the trees, trying to make out anything. Anyone. I didn't want to shout again and I was almost certain they were playing a joke on me.

"Come on guys," I protested loudly. "Joke's over. Ha ha. Let's go back to camp."

Nothing but the dull roar of the Borjomula River in the distance, pouring over the rocks and fallen tree trunks in a rush towards the town.

· I turned, walking in the direction Sarah and I had been heading in, remembering Nina's advice that I not get stuck alone with the Morgan sisters.

To my delight, Toma had made it clear he wasn't interested in Sarah, being polite but cool to her flirting. *A demon with morals,* I'd thought, amused. *Doesn't date other guy's girls...* A memory had stirred, then- him standing at the bar in Night Office talking with Susan- then faded. We'd set up the tents and cooked sausages, meat and fish- *kalmakhi*- for me and the triplets. If it'd just been me, there would have been teasing but in this case, we were left to our own devices. It made a nice change. We drank some beer, talked about school and our future plans, then, with the fire getting

111

low, we'd headed off in pairs and threes to get more firewood. I'd gone with Sarah and Emily. And lost them both.

I heard a rustling in the bushes beside me and stopped, staring at the night-black leaves intently. For a split-second I thought I saw two red eyes staring back at me, then they were gone. I gasped and turned away, stepping up the pace, clinging tightly to the wood against my chest like a shield against the dark. I heard a howl on my left; an answering shriek somewhere off to my right. Another crack and rustle behind me sent me stumbling forward in a panic. Cackling hyena-like laughter echoed through the wood. I tripped on a root, staggered and righted myself. I swore and threw the wood down and began to run; crashing through foliage, thorns, ferns- all sense of logic lost to a pounding fear.

I thought I saw a flickering light at my ten o'clock and adjusted my direction. Not five seconds later I came stumbling into the circle of the campfire, panting, my heart thumping hard in my ribcage.

Where's Ilia when you need an angel?! I wondered, then tried to laugh at myself for being afraid of the dark. The laugh came out hollow and lonely. *Where is everyone?*

My heart beating fast from the run and fear, I sat on a log by the dying fire and curled my knees into my chest, hugging them and shivering- equal parts shock and cold as I stared at the flames.

I heard the cracking approach of feet over dry wood and shrank back, eyes wide, blinded by the light of the fire so that the negatives danced over my vision, making it impossible to see into the dark.

I got ready to scream as a tall shape strode out of the trees and stopped beside me.

Toma!

He dumped his wood collection, considerable larger than mine had been, on the pile and crouched down by the fire, elbows on thighs, hands hanging between his knees; casual, unaffected, as I tried to steady my breathing. He picked up a stick of pine and fed the fire with it. After a moment, the small pine cone on the end popped and I jumped.

He turned and looked at me with amusement, the light of the flames dancing in his eyes and casting flickering light on his raven hair.

"Did you see anyone out there?" I asked. "No-one else is back yet. I lost Sarah and your sister..."

"Oh, I doubt Emily's lost," he said with a smile. "And the last I saw of Sarah...well, let's just say Mate will be keeping her warm tonight."

"Gross," I said in distaste, even as I blushed, remembering how this summer Toma and I had... I shook the memory away and reached my hands towards the fire, trying to let its warmth sink in.

"Your hands are shaking," Toma observed. "Did something scare you?" I frowned. "Or are you frightened of the dark?" he asked with a barely supressed grin.

"Of course not!" I said, trying to sound offended.

Toma raised his eyebrows.

"Hey, about Night Office..." I started.

"We're baaack!" Emily and Arabella sang out at the same time, emerging from the trees behind us. "And we come bearing gifts!"

Emily pulled out a bottle of Coke and Arabella threw Toma a two-litre bottle of vodka.

"You were supposed to be collecting wood!" their brother told them.

"This'll keep us warmer," Arabella said, lightly dancing her fingers over his shoulder as she passed and sat down beside him.

"Where'd you get that?" I asked.

"Does it matter?" Emily asked coolly.

She handed each of us a plastic cup and Toma poured the alcohol while Emily added the soft drink.

"Shouldn't we wait for the others?" I asked when the smell of the vodka hit my nose, reminding me of my Night Office blackout.

"Like- duh! They can get their own," Emily said. "And Saba looks like he'll be gone all night, anyway," she added.

"Oh Ana...," Arabella said, crudely mimicking Saba's voice.

"Yes, oh, yes, Saba, don't stop..." Emily joined, pretending to be Ana, and they collapsed into giggles.

"Cheers to...what?" I asked, not joining in their laughter.

"To not being afraid of the dark," Toma said, with a meaningful look at me.

His sisters glanced at each other, grinning as if at a shared joke.

"Cheers!"

"Cheers!" I said quietly and then sipped.

"Down in one," Toma said, wiggling his empty cup at me.

I frowned and glanced over his shoulder to where Ilia had appeared, his arms crossed, under the tree. He was shaking his head.

Now he shows up! Where was he when the Hound of the Baskervilles was chasing me through the woods?! I thought angrily.

Seeing my dark look, Toma looked in my angel's direction and smiled wickedly. "Sure you're not scared of the dark?" he teased.

"No!" I answered stubbornly, raising the cup to my lips and downing the contents. The heat of the alcohol hit me even to my toes.

Toma was already refilling his sisters' cups before I'd finished, then he poured for me.

"To avoiding temptation!" Emily sang out with a heavy look at me.

I blushed and avoided Toma's gaze instead as I drank it down.

Arabella rummaged in her rucksack and pulled out a speaker, then flicked through her phone until she found some deep progressive dance. She put it on full volume and pulled her sister to her feet and they started gyrating against each other.

I glanced at Toma and saw him watching them with a smile, which he then turned on me. I frowned and focused my attention back on the girls, wishing that our camp-mates would come back.

Toma got up and refilled his sisters' glasses, this time without Coke, and then started dancing with them. They all emptied their drinks and dropped the cups.

I watched them, my heart beating in time to the music, a beat that went down to my stomach. I remembered how Toma had danced at Susan's party- his speed, his muscles, his power. I remembered the night in the beach bungalow, the smell of his sweat and the way our bodies had moved together. My whole body suddenly throbbed with the need to touch him again.

Demon...they're all demons... a voice whispered in my mind, trying to see beyond their good looks, to imagine a movie transformation where their faces melted into something red and hideous. But looking at Toma, I just couldn't. *I want him!* I thought achingly. *I need to be with him.*

I watched his hands on his sister Arabella, sliding over her belly- pierced, I saw now, a red gem glowing from her bellybutton- as she lifted her hands and shook her head side to side in ecstasy. Emily stepped in front of her, between her legs, and started to kiss her. Like, a full-on kiss; sliding her hands over Toma's, up his arms, then back to Arabella, cupping her face then moving her lips down to her neck. Arabella turned her head and- *oh my God!* –kissed Toma. Actually kissed her brother. Tongues and everything! Just like we'd kissed...

Emily now slid round behind Toma and pulled him away from Arabella. For a minute, I thought she was angry with him, but then he grabbed her hair, pulled her head back and put his lips to hers and they embraced passionately, still moving to the music.

I didn't know where to look, so I looked back at the fire and gulped my drink down, hoping it would numb my embarrassment. Again, I wondered where the others of our group were, why they weren't coming back *now*. I could feel the vodka working on me as the fire danced. I looked over to where Ilia had been but couldn't see him.

Then I felt Toma crouch down behind me, close; his thigh against my back, his left hand on my shoulder. In his right hand, he held the vodka bottle. He quarter-filled my cup and leaned forward to whisper in my ear: "Dance with me."

I shivered, my skin bursting out in goosebumps of anticipation.

"Wouldn't you rather dance with your sisters?" I asked, my voice coming out weaker than the cutting tone I'd been trying for.

"No," he said, standing.

I looked up at him, wanting to hold on to some sense of dignity. But I fell into the intensity of his eyes. The music was suddenly everywhere, flowing through me.

He held out his hand and I downed the drink and dropped the cup.

He led me close to the girls, who were totally into each other, lost in the dance and each other's bodies. I fixed my eyes on Toma's collar, very aware of his hands on my hips.

Demon, demon, my mind hissed.

"Let go," he whispered, his breath hot in my ear.

Confused, I took my hands off his shoulders.

He laughed and moved around me, stopping behind me and lifting my hands up, his fingers linked with mine.

"I mean close your eyes and *let go!*"

I tried closing my eyes and immediately felt myself falling into the depths of the music as it boomed out of the speaker. Not having to see Emily and Arabella at it, I could concentrate on myself- my own body, and Toma's hands on me as we moved together.

He turned me around so I was facing him again and lifted his hand to the back of my neck, bringing my face closer. He hesitated a tantalising moment, his lips next to mine; his breath merging with mine. And it was me who bridged the gap between us.

CHAPTER 28

Dancing, drinking, no time to ask the questions I wanted to ask as the others finally arrived back- more dancing, joking, ghost stories in the dark, holding hands with Toma, our fingers sliding against each other, kissing, as if the months since August had never happened, and then smoking something which first made my head spin, then made me sleepy.

"E-la..." Toma called softly, and I woke to find myself sitting on the ground between his legs, my head on his knee, the flames dying - flames which I swear had been burning hot and bright only seconds before.

I sat up, groggily squinting my eyes, looking around and trying to make sense of what was happening. Toma was behind me, sitting on a log and I saw his sisters sitting giggling nearby, two empty bottles of vodka on the ground at their feet. Our friends were gone, though I could hear them in their tents and see torchlight shining through.

"I guess I dozed off," I said with a shy smile, blushing.

He gave me a half smile. "I guess you did."

I stood up and swayed, automatically reaching out for him.

"Feel sick?" he asked, sounding worried.

I shook my head. "I think it'd be a good idea if I just went to bed now."

"And miss the party?" Emily pouted, sending Arabella into raucous laughter.

I frowned, not getting the joke- even Toma was smiling.

"Whatever. Thanks for the, you know..."

117

"Drink?" Arabella suggested, flicking a look at her sister, who fell back holding her hands over her mouth to stifle the noise of her cackling.

"Er, yeah," I said. "Goodnight."

"Goodnight," the girls chimed.

"'Night," Toma said.

I ducked my head, embarrassed at my lack of stamina- the triplets were clearly expert in holding their drink and joints, whereas I...

"Lightweight!" I scolded myself as I stumbled over to my tent. I sat in the entrance to take off my shoes, then realised I was already barefoot. "When did that happen?" I giggled and collapsed backwards onto the soft sleeping bag.

I lifted my head once and looked out through the gap in the tent flaps. The triplets were arguing quietly and the girls seemed to be angry at Toma. I saw Emily cross her arms and turn away and Toma shook his head at her.

I was too tired to try and figure them out anymore. I let my head drop back and closed my eyes.

CHAPTER 29

I woke up, my heart thumping hard against my rib cage, much more alert after a few hours' sleep.

"Hello?" I whispered.

Nothing.

Just the wind.

I heard a footstep outside and sat up, ears straining, holding my breath until I thought my lungs might burst.

Then my door flap- which I'd forgotten to zip- opened and some-one came in.

I made to scream but a hand covered my mouth.

"It's me," Toma whispered.

I swallowed the scream and he took his hand away.

"What are you doing?"

He reached out and brushed back the hair from my face.

"This," he whispered.

Then his lips were on mine, tasting of cigarettes, alcohol, copper and chocolate. Bittersweet memories of summer came flooding back.

I swooned. I swear I've never done it before, never thought I was capable of it, but I genuinely felt my whole body melt as I opened my lips to his.

He pulled back for a second, both of us panting. I reached out to pull him back to me, wanting more, my whole body on fire from his touch. My hand on his muscled shoulder told me he was topless.

I stopped.

"Are you naked?" I asked incredulously.

"Not yet," he whispered, laying me down.

"Eliso, you have to stop."

Ilia's voice from outside the tent.

I ignored him, wishing he could read my mind telling him to leave me alone.

"Don't let him do this to you. You know what he is..."

But I want him to, I thought, feeling the heat of Toma pressing against me. He pulled back and yanked my t-shirt over my head.

"Ela!" Ilia hissed.

I broke away from Toma's kiss, ready to growl an angry reply, but Toma put his finger to my lips.

"Just ignore him," he breathed in my ear.

I jerked, looking him in the face, though I could see nothing.

"You can...?"

"Shh..." he said, covering my mouth with his once again and pushing me to the ground.

CHAPTER 30

I woke up with my hair smelling of smoke; naked, snuggled in the sleeping bag. The tent was still warm with the smell of adrenaline, though the door-flap was open and Toma gone. I pulled on some clothes and pulled my hair up into a quick knot. Then I peered out, breathing in the mid-morning autumn dampness: moss, earth, greenery.

The circle of tents was quiet, the only sound an occasional snore or snuffle.

Toma appeared like a ghost out of the woods, wearing jeans and an open shirt.

"What happened?" I asked quietly, my voice coming out croaky.

Toma smiled. "If you don't remember, then either you drank too much or I'm losing my touch."

I scowled at him, then laughed and shook my head.

"Here," Toma said, handing me a water bottle.

"Thanks," I said, standing up and gulping it down. Then I poured some into my hand and rubbed my face.

My hand came away pink.

"What the...?" I looked at Toma and he shrugged, moving over to the fire- now a pile of cold ash.

I sniffed my hand. "Is this...blood?" I asked.

"Yes," a disapproving voice said from my left. I turned and saw Ilia standing; white, pure and inviting, in the first line of trees.

I glanced at Toma who had crouched down and was poking the ashes with a stick, burying three bottles of Gomi vodka. Had I imagined that he'd heard Ilia last night? I frowned, struggling to remember, and failing- it was all so fuzzy.

121

"What happened?" I asked them both, grabbing my compact from the tent to inspect the damage- just some blood at the corners of my mouth, though the inside of my mouth felt fine- no cuts.

"We had fun," Toma said, grinning up at me.

Ilia remained stubbornly silent.

"Whose blood is this?"

"Mine," Toma told me.

"What?!"

"And theirs," he added, pointing the stick to his right. For the first time, I noticed his sisters, lying, limbs tangled, asleep in the circle. They were naked, though someone had thrown t-shirts over them as too-small blankets.

I swore and Toma laughed.

"Why do I have your blood on my mouth?" I demanded.

Toma shrugged and smiled.

"What does it mean?" I said, looking directly at Ilia now, trying to fight the panic at the realisation that I couldn't remember it happening, and that I had clearly drunk the blood of three demons.

"Apart from the fact you acted like an idiot, you are now stuck..." he stopped, glancing at Toma.

I looked and saw him poking at the fire again, in all appearances ignoring us.

"Maybe we should take a walk," Ilia suggested.

I nodded. "I'm going for a walk."

Toma nodded but didn't look up. "You might wanna put some shoes on," he said- nodding to where my boots and socks lay near one of the logs.

I sat down as I did up my laces, too shy to look at him, my gut twisted in nerves, uncertainty, confusion, and yes- still hot from that hour in the tent with him. Ilia was going to kill me.

CHAPTER 31

"So, what does it mean?" I asked Ilia again as we walked away from camp.

"It means that you're now bound to them."

"That sounds very medieval," I said grimly.

"It's as old as time," Ilia retorted. "Blood exchanging is one of the most powerful binding magicks there is."

"Hang on- *exchanging*?! You mean to say they took my blood from me?!"

"It didn't look to me as if you put up much of a fight."

"I was drunk!" I protested.

"Clearly," he said. "And stoned."

I blushed and bit my lip.

"So, was it, like, a vampire thing?" I wondered, images of neck biting and sucking on veins surging into my head. I touched a hand to my neck and found the skin there smooth and thankfully unbroken.

That got a smile out of my angel.

"Hardly. They bled your arm into a cup, mixed their own blood in and you all drank from it."

I looked at my arm and saw a tiny healed cut, halfway up my forearm. As soon as I noticed it, it started to sting.

"That's disgusting."

"I tried to stop you. Several times."

"I know," I said, frowning. "I guess I just got carried away...again."

"You're a teenager. It happens," Ilia allowed.

"Were you this wild when you were a teenager?" I teased.

"I lived in a farming village in mountainous Svaneti," he reminded me dryly. "There weren't so many opportunities to make deals with evil spirits."

I blushed again.

"Are you sure they're evil?" I asked him, shivering and hugging my arms around myself- more at the thoughts in my head than the chill of the shadows. Apart from the blood drinking, which I didn't remember anyway, the evening had been a lot of normal fun- drinking, dancing...

"As sure as I know that I'm good," he answered.

I groaned.

"I told you they like to hurt people- that's their sole mission as far as I can see."

"Why?" I wondered.

"Do demons need a why?"

I didn't answer as my mind fought his reasoning: *But Toma seems so normal. And that body...!*

"So, what do you think they want out of this bond? Will they be controlling my mind from now on? Stealing my project ideas? Cheating in tests?"

Ilia shrugged. "Who knows with demons?" he said. "Probably all the above. I guess it'll fade over time. Unless you do it again..."

"Bleurgh! No way!" I protested. "And no more drinking!"

"Good," he said, unsmiling.

"What's the worst that could happen?" I wondered.

"We'll see," he said grimly. "And if you listen to me, I'll do what I can to protect you."

I stopped, reaching out to him automatically, feeling my hand pass through his arm as if nothing was there, though to my eyes he was solid.

"I'm sorry," I said.

"For what?" he asked, frowning, still grumpy.

"For not listening to you," I said, my voice small with the tears that suddenly rose to burn my throat. "For letting you down. Again."

He sighed and frowned in concentration. I felt the air vibrate around us and then he reached out and pulled me into a very solid and comforting hug.

I refused to speak to or even look at Toma and his sisters all through breakfast, deliberately focusing my smiles and jokes on the others in our group. Saba noticed and stuck up for me, though: as we all climbed into the minibus, he pulled Toma to one side.

"What did you do to Ela?" he asked.

I was at the back, putting my rucksack in the luggage compartment. I peeked around the corner but they were in profile to me and couldn't see I was listening in.

Toma brushed him off.

"Nothing, man." Then he smiled, the picture of cool. "I tried but she passed out. Now she's hungover and pissed off at us for making her drunk. Seriously- nothing happened."

I growled low in my throat in indignation and made to go out and hit him, but Ilia's hand on my arm held me in place. So, I had to watch as Saba took it hook, line and sinker and, after slapping Toma companionably on the back, climb into the minibus without a care in the world.

As Toma put a foot up on the step, he looked at me and winked, as if he'd felt me there all along. Before I could react, he was inside.

"How dare he?!" I complained to my angel, my blood boiling.

"Ela, just let it go," Ilia advised. "They want to provoke you. Take the high ground and steer clear," he said.

"Another two hours till I can do that," I pointed out.

"Then plug your earphones in and pretend to sleep- you look like you missed out on some last night."

I scowled at his smile and made to nudge him, but he'd already dematerialised and I pushed nothing but air.

125

CHAPTER 32

"So...what happened?" Nina asked me, cornering me as soon as I stepped out of Levan's car onto the pavement on Monday morning. "Why wouldn't you answer my texts?"

"I did."

"'Back, see u tomorrow' is not an answer!" she complained.

I glanced around, saw Toma and his sisters getting out of the black limousine behind me, and grabbed her elbow, shaking my head.

Nina opened her mouth but I shut her up with a sharp look and steered her through the security point and instead of turning left to reception, I pulled her right, towards the sports hall.

She frowned, curious, but kept quiet until I'd slumped down on the top-most bench. I put my head in my hands as she sat down next to me.

"What happened?" she asked again, this time her voice soft, sensitive; realising that the news wasn't good.

"Where to start?" I mumbled.

"How about: I slept with Toma and did evil blood rituals with his Coven of Demons, totally ignoring the advice of my Guardian Angel," Ilia suggested.

I glanced up at him through my fingers- leaning against the railings, his back to the court- and shook my head.

"El- you're scaring me!" Nina said now.

"Me and Toma... you know..."

"You what?! Seriously?" She was grinning.

"Unfortunately, not."

Her phone beeped.

"It's Mari- on Skype."

"Don't..." But it was too late; she'd answered.

"Nina and Toma's girlfriend speaking," she sang out, sitting and holding the phone at arm's length so our best friend could see us both.

"Tell me you didn't, El?"

I glared at Nina.

"Didn't what?" I asked, trying to fend her off.

"Sleep with The Bastard!"

"What was she supposed to do?" Nina asked.

"Er...I dunno, Ni. Maybe...tell him where to stick it!"

"Well, actually..." I began, giggling.

"Stop, stop...bad choice of words," Mariam said putting a hand to her forehead. "But I am so pissed at you, Ela. The guy sleeps with you in the summer, then dumps you, sleeps with God knows how many other girls, then joins our school and dances with you like he's crazy about you...then practically ignores you and now makes you sleep with him again."

"She's talking like you had no part in this," Ilia commented.

"Yeah, well, I feel guilty, ok!" I told him.

"He's the idiot, not you," Nina answered. "Hey- you haven't, like, actually become boyfriend and girlfriend, have you?"

I frowned. "I don't know. I don't think so."

"I mean, he may be an idiot but he is hot, right?" Nina said with a smirk. "So, was he as good in the sack as last time, or...?"

"Nii," I moaned.

"You're not helping, Nina," Mariam said.

"Sorry, mum," she retorted. "But I don't see what the big deal is. He didn't think he'd see her again, which is why he left her. But now he's said sorry-" she glanced at me. "He said sorry, right?"

I shook my head. "Not exactly."

"But you blasted him about dumping you like that, right?" Mariam demanded.

"Well..."

"Urgh! You're too soft, El!"

"Just because I didn't threaten to cut off his vitals doesn't mean I can't handle him!"

"Clearly, if this weekend is anything to go by," Mariam said, sounding put out.

The first bell rang.

"Gotta go," I said, relieved to be able to have a legitimate reason for getting out of the grilling.

"Get online tonight! We need to talk!" Mariam told us.

"Sure. Bye. Love you!"

"Love you, too!"

"Jeez," Nina said as she tucked the phone in her pocket and we headed for the door. "What's her problem?!"

"She's just being overprotective, I guess," I said, looking Ilia straight in the eye.

He raised his eyebrows, unimpressed with the challenge.

MARIAM: Any news about Susan?

ME: No. No body. No clue.

MARIAM: The video?

'We haven't heard anything,' I said, feeling a cold sweat break out down my spine as I thought of it. Thankfully, she changed the subject.

MARIAM: So, did the Morgans say anything today?

ME: No. But they looked V.superior.

MARIAM: Why? I thought E+A hated u being w their bro?

I realised I hadn't told her about the whole angel-demon thing going on in my life. *So how could I talk about the blood drinking?* My fingers hesitated over the keys. Then I shook my head.

ME: I guess I made a fool of myself when I passed out. Toma probably had a good laugh with his mates about it.

MARIAM: But Saba was looking out 4 u, right?

ME: Yep. But boys are boys...

MARIAM: Well, stay away from The Bastard- that's my advice.

ME: What if I can't? It's a small school. I feel like the three of them are watching me all the time.

It was true- Emily always chose to sit behind me, or when in a semi-circle directly opposite me... and I'd see cold analytical curiosity in the way she looked at me when I caught her at it. And Toma... well every time I saw him smiling at me across the corridor, my stomach burned with longing. But today I'd done my best to ignore them all.

MARIAM: Creeps. You be careful. You don't wanna end up like Susan.

ME: There's nothing to say they were involved.

MARIAM: Nothing to say they weren't. Trust me, STEER CLEAR!

ME: Yeah.

And who knew what could happen with the blood link, I thought.

MARIAM: Anyway, you're in 11th grade- you have exams to study for.

ME: You're saying hide in the library?

MARIAM: Whatever it takes. He's not worth messing up your studies for. Not with your dad breathing down your neck.

ME: R we walking about me or u here?

MARIAM: Maybe both.

I knew Mr Walker, like my dad, was a stickler for top grades. But his pushing sometimes got extreme: once Mariam got 90 out of 100 and her dad had thrown her new laptop out the window. Ever since, she'd been the one to push us all to study hard. But without her, and with the triplets, I wasn't so sure I could tow the line like before.

ME: Is everything ok?

MARIAM: I miss u.

ME: Miss u, too.

She hesitated and I turned to grab my water bottle. When I put it back down, Facebook pinged with her next message.

MARIAM: I think my dad's into something heavy.

ME: Like what?

Drugs was the first thing that came to mind, though I couldn't imagine it of him.

MARIAM: That Zoroastrian stuff he's always liked. He hooked up with a group here- actually, I think that's why he came. But I looked into it- these guys are not the way they should be.

ME: What do u mean?

MARIAM: I think it's something...arghh I don't wanna say it but... satanic.

I felt myself go cold.

MARIAM: They do the regular Zoroastrian stuff like keeping the fire burning in the Temple...though they're not actually Zoroastrian because they weren't born into it...

My mind flashed to Toma, lighting the fire with his bare hands.

MARIAM: ...And he goes on about the Ahura and Ahriman- good and bad forces which influence humans- but then I found a file on his laptop about demon possession and exorcism...

ME: Where's he getting this stuff?

I sat waiting for her answer, chewing on my thumbnail nervously as she typed. *Was this just crazy coincidence? It had to be.* Facebook pinged.

MARIAM: Reading books, talking to people. It started out as a hobby but now when he's home he spends most nights shut away in his study. Mum's going crazy. When he's not there or at work, he's with the group doing God knows what. But he's as obsessed with me getting top score as ever...maybe he wants me to become High Priestess or something.

'What do u know about the those "forces"?' I asked.

MARIAM: Not much. I just found a few open books on the coffee table yesterday but didn't have much time to read. Why? YOU don't believe, do u?

ME: No, no. Ofc not. What can I do to help?

MARIAM: Nothing. Stay safe.

ME: I'll do my best.

MARIAM: And stay away from the Morgans.

ME: Mmm, can't promise.

I heard Ilia shift on the chair and quickly blocked his view of the screen.

ME: I gotta go. Speak tmrw?

MARIAM: Sure.

We sent hearts and kisses and I signed off.

"How is she?" Ilia asked as I stood and stretched my back.

I told him about Mariam's dad.

"Strange," he said. "You know, there are ruins of a Zoroastrian temple here in Tbilisi. One of the oldest buildings in the city."

"I think that's where he first got interested," I said. "But now she's worried her dad's going satanic."

"More demons by the day..." Ilia said, his words making my skin burst out in goosebumps.

"Well, I didn't notice anything particularly demonic about my day, apart from the surprise maths test," I said, reaching my homework out of my bag and piling the books on the desk.

"Glad to hear it," he said. "Stay alert."

Alert was exactly how I felt, but not for homework.

I slid my finger across my mouse pad, waking up the screen again. Then I took a deep breath and typed the word 'demon' into the search bar. I didn't like what I saw. I went off on a few different definitions. I could easily believe Arabella was a succubus, maybe Emily, too. But Toma was hard to place. Mainly because I'd never seen him do anything worse than mess me around and possibly light a fire.

I looked up Ahura and Ahriman. One was all about light and wisdom, the other was an evil force of anger, greed and hatred. Still nothing I could connect to the demons- I hadn't seen any of those things from Toma.

There was a knock on the door.

"Come in!"

Geta came in carrying a small white envelope. She handed it to me and I saw my name scrawled across the front.

"Who gave you that?" I asked.

"It was in the mail box," she replied, then walked away.

"Love letter from Toma?" Ilia wondered dryly.

I rolled my eyes at him, though my insides lit up at the thought.

There was a simple white card inside with a hand-written message: *'You left something at the scene of the crime.'*

Frowning, I tipped up the envelope and a small, familiar gold earring fell out onto my palm. It was a delicate twist with a tiny gem on the end- blue, like her eyes...

I swore.

"What is it?" Ilia leaned over, curious. "Hey, isn't that like the earrings you gave Susan for her birthday?"

I nodded, feeling cold. "Yeah- and she put them straight on."

"Coincidence. Could be from another pair," he said, reading the card and my expression.

"They were hand-made," I said. "The woman at the Flea Market promised me they were unique."

"Put it back. You have to take it to the police," my angel told me decisively.

"They'll think I did it!"

"But they'll be wrong and they can find out who sent you this."

"I'd rather burn it and forget about it!" I told him, standing.

132

My phone beeped. I dug it out of my pocket and unlocked it. Another message from 'Demon,' or rather, another song.

"Get Scared – Don't You Dare Forget the Sun."

I read the lyrics as it played. *…better off looking alone…look at what you've done…you just wanna stab again…your mind was dark…*

"He's saying I did it," I said, feeling claustrophobic panic bloom in my chest.

"Come on, Ela, this song can be interpreted in so many ways," Ilia said. "Take the earring to the police and show them the messages," he added. "I'll come with you."

I shook my head. "I know what he's saying. And I'm not taking this to the police," I said, holding up the card.

I rummaged in my bedside drawer until I found a lighter at the back.

"Don't, Ela," my angel begged. "Honesty's the best policy every time."

"Ilia- I don't remember what happened that night!" I told him desperately. "I'm too young to go to jail for murder."

"You didn't…"

"But what if I *did*?" I asked.

"They haven't found a body."

"But those boys- those demons- said I'd killed someone. I'm not risking it." I shook my head, deciding. Before I could hesitate, I set fire to the envelope. I held it as long as I could, then opened the balcony door and threw it out to burn up in the courtyard.

The next morning there was a fresh envelope outside our apartment door. Inside was Susan's earring and a card with the words: 'Drop something?'

I threw it in the dumpster before getting in Levan's car, my hands shaking.

CHAPTER 33

We climbed up the rocky path, slipping and sliding on the worn brick fragments and pebbles. The wind whipped us as we rounded the crest, blowing southwards through the valley of the Botanical Garden below. Then we were nestled between the remains of the castle walls with their red bricks and stone blocks- the sheer drop to the gardens at our backs; the spread of the city beyond the low wall in front of us.

It was Mtskhetoba, a national holiday celebrating the first Christian church in Georgia. A lot of people had headed to the nearby old capital Mtskheta to go to the Svetitskhoveli Cathedral. It was one of my favourites in Georgia, with its frescoes and warm smell of incense... but the wild appeal of a picnic with friends grabbed me more than the idea of fighting the crowds there.

We chose a flat grassy spot to lay out the blanket. Lasha and Saba took out the vodka and juice, and Emily and Nina got some music going while me and Arabella laid out the food. I helped myself to juice, rejecting vodka when Toma made to pour. My angel smiled in approval to see me keeping my word.

I'd been deliberately avoiding Toma, both angry at him using me on the camping trip and psyching myself up to ask him all the questions brimming inside me. He didn't seem bothered by my cold shoulder, though- on the contrary, he seemed to find my attitude amusing. Which annoyed me more.

I sat and flicked through Instagram.

"Hey, look at this," I told Nina, showing her something one of our school friends had posted.

"No way!" she said, taking my phone and showing it to the others.

We started up an animated conversation about our classmates and, after a while, the alcohol started to take effect and the mood became playful.

"Let's play truth or dare," Emily suggested, turning the empty Gomi bottle between thumb and forefinger suggestively.

"What are the rules?" Nina asked.

"No rules," Arabella said, flicking a look towards her sister. I noticed Toma frown and look my way.

"Ela- you in?" Emily asked.

I hesitated. Ilia shimmered semi-formlessly behind them.

I nodded. "I'm in."

Arabella handed out pieces of paper; Emily gave out pens. We wrote down dares and piled them up face-down in front of Arabella, under a stone, then put the bottle in place in the middle of our circle.

Saba lost the first spin. Nina, sitting on his left, came up with a question when he chose Truth.

"What's the most embarrassing photo of you?"

"Me on the loo. But Mate put it on SnapChat so it's already gone- you'll never see it," Saba said with a confident grin.

"Don't be so sure!" Mate said, waving his mobile. Saba made a snatch for it, swearing at him.

They fought and tumbled on the ground and we egged them on.

"Ok, ok," Mate said after a minute of this. "It was a joke. I deleted it."

"You'd better have done!" Saba growled, pushing him good-naturedly.

The bottle spun.

It hit Nina and I gave her a wicked grin when she chose Truth- it was my turn to ask.

"If you had to choose one, which teacher would you make out with?"

She scowled. I knew she had a crush on Mr Michaels, the maths teacher, even though he had a huge nose and jug ears that made him the butt of a lot of jokes.

"Can I change to Dare?" she asked.

"No!" we all said unanimously.

"Michaels," she mumbled, setting the group off in raucous laughter.

The next landed on Toma and I felt my stomach heat up.

"Truth or dare?" Mate asked from his left.

"Truth."

Oh, what I wouldn't give to ask him the question, I thought.

"How many girls have you slept with?" Mate asked. Everyone whistled and cheered for the answer. Only me, and Toma himself, weren't as amused as the rest.

"I'm not answering that," he said, flicking a look at me.

"You have to take a dare, then," Saba challenged.

"Ok."

"Hey! That's not fair!" Nina complained. "You didn't let me!"

"No rules!" I reminded her with a nudge.

Emily picked the first piece of paper off the pile and her expression soured.

"What is it?" Nina asked.

"Read it," Toma told her.

Mate took it out of her hand. "Spin the bottle and spend two minutes kissing the person it lands on," he read. He looked around at us. "Gross, man, what if it lands on his sister?!"

"What if it lands on *me*?" Saba asked, sounding ill. Everyone laughed.

"Dare set," Arabella said, clicking the lighter so the paper glowed orange and drifted into the sky as ashes. She caught my eye as the dare burned. I knew she'd have no trouble kissing her brother for two minutes. But if it landed on me...my stomach squirmed- if it landed on me, I'd be in a world of trouble.

"Wait, wait!" Saba said as Toma reached for the bottle. "Shots first. We have no idea how this could turn out."

We cheered and he poured into the disposable cups and we all downed in one.

"Ready to get this over with, darling?" Toma said with a wink at Saba, making us laugh again.

Saba, pale, swallowed and nodded.

Toma placed his fingers and thumb on the clear glass, paused, and then spun it.

The bottle passed us all in a blur, then slowed down, turning... turning.

"Eliso."

There were wolf whistles and cat calls. Emily huffed and stalked off, bringing more laughter, while Ilia frowned from his seat on the rear wall.

"Lucky escape," Toma told Saba with a smile.

"Two minutes, guys," Mate told us.

I glared at him and he shrugged, grinning.

"Can we get some privacy?" Toma asked the group.

"All dares on show and it specifically said kissing- no other fooling around!" Nina warned.

"Come on, guys," I said, blushing.

"Fine," Nina relented. "Get out of the circle but go sit on the wall over there where we can see you but not hear the actual face-sucking."

"Gross, Ni," Saba said, smiling as he filled her cup.

I got to my feet and stood with my hands in the back pockets of my jeans.

Toma also stood, then tilted his head and I followed him over to the wall, followed by more whistles, cheers and crude comments.

"Shall we sit?" he invited when we reached the curved part of the ramparts overlooking the city.

I sat cross-legged and he took off his coat, laid it on the rock, and rolled up his sleeves.

"Won't you get cold?" I asked.

He gave me a crooked smile and shook his head, mirroring my position, his knees touching mine.

"I doubt it."

"I'm still angry at you," I told him as he brought his face closer.

"I know," he replied.

Then we kissed.

"Hey- time's up, guys!"

I made to pull away but Toma leaned forwards so we carried on for another few seconds before the shouts from our friends got too much and I had to stop for laughing.

"Forgiven?" he asked.

I realised our fingers were linked.

"That depends on what happens next," I said, getting to my feet.

"What do you want to happen?" he asked, standing close.

Before I could answer, Arabella appeared below us, looking up at her brother and pointedly ignoring me.

"We have to go," she said.

"Why?" he asked, looking annoyed.

"Father," she said.

I raised my eyebrows- if daddy demon was calling, they would surely go running, though I had trouble imagining the triplets being controlled by anyone.

But Toma was putting on his coat already and walking away as if the intimacy of the last few minutes hadn't even happened.

As the triplets said their goodbyes, I re-joined the circle and the game, feeling the cold absence of Toma settle over me once more; the knowledge that my burning questions would have to wait again dragging my mood even lower.

Then Emily came back and sat down on my left and I knew I was in trouble.

CHAPTER 34

I watched as the neck of the bottle slowed at Nina, passed me and looked all set to land on Mate opposite me. Then, suddenly, it accelerated and the bottleneck ended up pointing at me.

There was no way that happened naturally, I thought, glancing at Emily, though no-one else seemed to notice anything amiss.

"Truth or dare?" Emily asked me with a smile that made it look like Christmas had come early for her.

I swallowed.

A dare from her could mean death. Truth would be easier- she barely knew me, so how could she possibly embarrass me?

And, anyway, you can always lie, I thought. *Better to play it safe...*

"Truth."

Emily grinned. "True or false: you were once locked in a loony bin by your parents because you thought your imaginary friend was real."

Everyone was watching me with their mouths open. Only Nina knew the truth.

"You have to tell the truth or take a dare," Emily said lightly.

Nina shook her head infinitesimally and I prepared to lie and deny the charge. But when I tried to form the word 'false,' I was unable to get it past my lips. I couldn't even shake my head: all my muscles screamed against the instructions my brain tried to send.

"No answer?" Emily asked. "Then it'll have to be a dare," she said with a smirk, delicately picking a piece of paper off the top of the pile. She read it and the smirk stretched into a "cat that got the cream" smile of satisfaction.

"Walk the wall from the tower to the end and back," she said, pointing at the wall behind us.

I breathed a silent sigh of relief. It was windy, but my balance was good, as was my head for heights.

"Sure," I said, getting to my feet again.

"I'm not finished," she said.

I stopped, frowning, and out of the corner of my eye saw Ilia sit forwards.

"You have to do it blindfolded."

"No!" Nina protested, looking around at the group. "Who put that? Show it to me!"

But Emily had already burned it.

"Dare set," she said, smiling at me, holding out her black silk scarf.

"You don't have to do this," Nina said as I took it from her. "Guys, come on. This is crazy."

"Arabella said no rules," Sarah pointed out. I knew she wasn't my greatest fan after the Toma rejection, but surely she didn't want me dead?

"I can do it," I said.

"Yeah. I'm sure divine intervention will keep her alive," Emily said quietly.

I looked around but couldn't see Ilia.

Nina came up to the wall with me via a pile of rubble that had been cemented into place as crude steps by time and weather.

We stood looking down at the sheer drop into the Botanical Garden. The other side of the 20-metre length of wall, where we were picnicking, was just a six-metre drop. But I didn't fancy that either.

"You can ask for another dare," Nina whispered as I studied the shape of the rampart- its curves, bumps and drops, trying to memorise it. One thing I was good at, at least, having a photographic memory.

I shook my head. "From Emily? The next one would be worse!" I told her. And with her medieval blood magick working on me, I probably wouldn't be able to say anything anyway.

"Jeez, Ela," she said, and I felt her hands shaking as she tied the scarf over my eyes and manoeuvred me into position.

"Why are you doing this?" Ilia asked me.

"I have to prove I'm not scared of her," I told him.

"Not by risking your life, surely!?" Nina answered, thinking I was talking to her.

"I told you what they are," my angel reminded me. "This is not a game to her. She's jealous of you courting her brother."

"It's not her choice to make who Toma dates," I said through gritted teeth.

"You think she set this up out of jealousy?" Nina asked.

I nodded and stepped forward.

"Just walk straight," she said. "Slowly."

The group lowered their voices to whispers as I began to feel for my footing. Loose pebbles slipped under my sneakers, some rattling down over the edge. The first few metres were flat and around 70cm wide, but then the centre dropped away, which left me to walk an uneven edge of just 15cm.

"I can't watch!" Nina squeaked behind me.

"You'll catch me if I fall, right?" I whispered to Ilia.

Silence. I stopped walking.

"Ilia?"

"I'm here," he said from behind my left shoulder.

"No cheating!" Emily's sing-song voice called up. "You have to do it alone- no help or there will be consequences. Nina come down!"

The wind buffeted me and for a moment I teetered, arms thrown wide, and all sound stopped. But the wind pulled back and I bent my knees and started forward again, feeling each step before I put my foot down.

"You're making up the rules as you go along!" Nina complained, but I heard her start down to the grass.

"You're crazy," Ilia said. I could tell that he'd stopped moving with me, scared of whatever consequences the demon girl had in mind.

"Ten more metres, El!" Saba called.

I grimaced. He might as well have said a hundred.

"Quiet!" Emily snapped.

I reached out one foot and felt nothing there. For a moment, I panicked and heard gasps below, but then I remembered the right turn and bent my leg, feeling across.

There.

I stepped and turned, started straight again, then turned left.

When I got to the end, my friends clapped and cheered. I started to reach for the blindfold.

"Now back again," Emily reminded me.

I stopped.

"You're kidding me?!" I threw in her general direction.

"Can't complete the dare, you get another one," she said, and I could see her smirk in my mind's eye.

"Fine," I said, turning to face back the way I'd come. But because I'd lost concentration, I wasn't totally sure I was facing straight. I reached out my hands to balance and felt slowly with my foot, identifying the inner edge of the wall. I started to follow it.

The wind picked up, blowing me towards the Botanical Garden side and I leaned against it. For a brief moment, I caught the scent of sulfur, picked up from the bath-houses in the streets beyond the castle walls.

Then I heard a whisper on the icy wind.

"He's not yours! I warned you!"

I frowned, tilting my head, thinking I'd imagined it. I was freezing cold now, and terrified.

"Stop this, Ela," Ilia said.

"I c-can't." I said, teeth chattering.

My toes hit a brick sticking up and I went down, grabbing the wall with both hands. I heard Nina scream but I wasn't falling- I was steady, balanced like a cat on all fours.

"I'm ok," I called out.

But as I went to stand straight, I heard the voice again.

"Die!"

The word of hate was carried on a hard gust of wind which beat at me before I could spread my feet to balance. I felt myself tilting back towards the abyss, unable to fight it. I heard screaming and wasn't sure if it was me or my friends, or both. I cartwheeled my arms and bent my knees, not able to believe this was happening. Then a strong hand grabbed my wrist and jerked me forward. I bumped my shins painfully on the edge and fell head first. I brought my arms instinctively out to break my fall and hit the ground hard. It was mostly grass but my right arm hit a rock- with the full weight of my body behind it. White hot pain travelled up my arm, across my shoulder and exploded into my brain as I rolled twice and lay blindly facing the sky, screaming silently, the pain too much to voice.

CHAPTER 35

"Careful. Don't move her. She might've hurt her back," Saba said.

"Don't be an ass- she fell on her arm," Nina replied, though her voice was strained.

"Ela?" she asked, lifting off the blindfold.

"Ela, tell me where it hurts!" Ilia's voice said.

I looked up at them leaning over me and my eyes fixed on the sky blue of my Guardian Angel's.

"My arm...You saved me," I said.

"Barely," he replied, turning to glare at Emily who was hanging back from the group looking sulky.

I sat up and struggled to hold onto my stomach as the pain pulled hot bile halfway up my throat. I swallowed it down as my friends told me to go easy.

"You tried to kill me!" I accused Toma's sister.

She narrowed her eyes.

"You took the dare," she said, taking an unconcerned swig from the vodka bottle.

"I heard you up there!" I accused. "You pushed me!"

"She's delirious," Mate said.

"Must've hit her head," Saba agreed.

"No!" I argued. "I heard her up there on the wall with me!"

"She was with us the entire time," Nina told me softly. "The wind pushed you. We saw it."

"Jeez, Ela," Saba said, looking as pale as I felt. That's when I realised I'd genuinely nearly died.

"Let's get you down to the road," he said, helping me to my feet. "We'll take a taxi to the hospital."

"Can't we get an ambulance to come up here?" Nina asked.

"It'll take too long, trust me."

Last year Saba had impaled his leg on a piece of rebar sticking up from a broken wall he'd been messing around on. The ambulance took nearly 25 minutes to get to him and he was bled to paper-whiteness by the time they got him to hospital. He'd been left with a scar at the back of his thigh and a deep distrust of the medical service.

"Can you walk?" Nina asked, her hand on my good elbow.

I pressed my bad arm gingerly to my chest.

"They need to tie it up," Ilia said. I repeated the instructions to my friends and, much to Emily's clear disgust, Nina used her scarf- my blindfold- to fix my arm still. I bit my lip to bleeding not to scream.

"Sorry!" she whispered as she tied the knot and I swayed dizzily on the spot.

"Let's go," Saba said.

He and Nina helped me down the path- the most painful walk of my life- while Mate and Emily held back to pick up our leftovers and rubbish.

That night 'Demon' sent me a song called "Broken Bones." The key line: *The Devil got him good for sure*. That he did, I thought, swallowing another painkiller.

'Leave me alone Emily!' I typed.

DEMON. Wrong.

ME: Arabella?

DEMON: Wrong again.

CHAPTER 36

"There's a boy here to see you," Geta said, appearing in my bed-room doorway with pursed lips.

"Who?" I asked, pausing the re-run of Lucifer I'd been watching to try and get a sense of what Toma might be. It wasn't very applicable to my life but Ilia was enjoying the series and we'd spent a few lazy hours side-by-side watching.

Geta shrugged. "Your father said you can have him visit for five minutes, door open," she said, turning away. Before I could reply, Toma filled the space she'd vacated.

"Jeez!" I said, blushing and glancing at Ilia, who stood and moved away, glaring at the demon. "You could've called first!"

I didn't have make-up on and I was in my old baggy Blood Omen t-shirt. Plus, I had nothing but underwear on under the bedsheet and I hadn't washed or brushed my hair in two days.

Toma produced a handful of dark pink flowers and a bunch of juicy green-red *tita* grapes, my favourites, from behind his back.

"Peace offering?" he said, waving the flowers. "These're called 'Cosmos'- a symbol of order, peace, and serenity."

"Peace and serenity?! Your sister tried to kill me," I pointed out.

"And she feels very, very bad about it," he said with a smile, invit-ing himself in and putting the flowers and fruit on the bedside table.

I wished I had at least foundation on. Or a splash of perfume. But there was nothing I could do now.

"Lucifer?" he asked with amusement, glancing at my laptop. "Isn't that about the devil in human form?"

I blushed and quickly shut the laptop, wincing as my broken arm moved.

"Is it bad?" he asked, nodding towards my plaster cast.

"Let's just say my ski season is cancelled before it started," I said grimly. "Want to sign it?"

He nodded and I handed him a marker as he sat next to me.

'Ela, our angel, get well soon,' he wrote.

I blushed. Ilia, reading over his shoulder, glowered.

"Thanks," I said.

"When are you back at school?"

"Monday," I said. "Not that I can write much."

"No ambidextrous genes in your family, then?" he asked.

"Even if there were, I'd hide them to get out of that atrocious maths test Michaels has planned for us," I confessed.

He laughed. Then he just looked at me.

"What?" I wondered, again wishing for makeup.

"Why'd you do it? Walk the wall."

"Because I didn't want your sister to win."

"Win what?" he asked.

The battle for you, I thought, but didn't say. I shrugged. "The dare. And I was worried what she'd come up with next."

"You never give up," he remembered.

I smiled.

"Don't you want to get revenge on her?" he wondered, his expression serious.

"You're asking me if I want to hurt your sister? Would I tell you if I did?" I asked, laughing. "But, actually- no. I just want her to leave me alone. I guess that makes me a chicken."

The corner of his mouth tilted up in amusement.

"You are so... good," he said, and I heard something like wonder in his tone.

"So back away!" Ilia growled. "Because she's way out of your league."

I frowned at him and Toma's smile grew.

"I like a challenge," he said.

My eyes widened.

Had he heard Ilia? Or was he saying that me being good was his challenge to change?

"What do you mean?" I asked him.

"Nothing." He got to his feet and adjusted his jacket. "I'll see you at school, ok?"

"Yeah," I said, trying to bite back on the crushing disappointment that he was leaving so soon.

He hesitated in the doorway and smiled again. "Sweet dreams."

"Toma?" I asked, stopping him.

He waited.

"About Night Office..."

"What?"

"Do you know what happened?" I asked, my stomach a tight knot of nervous tension.

"You still don't remember?" he asked, leaning on the doorframe.

I shook my head.

"I went outside for a smoke and found you collapsed on the ground."

"Did you see me leave the club? Did you see Susan?"

He hesitated then shook his head.

"No. Look, I have to go..."

"Ok. Thanks for the flowers and grapes."

"Welcome," he said with a smile.

"Do you believe him?" Ilia asked once we heard the front door open and shut again.

I shrugged. "I was hoping he knew something. Because I'm still my own suspect for Susan's murder."

"I told you-"

"You don't know!" I insisted. "No-one does. I have at least three people accusing me of killing my classmate and I can't remember if I did or not!"

"Well, the demon seems to think you're good," he said, nodding towards the doorway. "That must stand for something."

"You mean my angel and demon are thinking alike? Miracles do happen!" I joked.

He stuck out his tongue and made me smile.

"How about we finish Lucifer?" he suggested.

CHAPTER 37

"What's your obsession with this girl?!" Arabella growled at her brother as he came out the door of Eliso's building.

"You followed me?" he demanded angrily, stopping as she blocked his path.

Emily came and stood behind him, wrapping her arm around his shoulders. He held her hand and looked at Arabella defiantly.

"Why did you come here?" she asked.

"I don't know," he told them honestly. "But I can't bring myself to hurt her." He glanced back at his youngest sister. "She has no desire to get revenge for what you did to her. Don't you think that's strange?"

"I don't care. She still deserves to be Judged," Emily answered with a scowl.

"I don't know...there's something about her," Toma said, sounding uncertain.

"You know what she is! What she did! And then there's her guardian...She has to be punished for it," Emily said.

"You know it's not so simple," he argued.

"And when are you going to tell Father?" Arabella asked.

Toma's face turned stony. "We'll tell him when I'm ready."

"Aren't you worried the others will let spill?" Emily asked. "Father will be so angry."

"If they dare..." he clenched his fists. "But no- I need more time with her. I need to understand what this feeling is, why she's guarded..."

"Why bother?" Arabella demanded. "It goes against your nature to resist the pull to Judge," she said.

She stepped forward and took hold of his face, her lips close to his, her eyes pleading as he looked her steadily back.

"Don't change for her. Father will know it," she said.

"I'm not afraid of him."

"You should be," Emily whispered in his ear.

He squeezed her hand and pulled Arabella close, kissing her lightly on the lips.

"Don't worry about me."

"I'll kill Eliso before I let her change us," Arabella swore.

"She already has," Toma told her, pulling away from both his sisters. "And you will not touch her again."

Both girls clung to him, begging, "Please, Toma..."

"Leave me alone," he said, extracting himself from their clinging hands. He walked away, not looking back at their shocked and betrayed faces. But Nina saw them as she hid in the doorway. Luckily, they didn't see her.

"Nina! Some sanity at last!" I said, throwing back the covers as my best friend came into the room and shut the door behind her.

"No, no, stay in bed!" she insisted, laughing and giving me a gentle hug, being careful not to bump my arm.

She held up a cute bear with a heart in its paws.

"Aww," I said. "Thank you!"

Then she pulled a Barambo caramel bar out of her bag and I made a hungry grab for it.

"You star!" I told her. "Mrs B's soup is killing me!"

We laughed.

"I wasn't sure what to bring," Nina confessed. "I see you already got grapes and flowers."

I nodded, moving my legs so she could sit.

"How's school?"

She dug in her bag again and pulled out some books.

"Your homework," she said.

I rolled my eyes. "No sympathy vote for me, then?"

"They said you could dictate it onto your laptop if you can't write."

"Clever," I said grumpily. "Want some grapes?"

She shook her head. "Not if they're from The Bastard," she said.

"His name's Toma and, yes, they are. How'd you know?"

"I saw him leaving," she said.

"Well, we're kind of friends now."

"I think you should watch out for his sisters."

"Yeah, I kinda got that seeing as Emily did this," I told her, lifting my arm and cringing.

"We were all there," Nina argued. "She was sitting right by me."

"Well, you remember how convinced you were Arabella held you underwater at the beach?"

She nodded. "But I obviously imagined it- you saw how far away she was."

"Hmm," I said.

"Ask her if she saw Emily mumbling any words," Ilia told me.

I passed on the question and my friend shook her head, though I noticed she paled. "I was glued to your crazy stunt. Why? You think they're witches or something?"

I glanced at Ilia then shrugged, really wishing I could tell her.

Then she told me what she'd seen downstairs.

"Two things disturbed me," she said. "First, most obvious- Toma kissed his sister."

"I've seen it before," I said. "It *is* kind of gross."

My friend pursed her lips, then let it go.

"Secondly, that Emily and Ari think you deserve to be hurt. Toma said he didn't want to but they're pushing, threatening him with his dad..."

"And they mentioned a guardian?" I asked.

"That's what they said," she confirmed. "I guess they mean Levan..."

I looked over at Ilia and saw him frowning.

"What are you going to do?" Nina asked.

"Stay away from the Morgans," Ilia spoke for me.

"Stay away from Emily and Arabella," I said, compromising.

"Well, don't let them catch you with Toma, then," she advised.

"I'll do my best," I agreed.

CHAPTER 38

"Help me!" I begged Toma as his sisters dragged me up to the wall. Tbilisi was spread out below me and the wind whipped my hair. But Toma just stood watching us, his hands behind his back, his face expressionless. A figure approached behind him as I fought Emily and Arabella. He stopped beside Toma and Toma smiled up at him. It was the devil- a dark horned beast of a man, with bulging red muscles and a thick mane of black hair. He put a gnarled, long-fingered hand on Toma's shoulder and Toma nodded at his sisters.

"Punish the killer," he said.

"No!" I gasped. They released me. I fell, turning to see the rocky ground come rushing up and, below me, Susan's bloody, broken body; her eyes open and staring at me accusingly.

"Wah!" I woke up, my heart hammering, as I smashed into her. Ilia was instantly by my side.

"What happened?" he asked.

I shook my head and clung to him as, body shaking, my mind fought to let go of the feeling of impending death. He wiped the tears from my cheeks.

"It's ok, Ela," he whispered. "You're ok."

My phone beeped.

A Facebook message from 'Demon'- another music video.

'Why do you keep sending this stuff to me?' I asked.

'Because you have to pay,' he replied.

ME: What for?

DEMON: Watch it, then we talk.

I reluctantly clicked the link and began listening to "[FNAF SFM] You Can't Escape Me," watching the nightmarish robot creatures, reading the lyrics and feeling sick.

'Why are u hunting me?' I asked when the song finished.

DEMON: You know.

ME: I don't.

DEMON: Liar. Your time is running out.

ME: Until what?

DEMON: If he doesn't want to punish you, I will.

ME: He who? Toma?

DEMON: The party's just begun. You can't escape me!

The green light went out.

I threw the phone across the room in frustration and it hit the door.

"What was all that about?" Ilia asked.

I shook my head. "Nothing."

"Doesn't look like nothing."

I turned the light out and laid on my side, my back to him, feeling anything but tired, but not wanting to talk, either. If only I could remember what happened that night. Was I really Susan's killer?

I bit my lip and closed my eyes, hot, helpless tears squeezing out.

CHAPTER 39

As Levan drove, I looked out at the early morning Tbilisi streets, mostly empty save for the orange-clad street sweepers and the odd street vendor setting up or commuter heading for an early start at the office. I thought back to the dream, the threat from 'Demon', the fact that I had so many questions that Toma was never around to answer...and made a decision.

ME: I dreamed about you last night. And your sisters.

I added Toma's number, pressed 'Send', then sat back and waited. The reply was almost instant.

TOMA: Was it fun?

ME: You all tried to kill me. I think your sisters are messing with me. I know they have the power to. Because of the blood.

I hesitated, then sent it, feeling both hot and cold.

TOMA: We need to talk.

CHAPTER 40

We all walked along Kipshidze Street and entered our usual block of flats, took the lift to the top floor and climbed the stairs onto the roof. No-one else was there; strange, considering the nice night: warm with clear star-lit skies. No-one would believe it was late October. The city- Vake on one side, the mount separating us from Saburtalo on another, and the Varaziskhevi gorge below- shone in numerous twinkling lights.

"Drink, anyone?" Mate offered, digging vodka out of his bag.

"Only if you've got juice!" I said with a laugh, pointing to my cast. "I'm still on pain-killers."

Saba got out some one-use cups and me and Nina started serving.

Lasha took out his phone and put some music on, then we sat and talked and gossiped, comparing Facebook posts and looking through Instagram. We made plans to go to the cinema the next evening, looking online to see what was on at the Amirani Cinema where they usually showed films in English when they first came out.

Then I noticed Toma had drifted away from the group and was stood near the edge, looking out over the city beyond the gorge. We hadn't spoken on the way here, not since today in the canteen when I'd stopped him on the way out.

"Tonight," he'd said, glancing around, perhaps checking for his sisters, then walking away.

"Go on!" Nina whispered, nudging me. "While he's free from his evil kin."

I gave her a death look that no-one but her saw, then reluctantly got to my feet and went over to stand next to him.

I hugged my elbows, unsure how to start.

"I know you know," he said quietly, eyes still outward.

"Know what?" I asked.

"What I am."

"I don't…"

"Your ghost would have told you by now," Toma said.

"My what?" I asked shakily.

"Ilia."

I stopped, glancing at my angel. He eyed me, his mouth shut, his expression pained but watchful.

"How do you know his name?"

"Because I hear you talking to each other. And sometimes I see him. But you knew that already."

I stayed quiet, suddenly realising how far away I was from the others, realising that he could easily kill me- throw me over the edge before they could get to me or stop him, just like in the dream. Would he kill us all to keep his secret? What I knew was no small deal, after all. I wondered if I could get to the door before he caught me, whether Ilia would be able to help me if he did…

"I'm not going to hurt you," he said, and I looked at him in surprise. He moved back to sit on an upraised part of the roof.

"You read minds?" I asked.

He shrugged. "You went quiet and tense. And you sound scared," he said. "You don't need to be."

Ilia, some metres away, began to fade and I felt myself relax, helped further when Toma laid back, his head supported by one arm, looking up at the sky.

Not so easy to throw me off the roof from horizontal, I reasoned.

"Sit," he invited, his eyes fixed heavenward.

I hesitated and then sat down beside him.

My phone beeped and I slid my finger across the screen to see a rude picture with Ela + Toma scrawled across it.

I scowled over at my friends and they laughed, then went back to their conversation.

Feeling bold, I laid down next to Toma, careful not to touch him.

There were immediate catcalls and whistles from the group. I sat up and laughed at them, blushing furiously and shaking my head.

Toma didn't move and when I looked at him, I saw he was watching me expressionlessly, unaffected by the teasing.

My blush deepened and I looked away.

My phone beeped.

NINA: Get a room!

'F off,' I typed back.

More laughter from the group.

I turned the phone to silent.

"Your sisters didn't come tonight," I said, stating the obvious but desperate to fill the silence, more than half wishing I'd stayed with my friends.

"No," Toma agreed, once again looking at the stars.

"They really don't like me, do they?" I said.

"No."

"Why?" I asked.

"Because I do," he said.

I had no idea how to answer that, though it sent a shot of pleasure through me.

"Can I show you something?" he asked.

I shrugged. "Ok."

He sat up and put his arms on his knees, looking out at the city with its orange lights shimmering in the last heat of the day, broken here and there by white, or by the red-and-blue flash of an emergency car.

"You know why I prefer night-time over day?" he asked.

"Because it's dark?" I guessed.

"No. Because the voices stop."

"The voices?"

He looked at me sideways.

"What did your ghost tell you?" he asked quietly.

I swallowed but then lifted my chin. "That you're a demon."

"That's it?"

"That you're evil. That you take pleasure from hurting people."

"He makes it sound so simple," he commented dryly, looking back at the cityscape.

"He's wrong?" I wondered.

"He's not exactly right," Toma told me. Then he stood and walked back to the edge, looking down a moment before turning his back on it to face me. The lights made a silhouette of him; his face hidden in darkness, though I felt his eyes on me.

"Come here," he said.

I hesitated, narrowing my eyes- trying to make out his expression.

"You come here," I said.

"You don't trust me?"

"You're a demon," I pointed out. "And your sisters want you to kill me."

"We don't kill," he argued.

"Emily was pretty close that day at Narikala," I reminded him.

"She was out of line," he said.

"Insane, more like," I said.

He turned his head, his jaw tense, and I blushed, realising it probably wasn't a good idea to insult the sister of a demon to his face.

He came and stood in front of me, then took my left hand and gently pulled me to my feet.

I looked up at him, breathing in his proximity, waiting, very aware of our friends' eyes on us, though the gossiping and laughter went on.

"Close your eyes," he instructed.

"It's already dark," I said.

"Close your eyes," he repeated.

I sighed but did as he said, my shoulders tense.

"I'm going to show you what I hear," he said.

I waited. For a moment, I heard nothing but our friends, and beyond them the night-time city noises: a few car horns, laughter from a balcony, the buzzing of an air-conditioning unit, the bark of dogs, a baby crying...but then I heard a voice whispering:

"I'm going to kill her for this!"

I gasped and jerked back, opening my eyes. But I quickly realised it hadn't been Toma who'd spoken.

"Listen," he whispered, squeezing my fingers.

I closed my eyes again.

"I stole her purse. Deserves it, stupid old cow..."

"Your wife will never know...come here...kiss me..."

"Meh- just dump it over the wall, no-one will know..."

"Should get the car fixed- pouring out a ton of fumes. Nah, it can wait."

"Twist it, snap it off... well, done! Niko wanted a swing in his bedroom. The government'll put a new one in, for sure..."

"I want that iPhone! Why should she have so much when I got nothing? It should be mine..."

"I'll feed that dog rat poison if it doesn't shut up, did it before..."

I let go of his hand, backing up to sit down, the silence after their chatter leaving my ears ringing as if I'd just left the dance floor of a nightclub.

"Who are they?" I asked.

Toma sat beside me and waved a hand out at the city.

"Them," he said. "But that's just the people still awake. It's louder in the daytime."

"You hear that all the time?" I exclaimed, shocked.

"I can switch it off, but, yeah."

"Emily and Arabella, too?"

He nodded.

"But why?"

"So we can do our job."

"Which is?"

"To punish them."

"Why should you punish them?"

"Because we have to. It's why we're here."

"And you punish all of them?"

"Those we can get to."

"What if they don't do the bad stuff- only think it?" *Or don't remember doing it?* I thought.

"Then we wait."

"And do you enjoy it?" I asked cautiously. "Punishing?"

He smiled. "Would it make you feel better if I said no?"

"Of course," I said.

"Well, I do enjoy it most of the time," he confessed. "It's a relief to stop their sins."

"Sins?"

"Wanna listen to some music?" Toma asked suddenly, digging the latest iPod and a set of earphones out of his pocket.

"Sure," I said, frowning, confused at the sudden change in direction.

"Lay down," he said.

We laid shoulder-to-shoulder, looking up at the stars. I felt my phone vibrate but ignored it. He handed me one ear and I pushed it in. Deep trance pounded into my head, bringing my skin out in goosebumps. Looking up at the night sky with the music twisting my emotions, I suddenly felt like I was falling; falling into a vast black hole. For a moment, I got dizzy, but then I felt Toma's fingers linking with mine, anchoring me. I turned to look at him; he did the same.

"Who are you?" I wondered quietly.

He gave a wistful smile. "Just a boy."

"I don't believe that," I said.

He looked back at the sky.

"One thing's bothering me, though," I said after a moment.

"One thing?" he asked, amused.

"If it's in your nature to hurt people, then why are you protecting me? Your sisters? Those boys at Night Office? And actually, why did they want to hurt me?"

"That's two things," he said.

"And what's with the blood ritual?"

"Three."

"I was home from school," I pointed out, raising my plaster cast a little. "Lots of thinking time..."

"And watching Lucifer," he reminded me.

I blushed. "Research," I said.

"Really?"

"You're avoiding my questions," I pointed out.

He smiled. We listened to the music and I wondered if he was going to answer or not. Then he spoke, not looking at me.

"One- I don't know. We work on instinct and that's what I'm going with."

I kept quiet, watching his profile.

"Two- because you have a ghost and that makes you stand out."

"He's not a ghost-" I started, but before I could argue further, a hand reached between us and pulled the ear buds out of our ears. It was Saba.

"We're going to Subway," he said. "Wanna come?"

We sat up and I waited while Toma pocketed the iPod.

"And three?" I asked quietly as we started towards our friends.

"That was just for fun," he said, flashing me a grin.

"How so?" I asked, feeling faint nausea as I remembered not remembering drinking the triplets' blood.

"Touch your nose," he said suddenly.

I didn't want to, but my hand was already moving towards my face, Toma watching intensively.

No! I fought the impulse and for a second I thought I had control, but, like the day on Narikala, my mind was weaker than the one trying to control it. My forefinger bumped the tip of my nose and Toma grinned.

"Good fight," he said quietly.

I swore and grabbed his arm as he went to follow the others down the stairs. "So, you three can make me do anything you want, anytime?"

Or dream anything, I thought but didn't say.

"I doubt it," he allowed. "You're clearly a fighter."

"That is evil!"

He laughed.

Suddenly the lights flickered out and we were left standing in darkness. I felt Ilia's hand on my shoulder, holding me still on the step so I didn't fall forward.

"Electricity's gone!" Mate shouted. The boys cackled and Nina screamed as they made to scare her.

"Hey, residents! Dear neighbours," Saba shouted out. "Pay your f-ing bills!!!"

"Shh!"

"Saba!"

"Shut up!" my friends exclaimed.

Then Nina switched on her phone flashlight and the boys followed suit. She shined it up at me and Toma, a floor above them.

"You ok?" she asked.

I nodded. "Yeah."

"Looks like we're walking," Lasha complained, jabbing at the lift button in frustration.

"Come on," Saba encouraged.

They started down. I put my flashlight on and followed Toma.

"Can I make you do what *I* want?" I asked his back quietly as we turned onto the next flight of steps. "Seeing as we all drank from the cup?"

"No," he said, and my heart sank in disappointment.

He stopped and turned, blocking my path, one hand on the wall, the other on the peeling wooden bannister. The lights from below flickered around us and my friends' voices echoed up as they moved away.

"But say you *could*...what would you get me to do?" he wondered.

I looked up, thinking, then smiled at him.

"I'd...get you to tell me all your dark secrets."

He looked at me thoughtfully and then shook his head. "That you have to earn."

"Hmm," I said, biting my bottom lip as I thought again.

"Then...I'd...get you to kiss me and not stop till I said so," I said, blushing but smiling.

He leaned forwards and I felt his breath near my ear. "No need for blood magick for that," he said, putting a hand on my waist as I melted into his kiss.

The lights came back on and we heard whoops and cheering from our friends some floors down.

"Did you do that?" I asked, grinning.

"I'm a demon, not an electrician," he said.

"Toma, Eliso- come on!" Saba called.

We followed them down. My whole body was alight from that kiss, and from finally breaking through the barrier of his otherness and finding it not-so-scary. I wanted more of him and at the exit to the road, I grabbed Toma's hand and pulled him back towards me.

"I didn't tell you to stop," I pointed out.

He grinned and pressed me to the wall.

"El?" Nina called from the other side of the street. She sounded worried.

"You go on..." I called, then pulled Toma's lips back down onto mine.

"What are you doing?" a cold female voice asked.

I jerked and pulled away, though Toma didn't step back- just turned his head to the side.

It was Arabella, giving me a death look that may just have killed me if her brother hadn't been between us.

"Kissing Eliso," he pointed out.

"With her ghost watching?" she asked nastily. "Get off on that, do you?"

I saw Ilia beside her, his arms crossed, glowering at the demons.

Toma's expression cooled. "Maybe I do," he told his sister.

"What you're doing is *wrong*!"

He sighed and turned back to me, looking me in the eyes. He gave me a half smile, then kissed me again, gently. Then he pulled away and turned to face Arabella.

"You shouldn't be here," he said. "Father will miss you."

I noticed Nina was crossing back towards us with Mate. The others had already gone ahead to Chavchavadze Avenue.

"No," Arabella argued, ignoring the humans behind her. "*She* shouldn't be here."

And that's when I saw the knife in her hand.

CHAPTER 41

"Woah! Arabella, chill!" Mate said, walking slowly through Ilia, his hands up to show he wasn't going to hurt her.

"Mate- don't," I warned him, not so sure she wouldn't just lash out at him.

I saw Toma had lowered his chin. He looked furious. "You will not hurt her," he said.

"I *should*, though," she hissed. "And you know it."

"Ari," Nina tried now. "Please put the knife down."

But Arabella's eyes were fixed on Toma. Her fingers tightened, relaxed and tightened again around the handle of the blade- the white bones of her knuckles showing through as she decided how far she would take the argument.

"Ela- go with your friends," Toma told me, not even looking my way. "Me and Arabella need to talk."

"But..."

"Go," he commanded.

I frowned but headed down the steps, cutting a wide circle around the crazy demon girl. Nina grabbed my arm and clung to me, pulling me quickly away across the road. Ilia followed.

"Mate," Nina called. He was still there, looking ready to put some of his beloved martial arts training into effect to disarm Arabella.

He said something to Toma and Toma shook his head, tilting his chin at me.

Mate frowned and turned away.

"What the hell?!" he said under his breath as he joined us.

I looked back and saw Toma with his arms wrapped around his sister, comforting her.

"What the hell, indeed," I said with a sigh.

Subway was packed so we doubled back to Wendy's. I texted Toma and he replied he'd come soon- without his sister. And until he turned up, the talk was all about the Morgans.

"...so, what do we actually know about them?" Mate demanded.

Saba shrugged. "That the sisters are hot...er...headed," he said.

Nina punched him on the arm. "Good that you're not dating Arabella anymore," she pointed out. "At your rate of getting through girls, she'd have killed off half the city by now!"

We laughed as Saba sat up taller- proud rather than insulted by the insinuation.

"Toma seems ok, though," he said, biting into his burger. He looked around at us. "Right?"

Nina glanced at me. "I guess Ela's best qualified to answer that one."

I blushed and felt Ilia shift nearby. "He seems like the sanest of the bunch, at least."

"Talking about me?" Toma asked, making me jump as he slid into the booth.

Everyone exchanged overly friendly greetings with him, embarrassed to have been caught out gossiping; everyone except Mate and Nina.

"What's with your sister threatening Ela, man? That was not cool."

"I know," he replied. Then he looked at me. "Sorry. Domestic issues. It's sorted now."

"I hope so!" Nina answered for me.

I'd ordered a Veggie Burger meal without ketchup and Toma shared my fries. I wanted to ask about his sister...and to ask all the other questions bubbling in me, but with our friends there it was impossible, so we spent a lot of time smiling and talking about day-to-day things. Then he and the boys ended up competing in the Game Zone on the basketball hoops. Toma never missed. Then we paired off, me and Toma against Nina and Mate, on the pucs. Kids' stuff, but fun.

And all too soon the night was over.

"See you at school tomorrow," I said as he held the door open to Levan's giant 4x4 while my driver watched us in the mirror, pretending he wasn't.

"Maybe," he said.

"Maybe?"

"12th grade privilege," he reminded me. "Tomorrow's supposed to be home-study in my house."

"Ok," I said with a shrug, acting as if it didn't matter I wouldn't see him.

I got in and he wound down the window before shutting the door. Then he leaned on the frame.

"Ela," he said.

"Hmm?" I asked, leaning forwards so he could kiss me.

"Touch your nose."

Growling, I did as he said, fighting but failing.

"I hate you!" I said, smiling when I was finally able to put my hand down.

"No, you don't," he argued with a confident smile. Then he tapped the window frame and stepped away.

As Levan drove, I sat back against the seat and closed my eyes, a happy grin on my face.

Ilia sat, silent and disapproving, beside me but I couldn't talk to him until I was out of earshot of Levan and he knew it, so I had a whole blissful ten minutes to myself.

CHAPTER 42

It was Friday before I saw Toma again. I'd spent all week avoiding his sisters, and though Emily sent me laser-looks every time I caught her eye, I had so far escaped unscathed. Plus, I'd slept nightmare free and I hadn't got any new creepy messages from 'Demon'. Maybe the broken arm was considered punishment enough for the sin of loving their brother. I was desperate to talk more to Toma about what he was, about Ilia (finally someone who knew!) and about Night Office. I bumped into him at the end of school while I was waiting to meet Mikey. He was heading out, no rucksack- just a thin notebook rolled up in the back of his stone-washed jeans.

"Hey. How's your arm?" he asked.

I held it up.

"Getting better quicker than expected," I said with a grin. "I always was a fast healer!"

A shadow crossed his expression, gone as soon as it appeared, then he leaned forward impulsively and kissed me.

"I missed you," I confessed when he pulled away.

He smiled. "Walk you to your car?"

I shook my head. "I've got to wait for Mikey. He's at basketball practise. How's Arabella?"

He shrugged. "You don't need to worry about her..."

"What? Trying to slice 'n' dice me again?" I suggested. "What was that, anyway?"

He shrugged. "We're close..."

"I remember the camping trip," I pointed out, frowning.

He smiled. "Yeah, well, I mean we spend a lot of time training together," he stopped as some 9th graders went past.

"Training to punish people?" I asked quietly.

He nodded. "But we call it Judging. We're still in training. It takes a lot of time and energy. Father requires perfection. So does Arabella. The girls don't like it when my attention...wanders."

"Hmm," I said, smiling, liking what I was hearing.

"Least of all involving a human with a gho... hey, isn't that your brother?" he asked.

I turned to see Mikey coming along the corridor with his head down and his hood up. He would have walked straight past me if I hadn't grabbed his sleeve, and even then, he kept his focus on his feet.

"Mikey- what's wrong?" I asked.

"Nothing," he mumbled. "Let's go."

I frowned, sensing something amiss. "Mikey, look at me."

With obvious reluctance, he lifted his head.

His right eye was swollen to a slit, the skin there already beginning to bruise. I felt Toma tense beside me.

Shocked, I reached out to pull back my brother's hood, but he stopped me angrily.

"Just leave it!" he growled, glancing at Toma and away again, his cheeks reddening in embarrassment.

"Tell me what happened," I demanded.

"Nothing."

"We're not going till you tell me!" I said.

"Then stay," he told me, and made to walk away.

"Has Lazare done this to you before?" Toma asked my brother in a low voice.

Mikey stopped and looked at him in surprise, then quickly hid his reaction by dipping his head.

He shrugged. "It was an accident," he said.

Toma was looking at him, analysing. "But this isn't the first time you've had an 'accident' with Lazare, is it?"

My brother swallowed and glanced up the corridor towards the gym. He seemed nervous.

"Mikey?" I pushed quietly, touching a hand to his arm.

The look he threw me was hurt, shame, fear and anger all in one- a little boy lost and a teenager fighting to hold onto his dignity. It made me want to hug him- just like I would when he was little and lost a toy or banged his knee. But I knew he'd push me away, so I stayed put, lending him my love through that one point of contact.

"No," he told Toma.

I moaned, angry and sorry I hadn't noticed sooner.

"And where is he now?" Toma asked.

Mikey shrugged and nodded towards the door at the end of the corridor. "Still practising."

"Right." Toma turned and stalked off towards the indoor court.

"Wait!" I said, catching him up. He didn't slow down. Mikey was a step behind. "Toma! What are you going to do?"

"Teach him he could make better use of his fists than on juniors," he said.

"You'll make it worse if you beat him up," Mikey said, though I could hear hope in his voice that Toma would do it anyway.

"He won't know what hit him," Toma promised. He stopped as he opened the fire door and looked back at my brother and me. The sound of sneakers squeaking on the floor, the thump-thump of the basketball and the shouts of the players flowed out of the space around him.

"You shouldn't be here when it happens," he told us. "Go home. I'll sort it."

Then he turned and disappeared. The door closed behind him, leaving me and my brother in uncertain silence. We turned and headed slowly to reception. I bit my lip, frowning.

I was convinced Toma was going to do something demonic. Part of me glowed that he'd want to protect my baby brother that way. Another part remembered that conversation where he said he enjoyed dishing out judgments. The question was- how badly was Lazare going to get hurt? What punishment would the demon decide he'd earned with his bullying? I couldn't help remembering Arabella and that knife- all for a bit of jealousy. Was I sure Toma was the mentally stable one? And so, I decided to go against his instructions and watch.

"You go meet Levan," I told Mikey at the door. "I forgot my chemistry book."

"You're not going back to Toma, are you?" he asked, looking at me with suspicion.

"No," I lied. "He told us to stay out of it, so I will. Go- I'll meet you in the car."

I turned and started up the stairs. As soon as I heard the door swing shut, I crept down. I glanced to check Mikey was outside- and saw him at the top of the steps and heading down- then ran to the gym door.

I took a breath when I got there, then quietly opened it.

To my surprise, Toma was sitting below me on the bleachers, his hands clasped, elbows on knees, sleeves folded up, focused intensely on the basketball game. I'd expected him to be down on the court beating Lazare to a pulp in front of his friends, or burning him in some unholy fire. I felt hugely disappointed and annoyed that he'd lied to us.

"Sit and watch," he said quietly, making me jump- I hadn't realised he'd heard me come in.

"I'm not interested in the game. I thought my brother's tormentor was going to get a beating," I said angrily.

"We don't beat the guilty with our fists," he said.

"We?"

"Judgers."

"You mean demons."

He glanced at me and gave a half-smile. Then he stood and stepped to the railing and looked down.

I went and stood beside him, watching as Lazare laughed and joked with his friends. He was heavy for a 7th-grader, but lithe

173

on the court; dodging quickly between the opposing team. I saw Coach Tanner wave to Ms. Rostov, the Russian teacher, and while his attention was off the court, Lazare elbowed a boy in the face for taking the ball off him. The boy cried out and had to run to the changing room, blood streaming from his nose. It seemed he was too afraid to tell the coach what had really happened, because I heard him mumble the same excuse my brother had: "accident."

With a smug smile, Lazare took a shot and the ball sailed through the hoop.

"Whatever you're going to do- do it soon," I told Toma through gritted teeth, my stomach boiling in indignation.

"You want him hurt?" Toma asked.

"Of course- he punched my brother. And it seems Mikey isn't his only victim."

Toma smiled and opened his hands. I saw his lips move silently. For a moment, nothing happened- Lazare continued to weave and dodge, passing the ball back and forth to his team mates.

But suddenly he stumbled. It looked like he tripped over something, though there was no-one and nothing near him to make it happen. He went down with a tremendous crash, falling straight on his right arm.

We all heard the crack.

Then we heard him scream.

I looked down at him, wide-eyed. While his team hung back uncertainly, the coach ran in and tried to comfort him as he held his clearly broken arm to his chest and cried. I winced, my arm throbbing in sympathy, knowing first-hand the kind of pain he was in.

"Let's go," Toma said calmly.

"You did that?" I asked, shocked and almost reluctant to miss the revenge being played out in full.

He nodded and held open the door for me.

"How?"

"You're still asking me to reveal my dark secrets?" he asked, looking at me sideways as we walked back up the corridor.

I nodded, unashamed.

"Power of nature," he said. "We're elemental spirits. We can manipulate air, water, earth, aether-"

"What's aether?"

"Hard to explain. Let's just call it light and space. And also, fire."

"The fire in that beach house," I said excitedly. "I *knew* I didn't imagine it!"

He grabbed my hand and pulled me into the canteen, dark and empty, the snacks locked away for the day.

"What are you doing?" I asked, confused.

He dragged me over to the stainless counter and pulled the notebook out of his back pocket, opened it and tore out the centre pages. Then he scrunched them into a ball and put it on the counter.

"Watch this," he told me with a grin.

He held his hands over the paper and closed his eyes. I saw his lips moving. The pages began to smoke. Then they burst into flame.

"How did you do that?" I asked, shocked, stepping back as the paper blackened and shrank.

"There's more. Get me a cup of water," he instructed.

Eager to see what else he could do, I went to the water dispenser and brought back a cup half-full of cool water.

He put his left hand on the rim of the cup, palm down, again speaking silent words, his eyes closed. Then he slowly lifted his hand from the cup and I saw the water rising just under it, droplets spinning and dancing on the surface of his skin.

He turned his hand over and the water spun in a circle.

"Wow!" I breathed. "Can I touch it?"

He smiled and nodded, holding his hand up, palm-out.

I reached out shaking fingers. When my skin came into contact with the water, I felt small electric shocks zapping into my palms- Toma's energy. He felt me feeling it and his expression changed, softening from the child-like excitement of showing off a talent;

becoming something else. He slid his fingertips down against my fingers, and then pressed the whole length of his hand against mine. For a millisecond, the water drops resisted the pressure; remaining like soft bubbles separating us. Then they burst and the water ran down our arms. But, kissing Toma, I barely noticed.

My phone rang and I reluctantly pushed back from him, biting my swollen bottom lip.

"It's Mikey," I said, pressing OK.

"Where are you?" my brother complained.

"Coming," I said. "I...got talking to Mrs Foster," I told him. She usually stayed in the library until late sorting out our mess, so I was making a pretty safe bet that she hadn't walked through the carpark past him yet.

"Well, I want to go home and Levan's getting antsy. Wait...he wants to know if he needs to come up there and get you."

"No!" I said, shooting Toma a panicked look, but his attention was on scooping up the paper ashes. "I'll be down in a minute."

I hung up and gave Toma a reluctant smile. "I have to go."

He nodded and began to roll down his sleeves. "Shall I walk you out?"

"Er...better not. Levan also doubles as an unofficial bodyguard. He's already got his eye on you!"

"You think he can beat me?" he asked with a smile, again holding open the door.

"He's twice your height and width!" I said, laughing.

"But he's made of around 70% water..." he said, wiggling his fingers.

I shook my head, feeling amazement and warmth sending butterflies flapping in my stomach. "Best not. I'll see you tomorrow, though, right?"

"Weekend," he reminded me.

"Maybe the guys are meeting up..." I suggested.

But he was shaking his head.

"We're going away. Family thing," he said. I felt my heart sink. A whole two days without him.

"Oh, ok. Then Monday."

"Sure," he said. He frowned and glanced back towards the corridor as if he'd heard something.

"See you, then," I said, hesitating.

He nodded, his hands shoved in his pockets. "See you."

He made no move to kiss me goodbye and this time I was too shy to ask for it.

Red and blue flashing lights from behind me caught my attention and I turned to see the ambulance pulling into the carpark. When I turned back, Toma was gone.

Hot and cold... I thought grimly, stepping out onto the path.

Why do you bother? A voice whispered as the wood-glass door shut. *He'll kill you, you know. Eventually. It's in his blood. Leave. Him. Alone.*

I narrowed my eyes and looked around. Then I saw her, looking down at me from the library window. Emily. She waved and I stuck my finger up at her.

"What is it?" Ilia asked.

"She's trying to turn me against her brother," I said, turning my back on her and heading down to the car- the only one left in the carpark.

"Maybe you should listen to her," he said.

"Ilia! I can't help my feelings."

"He's a demon, El!" he implored.

"But he's not done anything bad to me- and he just stood up for my brother."

"Tricks to get you to trust him," Ilia warned me. "Of course you're interested in him- he can see me. It fascinates you. You feel connected to him by the fact. Don't be taken in by him."

But we were already at the car so I couldn't say anything else. I glanced back at him as we pulled away, standing on the pavement looking at me with an unreadable expression.

I looked in on Mikey as I was heading to my room that night. He was half in shadow as he sat reading a book in bed.

"How's your eye?" I asked.

He looked up at me and I saw the dark bruise now blackening his eye and cheekbone.

"Mrs B threw a fit, but some cold on it helped," he said. "Dad's away, so..."

"Well, that boy won't be punching anyone for a while," I said softly.

"Yeah." He grinned, then dropped the smile. "It almost messed things up for the team, though."

I looked at him, not getting it.

"Our tournament on Sunday?" he reminded me. "Against the Panthers? With Lazare out and the sub sick, we were one short. But then Toma sent me a message saying he could step in- Saba invited him."

I raised my eyebrows. "I thought Toma was busy this weekend."

Mikey shrugged, happy to have the game set and a senior on his side. "I guess he changed his plans. We're meeting at school early for him to get a feel for the court."

"Mind if I tag along?"

He shrugged. "Sure."

I smiled and turned to go.

"Ela," he said, calling me back. "Toma's a nice guy, you know. You could do worse."

"Relationship advice from my baby bro?!" I said with a laugh.

He shrugged and went back to his book.

Still smiling, I shut the door.

CHAPTER 43

I had a lazy morning, getting out of bed close to lunchtime. I went down, grabbed a coffee and was just getting into my Georgian History homework when the doorbell rang.

"I'll get it," Mikey called. "I'm off to the pool. See you later!"

"Ok!" I called.

Silence, then: "El, Toma's here!"

I swore and ran to the mirror. *What's with the constant surprise visits? Doesn't he know how to call first?*

I'd just put the hairbrush down when he knocked at the door. Geta hovered behind him, looking nervous.

"It's ok, Geta," I told her.

"Door open!" she told me.

Toma smiled.

"I thought you were going away on a family thing," I told him once she'd gone up the hall to tidy dad's room.

"Cancelled," he said, stepping forward and taking my hand. My stomach lit up in flames. "Want to come up to Turtle Lake with me?"

I started to nod, then cringed. "I have a pile of History homework to do..."

He looked at me incredulously, then pulled me closer. "I can tell you everything you need to know. Come with me." He touched a hand to my cheek and brushed his thumb lightly across my lips.

"Ela-" Ilia warned, sounding uncertain.

"You'll be safe with me, I promise," Toma told me.

"Magic words..." I whispered, shutting my history book decisively.

We walked the full circle, passing cyclists, joggers and parents with pushchairs, talking about school and our friends- little things, though the real topic we wanted to talk about hung over us like a cloud. We went to the water's edge and I sat on the grass watching while Toma threw stones into the water, skimming them 10, 15, 20 times across the surface of the lake while the frogs croaked in the reeds. I breathed in, feeling both peaceful and on edge, a crazy combination.

At last Toma glanced at me, smiled, and came and sat next to me, his knees up and arms resting on them.

"So?"

"So?" I asked back with a smile, blushing.

He nudged me with his shoulder. "If you don't want to know..."

"Tell me," I said, cutting off his teasing.

"First, tell me what you know," he said.

"Well," I blushed. "I looked up demons online but I had no idea where to start. The same with elemental spirits. There was nothing about demons being stuffed into babies whose souls have been ripped out...so I'm not sure exactly what you are..."

"Think of us like Phoenixes: reborn, growing, dying and born again. We're put into children who are promised to the Azruzai by their mothers.

"Azruzai?"

"Our sect. My father's the regional leader."

"And mothers actually choose to give up their babies?" I asked, shocked.

He nodded, his face unaffected.

"Then what? After they put you demons in?"

"Then we grow with our human hosts, maturing as they do. When they die, we return to spirit form until we're reborn in a new host to grow and learn again."

"Do you remember your past hosts?" I wondered.

"No. I get flashes of deja-vu or memories that might belong to others...but with all the voices I hear, it's hard to distinguish. I think Ariman does, though."

"Who's Ariman?"

"My father."

"Is he really your dad?"

"Of a sort- more a guardian. After our mum died, he took it on himself to bring us up."

"I'm sorry- about your mum," I said.

He nodded and we looked out at the lake. A breeze- a precursor of a storm going by the fast gathering black cloud moving our way from the north- lifted my hair.

"So, who am I talking to now? The other day you said you were just a boy- just Toma. But I know that's not true."

He looked down at his hands, then sideways up at me. "My name's Lilu."

"That sounds like a girl's name," I said with a smile.

"It's not. It's ancient. Google it, though don't believe everything it says..."

"So, you're a centuries old demon..."

"Who right now feels 17," he said with a smile.

"And what happened to Toma? Is he inside you?"

He shrugged. "I don't know where the lost souls go. But what's here within me is just me. I'm Lilu in the body of Toma, so I am Toma. The spirit that was born in this body is gone."

"That's sad," I said, frowning.

"That's life and death," he replied with a shrug.

"Why didn't God give you your own bodies? Why let you steal others'? Isn't that a sin?"

"The bodies are given, not stolen." He looked up at the sky. "But I don't know. We just keep on doing what we do."

181

"You never asked God?"

"I've never met Him. Maybe we had our own bodies once...but not within my memory." He looked at me. "Want to see some magic?"

I nodded and he picked some grass, opened my right hand, palm-up, and sprinkled the blades over it.

"Don't move," he said. I smiled, wondering what was going to happen next, but kept my hand steady, as he'd asked.

He placed his hand over mine, spoke some silent words and slowly lifted his hand upwards. Between our palms was a mini tornado of grass, swirling gently and growing taller as he widened the gap. I looked up at him in surprise, then laughed and shook my head.

"How are you doing that?"

He shrugged. Then, lightening quick, he brought his hand down, scooped up the tornado and threw it up. The scattered grass fell down on us, landing in my hair and on my cheeks. I laughed and he leaned forward and kissed me.

I think that was the first moment I thought I might love him.

"Tell me about Ilia," he said, pulling away.

I swallowed, the mood dampened. It was instinct that told me not to answer- my memories of the trouble it had caused: doctor visits, medicine, my mum leaving...but I realised of all the people I could talk to about it, Toma, a supernatural being himself, was the most likely to understand.

"I don't remember life before him- but he said he came when I was four."

"What happened?"

I frowned. "What do you mean?"

Out the corner of my eye, I saw Ilia appear, leaning on the old tree, watching us. He was shaking his head.

"Something pulled him to protect you, right?"

I frowned, catching the sense of something- warmth, darkness, pain. But I couldn't form any images, so I said: "I guess it was the trauma of my mum being a bit crazy. Or because when Mikey was born I kinda got pushed to one side, like I wasn't really hers and Mikey was...I don't know."

I shrugged and shut my mouth, pulling at the grass, feeling I'd said too much; opened myself too much.

"Do you get a lot of black outs?" he asked quietly.

"Black outs?" I looked at him.

He nodded. "Times when you can't remember."

I smiled. "Well, as you've seen, that's usually alcohol related!"

"Usually?"

I shrugged, feeling my cheeks colouring.

"Talking about black outs...about that night at Night Office..." I started.

"What about it?"

I glanced around and, seeing no-one close, went on. "I don't remember how I ended up out on the street."

"I think you were following me."

I nudged him and laughed, blushing. "Yeah, right!" I joked sarcastically.

He smiled but said: "Seriously. Emily told me you were wound up about Susan's flirting...so she sent Susan up to mess with me to upset you."

"You were with Susan before she disappeared?! You told me you didn't see her!"

The news was both a relief and a shock.

"Well, she was coming on to me..." My stomach jolted in jealousy at the thought and I swallowed it back. "But she suddenly switched off, said she was going home and walked away."

"That's it? You didn't see anything?"

He shook his head and lobbed a stone into the water.

"Did you tell the police?"

"Of course," he said.

"And those boys?" I asked. "They chased me..."

"They were interested in Ilia," he said.

"Do you think they had something to do with Susan's disappearing? Maybe...judging her...for something."

"Maybe," he allowed. "But they're still 17, so...I doubt she died because of them."

"You know she's dead?"

He wrapped an arm around me and I held his hand on my shoulder.

"It's a pretty sure bet, don't you think?"

I frowned, thinking of 'Demon,' the earring, the fact Susan still hadn't been found.

"Yeah," I agreed. I realised I wasn't ready to tell Toma about 'Demon's' threats yet. Not until I knew more.

He kissed me, then stood up and pulled up his hood- it was getting cold. I got the impression the Q & A was over. He reached out a hand and helped me up.

"One last thing," I said as we walked up the hill to the path.

"Shoot."

"The solstice you guys were talking about...."

"You understood that?" he seemed surprised.

I shrugged.

"I know the June one is my birthday. And it's some kind of important spiritual holiday, right?"

He nodded, but didn't return the smile. "It's when our kind are brought through."

"It means more babies are going to die?" I wondered.

"It means more of my brothers and sisters will have the chance to live."

I thought of what Ilia said- about the number of demons increasing.

"And what does that have to do with me? Those friends of yours seemed pretty sure I killed Susan...and that you had until the solstice to, what, judge me?"

His jaw tensed and he looked away.

"You didn't kill Susan," he said quietly.

I touched his arm. "You know who did?"

He looked down, scuffing his sneaker on the ground, then looked up at me. "No. But I'll find out soon."

I felt the first drop of rain land on my cheek. He wiped it away with his thumb, kissed me, then rested his forehead against mine.

"It'll be ok," he said.

I guessed he meant about Susan and, reassured, I kissed him back, ignoring the rain now falling more heavily on us.

CHAPTER 44

NINA: U still at the docs?

ME: Just got home. Cast off, arm free! Got a bad case of Skinny Arm, but all fixed.

NINA: Congrats! So soon! And you got to miss a Monday! Got good news. Ms Stevens volunteered to take us on an excursion this weekend.

ME: Srsly?

SUSAN: Yep- says it's her way of rewarding us 4 studying so hard.

ME: Nice! Where this time?

NINA: Timotesubani church.

ME: O...K. Could b worse.

I was remembering the last church excursion we'd been on- a pile of ruins, though the picnic after had been fun.

ME: But we're Grade 11- why do we need an excursion?

NINA: Why not? It'll be nice to get outta the city...And I heard Grade 12 might tag along.

I could picture her wiggling her eyebrows at me provocatively.

ME: I'm in. Shame u couldn't see the game yest. T was soooo hot in his bball gear.

NINA: I had a hot enough video call with Giorgi! What did u do after?

ME: He took me to Luca Polare for ice-cream.

NINA: Romantic- but cold!

ME: Totally needed to cool off...

NINA: Haha.

ME: I just thought- the trip won't be so fun with E+A there, too.

NINA: Don't worry. Me n Mate will protect you from Mad Ari.

ME: Yeah, borrow ur uncle's Taser!

Her mum's brother was a policeman. Last summer he'd let us shoot off a couple of his guns in the village. He'd refused to let us Taser him, though.

NINA: I might do, at that!

ME: Wanna meet at Subway tonight?

NINA: Deal. 8?

ME: C u there.

It was busy but we managed to snag a table just as a group was leaving.

"So, what's the latest with you and Mr Incest?" she asked.

"Don't be gross," I told her.

She shrugged. "He kissed his sisters."

"Yet you keep telling me to get in there," I reminded her, taking a bite of my salad sandwich.

"If you can deal, so can I."

I swallowed. "I can."

"Though the sisters still want to kill you. Literally."

"Yep."

"And that doesn't put you off?" she wondered. "These death threats seem pretty real!"

I'd not told her about the other phone messages from 'Demon'. The most recent followed mine and Toma's surprise date on Saturday- she'd (I was now convinced it was one of his sisters) serenaded me with Neyo's "Don't Fall in Love," no doubt trying to remind me of Toma's several summer romances, with the main point being that he'd ultimately hurt me. Of all the songs she'd sent, that one had hit the worst chord. But even that I kept to myself, knowing that, like Ilia, Nina would only push me to go to the police again.

187

I shrugged, trying to keep it light. "Adds spice to the relationship, actually. And Toma won't really let them hurt me," I said.

"Don't be so sure," Ilia warned from behind me. I ignored him. He'd been off with me since Saturday. He hadn't been as impressed with Toma's "parlour" tricks and "petty confidences" as me- he was suspicious and nothing would change that. Sad for him, he couldn't convert me: I was head-over-heels for the demon Lilu and we both knew it.

"So, are you two official now?" she asked.

"Hard to say," I said. "Him and the other 12th graders spend more time out than in, you know that. Can't wait for it to be us!"

"I know, right?" She took a sip of her Pepsi. "Tell me about him," she asked, leaning closer. "Any dark skeletons in his closet?"

More than you can imagine, I thought. I shrugged. "We don't speak much," I said with a grin, wiping my mouth.

"Miss Machabeli, you shock me!" Nina said prudishly.

"No, I don't," I laughed.

"Oooo- speak of the devil," she said.

I tensed and looked around. Toma had just walked in with Saba. My heart sank when I saw Emily and Arabella behind them.

I pushed my sandwich away and took a gulp of Pepsi.

The boys saw us and headed over.

"Hi," I told Toma shyly, kissing him on the cheek as I did the others.

"Hi," he said, smiling warmly.

"I see your arm's better," Emily said, stroking a finger down my skin. I pulled away, tugging my sleeve down self-consciously over my too-pale arm.

"Yes," I said.

"What a pity."

"Don't be mean!" Arabella scolded with a cruel smile. They went over to the counter to order and we moved our jackets to make space for them, grabbing a couple of free chairs from the table next to ours.

"So, my birthday's coming up," Saba said when they were back.

"Party?" Toma asked. He was sitting diagonally opposite me- he would've sat next to me but Emily and Arabella practically ran to put themselves between us. It was fine with me- I got a better view, though I loathed having Emily so close, awareness of the blood link sending tremors of apprehension down my spine.

"I won't let them hurt you," Ilia said from behind me, ever sensitive to my moods.

Emily glanced back at him and gave me a smug smile. I didn't look- my eyes were on Toma.

I'd had another dream last night. Perhaps Emily had got bored of being "nice" to me, or she'd been inspired to remind me what Toma was really capable of. I'd been running in a giant labyrinth. A dark force was chasing me- an evil cloud of maliciousness that chilled me to the core. I ran this way and that trying to escape it, the walls oppressively high above me. In the centre, I'd found a circle of snow and ice, Ilia lying bleeding in the middle, his limbs broken as if from a great fall. His head was cracked and bleeding but he was still conscious when I fell down on my knees beside him, crying.

"They killed me," he whispered. "They..." his eyes moved past me- looking up to the heavens. I followed his eye-line and at the top of the cliff saw the triplets looking down at us, their faces stony. I screamed up at them in fury and they turned their backs to me and walked away.

I'd woken up shaking with the certainty that Ilia was gone. Of course, he'd appeared as soon as I called him and enveloped me in a hug.

"You're in too deep with these demons," he said, after I'd told him what I'd dreamed.

"They can't hurt you, can they?" I'd asked him.

To my relief, he shook his head. "No. But by hurting you, they're hurting me," he said.

"Toma isn't hurting me," I reminded him, remembering Turtle Lake.

"But his sisters won't let his attention be divided. Their jealousy is dangerous, and your arm only just got fixed," he said.

I'd kissed his cheek and laid back down. He lay behind me, his body warming me, his arms making me feel safe.

"Will you really be with me forever?" I asked.

He made a positive noise.

"But why?"

"You know- to protect you."

"Why me?"

"Why not you?" he'd replied cryptically.

"Did you pick me?"

"No. I was drawn to you. It just happened, but I'm thankful for it."

"I'm sorry," I said. "I got myself into something here..."

"Well, I have to admit it's a harder one to solve than stubbing your toe, falling off your bike, drinking floor cleaner instead of lemonade..."

I blushed. "I was five."

I sensed him smile. "Even so, it was a close one! And I'm glad I was there for you. I'm still glad, Ela."

Toma glanced in Ilia's direction and away, seeming unconcerned as he chatted to Saba about his birthday plans- first dinner at a restaurant, then back to his duplex for dancing and drinks. Maybe Toma believed that him asking his sisters not to touch me was enough. I didn't feel so confident, and what Emily whispered to me next was confirmation.

"In about 30 seconds, lean back on your chair- as far as it'll go."

"No!" I hissed back at her.

"So, are you girls up for? I thought about making it a lads' night but..." Saba asked.

"It just wouldn't be the same without us, right?" Arabella said, sliding her hand onto his thigh under the table.

His breath caught and he nodded. "Exactly."

"We're in," Nina said, shrugging.

"Definitely," Emily agreed.

I nodded. And realised I was unconsciously tilting my chair back.

I tried to ground it but couldn't- my feet pushed back and up even with my mind shouting at them to stop. Emily kept the focus on her- telling some scandalous story about our school caretaker caught for stealing.

"Ela- be careful," Ilia said from behind.

I knew I was going to fall and that Ilia couldn't materialise in front of a crowd. I clung to the table but my fingers were slipping. My face wouldn't even show the fear- my expression remained blank, my eyes fixed on Emily as if I was interested in what she was saying. Toma glanced at me and smiled. I tried to communicate with my eyes but I was trapped within myself, screaming for help.

My feet left the floor and my hands took over the pushing.

No, no, no! I thought, desperately.

Arabella, her arm on the back of her sister's chair leaned towards me and whispered: "Now, let go."

I did.

CHAPTER 45

"Woah, there," a familiar voice said, hands catching my chair as I tipped the balance and began to fall backwards.

"Ilia!" I gasped, relieved, looking up at him as I was released at last from the mental grip of the demons.

He was solid, strong, helping me upright.

Nina's eyes were goggling, her jaw practically on the tabletop. Everyone had stopped and was looking at the new boy who'd just saved their friend from a nasty crash.

Emily and Arabella looked as if they would happily start stabbing at him with their plastic forks; Toma was watching him, assessing. This was, as far as I knew, the first time they'd seen him in the flesh.

"Ilia," my angel said, shaking hands with them all, including me.

"You already met, remember?" Nina pointed out to him. "At the banquet hall?"

"Oh, yes," Ilia said, eyeing me warmly. He was a great actor- 10 out of 10.

"Good catch," Saba said, nodding at me. "Where did you appear from?"

"Just walked in," he answered, tilting a thumb at the door. "I saw- Ela, is it? - leaning too far back in her chair."

"Thank you. I don't know what came over me," I said, looking at Emily and Arabella pointedly. Toma's green eyes narrowed and he raised his eyebrows at his sisters. They smiled demurely at him.

"You're welcome," Ilia replied. "So, see you around."

"Join us," Saba invited. "We were talking about my birthday. Why don't you come along?"

"Well, I..."

"Oh, do!" Arabella said, a hand on his where it had rested briefly on the back of her chair.

Ilia glanced at me. "Ok," he said, pulling up a seat in the only free space- the corner between Arabella and Saba.

"Where are you from?" Saba asked him.

"Svaneti," he replied.

"Land of medieval towers and glaciers!" Toma said appreciatively.

"Have you been?" Ilia asked.

"Once or twice," Toma answered.

"I haven't. Might go skiing there this year," Saba said. "Your accent isn't as strong as I would've expected."

"I tried to adapt to city-life," Ilia said, smiling at me.

"And you're studying in Tbilisi?" Nina asked him.

"Home school."

"Nice!" Saba said. "Going to school is such a pain in the backside."

"Seven months till freedom!" Arabella said, grinning.

"Not for me," Emily said glumly.

"So, about this party..." Saba said- and went into a long discussion. Ilia recommended a restaurant and they sat chatting about the best food to order, whether they could get away with bringing their own drink...blahblahblah.

The triplets, though joining in the conversation, never lost their expressions of fascination as they stared at my angel.

I looked at Ilia and saw him fidgeting, in that moment remembering how much energy it took him to stay solid.

"I'm sure Ilia has places to be," I said, interrupting a discussion on the best beer to order for the house party.

Nina shot me a confused look, as if to say: *Are you crazy?!*

"Oh, come on Ela," Toma said. "He just got here."

"Well..." Ilia said, shooting me a look.

"No, really," Toma said, getting to his feet. "What can I get you?"

"I'm not…"

"It's on me," Toma said. "You are Ela's Guardian Angel, after all."

His sisters grinned, sharing that greedy look I so dreaded.

I glared at Toma but he just winked.

"Yes," Emily said, turning to my angel. "Stay."

Ilia gave a nod and forced a smile. I saw a bead of sweat roll down his left temple.

I got up and rested a reassuring hand on his shoulder as I passed, then went to Toma where he stood ordering a sandwich.

"You have to let him go," I said.

"Why? He chose to interfere."

"He did what he had to do to stop me falling and cracking my skull open," I said. "No thanks to your sisters."

"But here he is and here he'll stay until he can't take it anymore."

"What's he ever done to you?" I demanded angrily.

"He's a sinner and must be Judged," he hissed at me, then switched on a smile and paid the cashier.

"What?! He's an angel. How can he be a sinner?" I hissed back.

"Go and get him a Pepsi, El," Toma answered. "He looks a bit hot under the collar…"

It was a blood command, and my feet forced me over to the drinks machine and my hands pressed the button while I watched Toma hand Ilia a sandwich I wasn't even sure he could eat.

I hurried back and put the drink down in front of him and bent to whisper in his ear: "You don't have to do this. Just go."

He smiled at me, though I could see the tension in his eyes.

"Thanks," he said brightly.

I frowned and unenthusiastically returned to my seat.

They talked about normal things, the triplets now lavishing attention on Ilia, forcing him to talk, eat and drink- and burn energy. He did it all with a smile, while I couldn't eat or drink a thing.

'*Wassup?*' Nina mouthed at me.

I shook my head, my jaw tense.

"Toma, wanna smoke?" Saba asked.

I could see the demon was reluctant to leave his prey, but his craving for tobacco was stronger.

"Sure. You smoke, Ilia?" he asked, his smile twisted in amusement.

Ilia shook his head. "No- you go ahead."

"We'll keep him entertained while you're gone," Arabella promised, sliding a hand over Ilia's shoulder.

As soon as they were out the door, Ilia wiped his mouth and got to his feet. His hands were shaking.

"Where are you going?" Emily asked. To Nina, it probably sounded like a pleasant enquiry- but I could hear the warning underneath.

"The bathroom," Ilia told her firmly.

Arabella glanced at her sister and I could see they were calculating.

"Not gonna try and stop me, are you?" he asked with a smile, challenging them.

"No, no, of course not," Arabella soothed.

Ilia winked at me and turned to go.

"But it'll be sad to have Ela left on her own without you," she added. "Unprotected," she emphasised.

He stopped, his shoulders tense, and looked back at me, the pain clear in his eyes.

"I'll be ok," I reassured him.

"Jeez- he's only going to the loo!" Nina scoffed.

He clenched his fists.

I nodded at him. "Go," I said.

He took a breath and nodded back, glared at the sisters, and headed to the toilet.

"Is it just me, or did things just get strangely dramatic?" Nina asked, finishing up her Pepsi.

Toma came back in and gave his sisters a look of annoyance, immediately realising Ilia was out of their grasp.

We sat waiting for a few minutes, then Saba went to the bathroom to check. He came back with a frown, shaking his head.

"He's gone."

Nina looked at me, puzzled. "He ran out the back way?"

I shrugged. I knew I wouldn't be seeing him for a while. He'd been with us for around half an hour. The most time he'd ever spent with me in solid form was half that.

I realised Emily was looking at me with a smile.

I looked pointedly at Toma and he told his sister in Russian to leave it.

"Let's go, Nina," I said, grabbing my bag.

"Where?"

"Anywhere."

We said goodbye to Saba- who was chatting with some 12th graders from another school he'd met in the recent basketball match- and headed out.

"Are you ok?" she asked. "That was super weird."

"I'm fine. Dad's away. Want to sleep over at mine tonight?"

She grinned. "Definitely. Let me just call mum."

CHAPTER 46

"There's something I need to tell you," I said.

Nina was standing with her back to me, looking in the mirror as she rubbed my face cream around her eyes and over her forehead. She nodded to show she was listening.

"You remember I told you that when I was little I had an imaginary friend and that my parents locked me up with a shrink for a week to make it go away?"

She frowned and turned to face me, picking up the hairbrush and brushing her long waist-length hair in smooth straight strokes. "Of course, I do."

"Well, I lied to them. He never went away."

"What do you mean?" she asked.

"He was never imaginary," I said. "He was real."

"You what?"

I took a breath.

"That guy in Subway tonight? Ilia? That was my Guardian Angel."

I could feel Ilia's disapproval in the air around me, but it seemed he was unable even to speak, so I was temporarily free from his condemnation.

"Ela- you're freaking me out," Nina said. "Ilia was very clearly there. No figment of anyone's imagination."

So, I told her the whole story- what I could remember of it.

"And there's more," I admitted heavily.

"Can I sit down for the next part, then?" she asked, sounding shocked.

I nodded and she sat down on the edge of the sofa bed beside me.

"Go for it," she said.

"The triplets are demons."

Then I told her what I knew about Toma and how Emily had truly pushed me off the wall, and how it probably was Arabella who'd held her underwater in summer.

"I know this sounds crazy..." I finished.

"Yeah, it does," she agreed.

"But it's all true."

"Are you sure it's not just exam stress or something..." she said, a stab in the dark.

I shook my head. "I just wish I could prove it to you," I said.

"Tell Ilia to show himself," she suggested, looking around the room.

I shook my head. "He used up all his strength in the café. He won't be able to materialise for days...You'll just have to trust me."

"What about Toma? He doesn't disappear. Can you get him to do a magic trick in front of me? Light a fire or something?"

I shrugged. "I don't know. I can try."

"Or make a video with your phone," she suggested.

"Won't you just believe me?"

"It's hard to believe," she admitted.

I sighed.

I heard the doorbell ring downstairs and ignored it, figuring Mikey or Geta would get it.

"So, say this is all true-" Nina began.

"Which it is!"

"-it means you should put a hundred miles between you and the Morgans!"

"Why?"

"Well, clearly they're out to get you and Ilia. They're crazy."

"It's not so simple."

"We're talking angels and demons, who said it was simple?"

"No. I mean about Toma. I think I..."

The doorbell rang again and I huffed out an annoyed breath.

"MIKEY!" I shouted.

No answer.

"Fine!" I got up and went to the door. "Back in a mo.," I told my best friend.

I bounded back up the stairs two-at-a-time.

"It's *him*!" I hissed, shutting the door behind me and running to the dresser to fix my make-up.

"Who?"

"Toma!"

"The demon Toma?!"

I nodded. "But he shouldn't know you know that!"

"What are you doing?"

"What do you think?! I'm ready for a girls' sleep-over! He can't see me like this!"

"Ela! You're crazy!" Mariam's voice said.

I looked back and saw her face on Nina's phone screen.

"Don't I know it!"

"Nina was just telling me the latest..."

"Which part?"

"All of it. I'm actually hurt you didn't tell me sooner..."

"Nii..." I complained.

"Don't 'Nii' her- you should've told me. I told you about dad..."

"Woah, wait- what about your dad?" Nina asked, turning the phone to look at Mariam.

"Oh, he's a demon-hunting exorcist fanatic," I said, being deliberately blasé.

199

"El!" Mariam complained. "I've actually been talking to him... some of what he says makes sense. You, though..."

"Look, I'm sorry," I told her. "It was never the right time..."

"The right time being after one of his demon brides killed you?" Mariam suggested sarcastically.

"They're his *sisters*!" I glared at Nina. "And how did you manage to tell her so much in the two minutes I was gone?!"

She shrugged. "I may have mentioned a few things before today..."

"At least you have the decency to blush!" I said, and turned back to the mirror to smear on some foundation.

"Are you sure he's what you say he is?" Mariam asked.

"I know he's got powers. I've seen it. And I trust Ilia."

"Your Guardian Angel?" Nina asked, glancing at Mariam.

"Yeah, go on, have a laugh," I told them. "Crazy Ela. Been there, had the treatment."

"We're not laughing," Mariam pointed out. "We're worried about you!"

"Well, when Ilia's got his strength back, I'll get him to appear right in front of you. Then that'll be one thing out the way."

Again, that shimmer of disapproval in the air around me.

"And how do we prove The Bastard is what you say he is?" Nina wondered.

"Let me talk to him," Mariam said. "I've got an idea."

"Why?! What are you going to say to him?" I asked, suspicious.

"He's dating my bestie- don't I have a right to ask a few questions?"

I wanted to argue with her but Nina had already called Toma's name and invited him up.

"I can't believe you're doing this to me," I told them through gritted teeth as I heard him climbing the stairs.

"I'll be back," Mariam said. "Don't hang up."

"What if he goes crazy and burns the house down?!" Nina suddenly asked in a panic, grabbing a dressing gown out of my wardrobe to cover the nightie I'd lent her.

"Then it'll be totally your fault for provoking him...and you wanted proof of his powers, so there you'll have it!"

"El..." she complained.

There was a knock at the door.

"Come in," I said, inviting the demon into my bedroom.

"Hey," he said, stepping in. He left the door open and shoved his hands in the pockets of his hoodie.

"Hi Nina," he said.

"Hi," she said, crossing her arms and frowning at him defensively.

He took in the mess of make-up, nail varnishes, CDs and snacks and gave me a crooked grin. "I can come back another time," he said.

"No, no. It's fine," I said, grabbing his hand and pulling him to the edge of my bed. "Sit."

"Our friend wants to meet you," Nina said, shifting to sit on the dressing table stool.

"Why?" he asked.

"Curiosity," I said with a shrug, sitting next to him, feeling my cheeks warming.

"Curiosity killed the cat," he said.

Nina's eyes went wide and I saw the panic there. Toma caught the look and frowned at me with a smile. "What's going on?" he asked.

"Nothing," I said.

"I'm back," Mariam's voice said from Nina's hand. "So, where is he?"

Nina turned the screen to face me and Toma.

"Hi," he said, waving at her. He looked totally at ease, whereas I wished I could crawl under the bedclothes and make the whole day go away.

"Mariam, this is Toma," I told her in English.

"Toma. I've heard a lot about you," she said with a friendly-enough smile.

"Have you?" he looked at me, his eyebrows raised.

I shrugged, blushing.

"I want you to meet my dad," she said. "He's like a second father to Ela."

"O-kay," Toma agreed.

Mr Walker appeared on screen. It was the first time I'd seen him since the airport and he looked very different. In fact, I'd describe him as haggard- his jaw and cheeks covered in two days of beard, his hair unkempt, his eyes lined and tired-looking.

"Mr Walker! How are you?" I asked brightly, trying to cover my shock at his appearance.

"Good to see you, Ela," he said, though his focus was on Toma.

"Hi," Toma said again.

"Do you mean them harm?" Mr Walker asked him abruptly in Russian.

Toma frowned.

"Answer me, Ahriman," Mr Walker demanded. "We know what your lot are planning and we will stop you. What do you want with Eliso?"

Toma showed a millisecond of surprise- looking at me, then back at the screen. Then his expression closed and he stood. "I'm going," he told me.

"Wait," I said. But he was already out the door and heading downstairs.

"Thanks a bunch!" I told Nina angrily. She shrugged, looking apologetic as I ran out the door after him.

Mikey came in the apartment door just as he was leaving and gave him a warm greeting. Toma ignored him and started down the stairs.

"Toma, please wait!" I called, stopping to put my boots and coat on.

"What's up with him?" my brother asked, dumping his guitar on the sofa.

"It doesn't matter. Listen- Nina's upstairs. Go talk to her, right?"

"Nina?" his eyes reminded me of a rabbit caught in the headlights of a car. It was cute but I didn't have time to indulge his teen lusts.

I punched the lift button and it opened. I jumped in and hit 'G,' hoping I could beat Toma down. My dream flashed, unbidden, into my mind's eye. *How angry was Toma right now?* I suddenly realised I didn't have Ilia to protect me.

The lift door opened just as Toma was leaving the glass entrance of the building. He turned and headed down towards Rustaveli Avenue- probably to get the Metro home.

"Toma, please," I begged. I ran forward and went to grab his arm but, sensing his mood, chose to fall into step with him instead.

"What did Mr Walker mean?" I asked. "What are you planning?"

He shook his head, clearly too angry to speak.

"I'm sorry," I said.

"How could he know what I am?" he asked, though from his voice I could tell he knew.

"I didn't know Mariam would tell him," I said, realising as I spoke how lame it sounded.

"I trusted you," he said.

"You never swore me to secrecy," I pointed out.

"Don't be childish," he said. "You know this isn't the kind of thing that makes good gossip with your girlfriends. This isn't a game. It's dangerous."

"I don't think you're dangerous," I said quietly. "Not to me, any-way."

"All sinners must be punished," he recited as if by rote.

"Am I a sinner?" I asked quietly.

He frowned but didn't answer, nor did he slow.

"I don't think you'll hurt me," I said.

"How can you be so sure?" he asked, a sharp edge to his voice.

I shrugged, pushing away the dream images. "I just am."

He narrowed his eyes thoughtfully, then scowled, shook his head and stepped up his pace.

Great, I thought angrily. *I'll kill Nina and Mariam when I get back! How could they do this to me?* I pictured smashing that damn iPhone Nina adored, unfriending Mariam...and them both twisting their ankles on those stupid clubbing high-heels they loved, maybe falling down a few steps. *Didn't believe that Emily was a demon, huh? Thought I was crazy?* Well, let *them* break an arm and...

"What are you doing?" Toma asked, stopping and turning so suddenly, I bumped into him.

I looked up at him, shocked.

"Nothing. Following you."

"You're projecting sinful thoughts. I can hear them. That's not like you..."

He touched a hand to my shoulder and for a moment the dark anger surged, then receded.

"Sorry," I said again. "I'm angry at Nina and Mariam...I had no idea they'd confront you like that..."

He sighed. "Don't be. I mean, you don't need to be angry."

I bit my lip. "I don't want to lose you," I blurted, then blushed, looking at my boots, feeling stupid.

He smiled and tilted up my chin. "I'm not so easily lost, Ela."

Relief flooded my stomach and I put a hand on his chest, feeling his heart beating there, and kissed him, once more feeling an overwhelming need to be with him.

"Why did you come round, anyway?" I wondered after we broke apart to move out of an old lady's way- hobbling past, complaining of the rude youth of today, kissing on the streets.

"To see how your ghost was," he said with a shrug.

"He's weak," I said dryly. "And with your sisters out to get me, that's not good."

"They won't kill you," he promised.

I gave a short laugh. "They'll just break every bone in my body?"

He frowned and stroked my cheek.

"So, what was Mariam's dad talking about? Are you guys planning some demon takeover or something?" I asked, smiling to show him I was joking.

But he didn't return the smile. His jaw flexed in tension.

"It's...elder business," he told me hesitantly.

"Your dad?"

"Not only him. But in any case, I don't take kindly to threats from your friends' parents. It's best you all stay out of it."

"I...want to be part of it," I said, my voice small, nervous. "I want to be part of you."

He frowned and hooked his fingers into my jeans pockets, pulling me close. Instead of answering, he kissed me.

I didn't head straight home after Toma left, instead sitting in the park near my building, breathing the cool evening air and watching the happy couples and groups of friends riding the funicular up to the restaurant on Mtatsminda mountain. The aerial glowed its standard white and red, just like the Georgian flag- no new EU agreement to celebrate or special country to recognise and change its colour for.

"Thinking about Toma?" a voice whispered: Ilia, still not at any strength to appear.

I nodded and, seeing the coast was clear, whispered back: "How are you feeling?"

"I've been better. It was my own choice to appear."

"Thank you," I said. "You saved me from a serious bump to the head!"

"Why do you keep up relations with the Morgans?" he asked after a moment.

I shrugged.

"They're no good for you, nor are their circle."

"So, you keep saying," I reminded him. "It doesn't change how I feel about Toma, though."

My memory flew back to the previous day, sitting over ice-cream with him, the warm smell of coffee and chocolate around us.

"Have you ever read the Bible?" Toma had asked me.

"Er...once," I said, flushing, for some reason embarrassed by my lack of dedication to my own religion. "You?"

He'd smiled. "I know it by heart. Do you remember the Ten Commandments?"

"The Old Testament? Thou shalt not steal...thou shalt not take another man's wife..."

We'd gone through the rest of them.

"Are those the sins you judge people for?" I'd asked.

He'd nodded. "We live by the principles: Humata, 'Good Thoughts;' Hukhata, 'Good Words;' and Havarashta, 'Good Deeds.' Obey them and eternal happiness is yours. Disobey them and suffer the consequences."

"And how do you decide how to punish?"

"It's up to our interpretation. Like I told you- it's instinct."

At that point, the red-head from Night Office had walked in.

He seemed surprised to see me and Toma together. Unhappy, actually.

Toma greeted him with a handshake.

"What's going on?" he asked Toma in Russian, frowning down at me.

"It's under control," Toma told him quietly.

Alastor narrowed his eyes. "She's dangerous," he said.

"Excuse me?" I asked, standing.

"Have you even told her?" he asked Toma, giving me a look of distain.

"Told me what?"

"You can understand us?" he'd asked, surprised.

I nodded and shrugged.

His face changed to anger. "You're teaching her our language now?" he accused Toma. "This is so wrong."

"Leave it," Toma advised him, then he took my hand. "Let's go," he told me in English.

Alastor gave him a smile, though it was far from friendly. "Sure. See you at the solstice."

"What's happening on the solstice?" I'd asked Toma, and he'd replied it was just a party they had every year around Christmas-time.

"Killing babies?" I dared.

"No," he'd replied.

"And what is it you haven't told me?"

"About us," Toma had answered quickly. "Demons."

"And why am I dangerous?" I wondered.

He pulled me around a corner into a quiet road and pushed me against the wall of the building.

"Because you're stealing the heart of the boss' son," he'd said and kissed away any other questions.

"You'll get hurt- literally," Ilia said, bringing me back to the present.

"I know there are...risks. But I think Toma genuinely cares," I told him. "You know he came to apologise, right?"

"To me or to you?"

"Me, of course," I said with a small smile. "I think it hurts him to even acknowledge you. Why is that? And he keeps calling you 'ghost'. Why?"

Silence, then, very quietly: "I don't know."

"Are you angry I told the girls about you?"

He sighed. "A little...disappointed. But I suppose it had to come at some point."

"Well, Nina is the 'I'll-believe-it-when-I see-it' type, and Mariam...I think her dad going a bit nuts is having an effect...which works in my favour as long as she doesn't keep provoking Toma."

"You think Mr Walker is nuts?"

"You think he's not?"

"Not sure," he said, then would say no more.

I found Mikey and Nina on the sofa, a movie playing on the TV. Nina had fallen asleep and Mikey was sitting with his arm protectively around her, looking one third proud and two thirds terrified.

I smiled. He was growing up too fast.

"Come on, Ni," I said, encouraging her up. "Bed's upstairs."

"Do you hate me?" she mumbled sleepily.

"No!" I said, remembering those dark thoughts of mine which had set Toma's judger-alarm going. Those thoughts were gone now, though- all forgiven.

"Mariam wants to talk to you. So, does her dad," she said.

"Tomorrow," I said.

"I broke my phone..." she said, crawling into her sleeping bag then holding the iPhone up. The screen was smashed and black, useless.

I froze. It looked exactly as I'd imagined it to look when I pictured the revenge I'd take on her for embarrassing me in front of Toma.

"What happened to it?" I asked, falsely casual as I pulled back my own covers.

Nina shrugged. "It was weird, actually. I was walking down the stairs with Mikey and just got this really strong desire to throw it. I didn't, of course, but my hand let go anyway. Your marble steps did the rest," she said sadly.

"Must've been a guilty conscience," I joked lightly, though I felt anything but light. "Just do me a favour- don't wear high-heels for a while, ok?"

"What?! Well, I'm sorry I told Mariam. I had no idea she'd get her crazy dad involved."

"You think he's crazy?"

"He believes in demons," she said, then stopped herself and looked at me, her cheeks reddening. "Sorry."

"It's ok," I said, swallowing my anger. "It does sound crazy."

"Maybe you should just let her forget it and go back to believing in a normal world," Ilia suggested, still invisible.

I shook my head. I needed Nina to believe.

"Can you show yourself?" I asked him.

"What?" Nina asked, looking down at herself in the covers, then back at me, confused.

"I was talking to Ilia," I said.

"Ohhh...."

"Are you sure?" he asked.

I nodded.

He sighed, then the air shimmered beside me and I looked to watch him emerge- not at full strength, but almost- just enough that Nina could see him, too.

Her mouth and eyes made three circles.

"Oh. My. God," she said.

"Hi, again," Ilia replied.

CHAPTER 47

At our special request, we got the minibus driver to pass Khashuri before turning towards the Borjomi area, and drive us up into the pine forest to buy some sweet cinnamon-raisin *nazuki* bread from one of the many road-side traders. I got out while the rosy-cheeked village woman bustled around in her hut getting our order out of the pit-oven, breathing in the heady scent of woodsmoke and winter pine. The first snow was yet to come, but the air was chill enough for me to need my jacket on.

"Ela," Toma said in greeting, coming to stand beside me, a cigarette in his mouth.

I smiled shyly and glanced around. His sisters were far enough away for me to take the risk and kiss him. I'd barely seen him at school this week.

"I missed you," I told him.

He smiled. "How's your ghost?"

"I'm fine," Ilia said from right behind Toma's back, making him jump, though he was invisible even to me- he'd barely had the energy to let me see him all week since Subway and then showing himself to Nina. And all week she'd been pestering me: "Is he here now?"

"Yes," I'd repeated for what felt like the hundredth time.

"Watching you?"

"He's always watching- that's how he protects me."

"Even when you're...you know... on the loo or...getting it on with a boy?"

"Nii!" I complained. "Come *on*."

"Save the chat for break time, please, girls," Ms. Rostov had told us from her place by the board.

"Has he seen you get it on with Toma?" she whispered a few minutes later.

I glared at her and didn't reply, feeling a dark hungry need tug at my body. *Toma, Toma, Toma...*

"Toma!" Arabella called from the minibus, glaring at me. "We're going!"

He stubbed out his cigarette and blew out an angry cloud of smoke. I turned away from the woods and went back to my class-mates, feeling Toma's eyes on me.

The next part of the drive was one of my favourites: from a wider valley along a tree-lined B-road into Akhaldaba and the gorge- the vast river on one side, criss-crossed with footbridges; sheer rock face on the other, the layers of rock pushed almost vertical. That natural wall would occasionally dip away to reveal small areas of grazing land and a scattering of houses with tin roofs and smoking chimneys. I saw a farmer leading his two cows along a muddy lane, the late morning sunlight barely warming the earth. A splash of bright yellow painted fences, then back to bare trees, their brown leaves shed and lying in unattended piles in the gutter; a few fields of dried corn stems, and, looking up, pine trees on the mountains. We entered the boundaries of Borjomi town and turned left over the first bridge, heading towards Bakuriani through another stretch of gorge, this one with the river on the right; with a few smaller settlements on the way. At the springwater village of Tsaghveri, we turned left- a cheer went up in the minibus when we saw the sign to the Timotesubani monastery. Two hours out of Tbilisi and we were ready to picnic!

As we walked through the renovated red-brick-wooden gate, some of our group kissed the frame, including Nina, and crossed themselves. I did the same, touching my forehead to the wood.

The triplets walked past us chatting loudly. Emily tugged gently on the bells at the top of the path, earning her a telling off from our teacher.

We headed into the side entrance of the 12th century church and I put the hood of my jacket up. Only Emily and Arabella didn't do the same or cover their hair with a borrowed scarf from the stand. The scent of incense and wax enveloped me and I closed my eyes, enjoying the warmth of it. I always felt at home in Georgian churches- the older the better.

"Are you ok?" a voice asked quietly, warm hands pressing to my shoulders. I turned to my angel and smiled.

"Peaceful," I said.

"Ilia!" Nina said, surprised, appearing beside me with a blue silk scarf covering her hair, white Georgian ornaments block-printed on it.

He smiled at her and she tried to smile back, but open-mouthed wonder won over.

"Earth to Nina," Saba called, clicking his fingers in my friend's face. "You said you'd buy me some candles...oh, hi, Ilia. Nice to see you again."

My angel reached out and shook Saba's hand.

"Let's...er...get those candles," she said, backing away, her eyes fixed on Ilia but pulling Saba's sleeve.

"See you around," Saba said. "And don't forget my party- Ela, take his number, will you? Nina- stop pulling me!!"

"Still struggling with the truth, is she?" Ilia asked, smiling.

I squeezed his hand and looked around at the painted saints; full bodies of faded red, blue, green, orange and flesh-coloured, framed in red- builders, warriors, scholars. There were animals, too, on the arches; crudely drawn elephants, birds and lions prancing around the exposed brickwork. In some places, only the heads of saints remained, their bodies having fallen away with the years of changing temperature. The walls boasted heavy-framed icons- the dark-skinned gilt Mary and Jesus, the elementary colours that made up St George on his horse... and there, looking down from above, the benevolent faces of Mary and her son painted hundreds of years ago onto the ceiling, Mary's face worn to an almost skeletal appearance by time.

Ilia bought candles and handed me three, then went over to stand in front of the icon of Saint Michael the Archangel.

The last time I'd been in this church was when I was four, with my parents. Mum was pregnant and in pain. My dad had persuaded to come here and pray- we were staying in Borjomi for the water anyway and a quick "Dear God, help me..." stop was no big deal.

I went to stand in front of the Holy Mother, bowing my head and thanking her for the protection Ilia gave me. I'd just begun to recite the words of a familiar prayer under my breath when, suddenly, something in the atmosphere changed. I glanced over at Ilia and saw he'd felt it, too, and was looking around the dull hall, confused. Everyone around us had stopped moving. Silence fell over the space, and for a second I could hear only the hiss and guttering of the dying candles. Then a cackle sounded to my right. I looked to see Emily laughing and pulling candles out of the sales box and scattering them on the floor. Toma whooped in delight and made his way into the darkest corner, while Arabella whistled and weaved her way through the people, peering into their faces, though they made no move in reaction. I felt I was watching through the sides of an aquarium- the people the fish in the bowl, me outside, unable to help them, and the Morgan triplets the sharks swimming between. I looked around for Nina and saw her bent over to kiss the centre icon; frozen, her eyes closed. Only me, Ilia and the triplets were able to move freely.

"What are you doing?" I demanded. "Stop it!"

The Morgans looked at me, and the sisters narrowed their eyes to see me unaffected by their dark magick. Toma gave a small frown, then turned away.

"Why should we? You don't believe in all this, do you?" Arabella asked as she reached past me to the framed icon of Mary and baby Jesus and touched her fingertips to Mary's eyes. When she slid her fingertips down, she left a trail of blood.

I gasped and looked over at Emily. She was dancing on the altar just in front of the priest, whose incense still burned, though the thurible remained frozen mid-swing. Her dance was erotic, wrong, and not just for the fact that no women, unless they were brides, were allowed on the steps. She went through the swing doors into the little rear-altar and hesitated, looking up at the cross on the table, resting on the red velvet mantle. For a moment, I thought she was praying, but then she spat a gob of phlegmy spit onto the gold. It slid down and dripped slowly onto the tabletop while Emily looked on smiling.

I looked around, horrified, and saw Toma dragging the intricately carved wooden cross of death, belonging in the west corner of the building, up to the altar. Emily giggled delightedly.

"Toma, don't," I begged quietly. He shot me a half-smile.

"They have to be Judged," he said.

"What have you done to everyone?" I couldn't understand why I was the only one who could see them being so mean.

"Time fluctuations," Arabella spoke in my ear. I jumped. "They'll catch up to us, see the damage, but we'll already be long gone."

"Please stop!" I said.

"Why do you care?"

I glanced at Ilia nervously. He looked distraught. "Because it's not right!"

"Who says it's not right? God?" Toma asked, now leading the oblivious priest over to the cross and putting him in front of the sand-filled candle stand beside it. "Him?"

At first, I thought he was referring to the priest, but then he shot a look over my shoulder and I realised he meant Ilia.

I looked back at my Guardian Angel and saw him with his eyes narrowed in dislike, looking right back at Toma.

I caught Emily sticking her tongue out at Ilia as she jumped lightly down from the altar step.

"Time to go," Toma said, steering her away.

I watched them skip out the door laughing. As she left, Arabella knocked the scarf stand to the floor, sending silk and cotton to the stone in disorder.

I went towards it as they disappeared back out into the sunshine, hoping to clear some of the mess up before everyone came to their senses.

"It's too late," Ilia told me sadly, then he looked back towards the priest as my ears filled with a rush of noisy air.

A shout of surprise, a scream, the thump as someone fainted against a candle stand and the clang as it was knocked to the ground. Then the scream of the priest as he realised his long grey beard was on fire.

He left a trail of acrid smoke behind him as he dashed passed me, out and down through the rose garden, slipped on the stone steps, then half crawled through the huge wooden gates into the carpark. We all heard the splash as he jumped into the icy stream the other side of the lane and sank his face into the water.

The church was in uproar; the black-clad nuns dashing here and there between pale parishioners, who sat, weak and shocked, on the floor as they cursed the devil and his minions for their blasphemy.

"*Vai, vai,* God help me," our Georgian teacher begged, fanning herself and leaning heavily on Saba as he helped her out of the church.

Two men went to pick up the death cross to take it back to its place in the western corner but a woman screamed, begging them not to touch it lest they be struck down. Then another woman saw the blood that Mary was "crying" and loudly proclaimed it a miracle, a breath later saying we humans had brought the demon attack on ourselves for some sin- the "tears" were a clear sign of God's disappointment in us. Another woman took up the cries. A third began to disagree loudly with her. Then everyone joined in with their own opinions.

"What the hell is going on?" Nina asked.

"Hell," I said, unable to think of a better word.

"They're saying the devil was here!" she said.

"I know."

"The Morgans?"

I nodded. "Let's get out of here."

I saw the triplets the other side of the carpark, standing around a grazing chestnut horse. They were laughing at the sopping wet priest, who was being dragged from the water by our science teacher and two heavy-set local men, alive but with his beard half-gone and his chin and right cheek pink.

I narrowed my eyes and set my attention back on the triplets.

"How dare they?!" I mumbled as I stormed towards them, leaving Nina to gossip with our classmates.

"Don't waste your time trying to understand them," Ilia said, now transparent for only me to see, matching me step for step.

"Why not? Maybe I can get them to stop judging us."

"They won't stop- this is what they do. They've been doing it for centuries."

"They disgust me."

Ilia smiled, pleased to see I'd come to my senses.

I thought how good it would feel to set *Emily's* hair on fire, or throw Arabella into the water, see how *she* liked it...

I walked up to the Morgans, half expecting to hear them torment-ing the poor horse, but instead I heard Emily whispering soothing words to it. Toma was looking at me frowning.

"You're doing it again," he said.

"What?" I snapped.

"Thinking sinful thoughts."

"Is it any wonder?" I exclaimed, "How could you?!" I asked them.

"Little Miss Perfect is angry at us," Emily lamented mockingly.

"Too right I am when you hurt innocent people like that!"

The girls laughed and I felt an overwhelming urge to start hitting them.

"Ela," Ilia warned.

"Calm down and look at this," Toma said, beckoning me forward.

He stepped aside and behind him I saw a sign: Keep your church clean, throw your rubbish into the water.

"No way!" I exclaimed, shocked.

"Yes way," Arabella said. "Your darling priest over there, the one who spent hours brushing his beloved beard while his nuns scrubbed the floors for him, painted the sign himself." I looked over and saw the priest sitting on the wall near the gate, surrounded by concerned parishioners. "He believes the blessed water will cleanse away all sin, as its flow will sweep all picnic leftovers downstream to be someone else's problem. And that honey they're selling over there?" She pointed to the little wooden hut containing a fat local woman selling candles, icons and golden honey.

"It's fake," Toma cut in. "Sugar. It costs them Tetris to make and they sell it for 15 Lari a jar, then spend the money fuelling their huge 4x4s." He pointed towards the monastery and in front of it two giant black Toyotas.

"*And* the priest owns a bakery in Tbilisi. Know what it's called?" Arabella asked.

I shook my head.

"'Holy Bread,' and he overprices it- even for poor pensioners who think they'll be cured of their rheumatism if they buy it, just because it has 'holy' water in."

"They're cheaters!" Emily concluded.

"In other countries, he'd be shut down for false advertising," Toma said. "Here, there's us."

"And that's why you set the man on fire?" I demanded. "You could've killed him!"

"Oh, we'd never do that," Emily said. "Daddy would never allow it."

"Daddy? You mean head demon daddy?"

"Yes," Arabella said. "Our father is quite strict about the order of things."

"Only the Elders are permitted to kill," Toma clarified.

"If that's the case, then I wonder what he'd have thought of your little stunt on Narikala!" I threw at Emily.

She glared at me.

"Maybe he doesn't know..." I pushed.

"Ela, stop," Ilia advised from behind me.

I ignored him. "Maybe I should tell him. That his crazy kids are going around trying to knock classmates to their death and burn priests at the altar."

Emily's eyes blazed. "Maybe you should listen to your ghost!" she spat.

"He's not a ghost!" I yelled.

"What's going on here?" Nina asked, walking through Ilia, tucking her scarf into her bag.

"Nothing," I told her.

"Doesn't look like nothing," she said, coming to stand squarely beside me, glaring at the triplets.

"Ela- tell your friend to f-off," Arabella said.

I opened my mouth, intending to throw the insult back at her. But instead I found myself turning towards Nina, the blood magick compelling me to follow through. I fought it.

No! I willed myself to stop as my lips formed the words. No! I pushed back at the demonic force but it was too strong.

Nina looked at me, frowning in confusion.

"Enough Arabella," Toma said. "Ela, don't."

And just like that I was released from the compulsion. Toma's sisters glared at him.

"Just give me a moment, Ni," I told my friend.

"But..."

"It's ok," I reassured her. "I'll meet you on the bus."

"You need to stop messing with me," I told them when she'd gone.

"Annoying you, is it?" Arabella asked innocently. "Should we be scared?"

"Ohh...don't want to upset her ghost!" Emily giggled, glancing in Ilia's direction.

"Or maybe we do," Arabella said. "Then we can find out what dirty little secrets she's been hiding."

"Why don't you tell me, 'Demon'?" I asked her. "All those messages you've been sending..."

"I've no idea what you're talking about," she said lightly.

I looked at Emily. She smiled and shrugged.

"What's she talking about?" Toma demanded of his sisters.

"No idea," Emily said quickly. "But ghosts come to people at their darkest hours," she told me.

"So, people with an 'Angel,' as you call him, usually have a dark secret," Arabella finished for her, twirling a strand of hair around her finger.

"What?!" I asked, glancing over at Ilia where he now hovered near the priest, watching us. "He's been with me since I was little. Nothing happened to make him come...I mean, life wasn't perfect but there were no great tragedies or anything..." I looked at Toma. "I told you that. There's nothing else..."

"I doubt that," Toma said quietly.

"Well, I don't have any 'dark secrets'. So, if the reason you came to my school is curiosity, I'm afraid I can't help you."

"Maybe you do and you're blocking the memory," Emily suggested.

Arabella smiled and nodded. "Oh, we know there's more to you than you show, Eliso. We want to know why you got a guardian when you were four."

"You're marked," Toma said softly.

Dark secrets? I thought of Susan, 'Demon,' and the nightmares I'd been having. But Ilia was in my life way before that. My mind, unbidden, flashed to my mother, her face lit by flame, though I couldn't place where I'd ever seen her like that.

I shook the thoughts away. "So, you're basically waiting around to find out what sin I committed- or my family...?"

"Oh, we have bigger fish to fry," Arabella replied breezily. "You're just the side dish."

I opened my mouth to give a sharp retort, but Saba appeared behind me and draped an arm over my shoulder.

"Can you believe that?!" he asked us.

"Crazy, right?!" Arabella agreed, switching on a cheerleader smile.

"They're saying it was demons," he said, running his fingers through his sandy blond hair, his cheeks flushed in excitement.

Emily and Arabella laughed lightly. Toma remained poker-faced, but, sensing me looking at him, looked back; a challenge in his olive-green eyes.

"Time to go!" Ms Stevens called out.

CHAPTER 48

"I'm sorry what we did upset you so much," Toma said, coming to crouch by my seat.

A few seats down, I saw Emily watching him angrily.

"Why say sorry to me? You should apologise to the priest."

Toma shrugged. "He'll live."

"I'll just go and talk to Saba," Nina said, getting up and squeezing past us.

I moved over so Toma could sit next to me. His proximity set my skin alight and aching for him. I fought it.

"I don't get it," I said in a low voice. "I don't get *you*. One minute you say you have to judge people, the next you're doing things which are just as bad, if not worse, than the people you want to punish..."

"We talked about the Ten Commandments," Toma reminded me quietly. "That's our basic guideline. How we punish is up to our interpretation."

"Sounds like a lot of grey area," I said, frowning.

He smiled. "It is- but practise makes perfect. That's why our father's training us."

"And all demons get trained?"

"From the day they're bound...if not, they lose control, kill..."

"What does 'bound' mean?"

"Our father bound us in these bodies- he's done it for hundreds of other demons, too, over the years. And there are others like him helping us through."

I frowned, again getting a flash-image of my mother's face, fire, an underground place. It made no sense.

"Do you ever punish someone unnecessarily?"

"No," he said. "We're not hateful beings. We act carefully."

I glanced sceptically in his sisters' direction and he caught the look.

"Well, with the exception of a few...emotional moments. We're humans, too, at the end of the day. But we learn to control our feelings, our anger, as our bodies mature."

"It must be hard hearing all those horrible things and having to sort out other people's messes...I guess I'd be surprised if you didn't get angry..." I sympathized.

He slid his fingers between mine and smiled.

"The training helps. As demons, hearing sin after sin on top of more sin, we can become too filled with anger. We can lose control. But the training teaches us to control the demon side using human compassion- that's why hosting with humans is so necessary. By the time we get to adulthood- 18- we have full control of our demon side."

"Are you allowed to, you know, love?"

He laughed softly and looked at me in a way that made my body tingle. Then he leaned forward.

"We can love," he said, and gently pressed his lips to mine, heating my insides right down to my toes. We parted a minute later panting, me realising how much I needed him, because he gave me something I'd never had; made me feel more intensely than ever before.

"Are you sure your sisters won't kill me for this?" I whispered, my forehead to his.

He laughed and shook his head.

"Well, technically, they're not my sisters. But...hey...don't worry. We're not allowed to kill and they wouldn't dare- they respect my choices."

"Your sister trying to push your girlfriend off a mountain is respect?"

"Girlfriend?" he retorted, one eyebrow raised in question.

"Whatever," I said, blushing. "You know what I mean."

He sighed and looked down at his hands. "We're kinda wound up right now."

"Aren't we all?" I pointed out. "We all have exams, you guys have uni applications coming up..."

He gave a wistful smile. "If only that's all it was!" he said.

"So, what is it?"

"Family issues," he said, then shut his mouth and looked away.

Before we got back to Tbilisi, I called Levan and told him I'd walk home from Rose Revolution Square.

"Did you clear it with your dad?" he asked.

"Of course," I lied.

"So, if I phone Mrs B at 8pm, you'll be home?"

I sighed and rolled my eyes. Toma smiled, puzzled.

"Sure. I'll be home." I hung up.

"Bodyguard problems?" he guessed.

"More like babysitter problems!"

"Guarded at every turn," he observed.

"My dad's a little overprotective," I said, then looked over at Ilia, standing at the front looking out the window. "So's Ilia," I whispered.

Toma smiled and kissed me again.

He slipped into a dark mood as we walked, seeming distracted.

"Hearing a lot of sins?" I asked, walking beside him, my cold hands shoved in the pockets of my puffa.

"It's the weekend in the capital city," he said by way of explanation. At the corner of the Opera House, he suddenly stopped, looking down the street.

"I have to go," he said.

"No- stay with me," I said, taking hold of his arm. I wanted to walk more, to get to know him better; to enjoy more kissing...

He gave me a small smile and put a hand to my cheek, leaning down and pressing his lips to mine. Just a second, then he pulled away.

"I can't," he said, his jaw flexing in irritation.

"What is it? What did you hear?" I asked.

For a moment, he didn't answer- and then he forced himself to look at me.

"A burglar. In a flat. Stealing."

"Is he hurting anyone?" I asked.

"There's no-one home," he answered hollowly.

"Then. Let. It. Go," I insisted.

"You don't understand," he said.

"I understand you could stay here with me, shut out the noise."

"That would be selfish," he said.

"So be selfish!" I said, holding onto his jacket and brushing my lips against his, smiling.

He took me by the upper arms and pushed me gently back.

"If the burglar empties that flat, the flat owner- a single mother with no job and no other family- will have no way to pay the rent. Her daughter needs new shoes for school. The electricity is about to be cut off. She's going to a loan shark tomorrow with her mother's gold. It's all she has and it's hidden under the mattress with her last money. If the burglar finds that gold and takes it, she and her daughter will be forced onto the streets. Then she'll have to start selling her body to support her daughter through school. She already knows the people who can help her but she's resisted until now. After prostitution will come drug addiction. She'll die in a horrible way and her daughter..."

"Stop, stop!" I said, turning away, hugging myself, not wanting to hear more.

Feeling my distress, Ilia appeared and stood watching Toma with narrowed eyes.

"I have to go," Toma told me again, ignoring my angel.

This time I let him.

"Demon is not the right word for him," I told Ilia, looking after Toma as he walked quickly away from Rustaveli Avenue, his hands in his pockets and his shoulders hunched. At the bottom of the street he turned right and disappeared from sight.

"I can think of a few alternatives," my angel said gruffly.

I smiled and shook my head. "I was thinking something like 'hero'."

"You think he's a hero?"

I shrugged. "Maybe."

"To some a hero, to others their worst nightmare," he said. "Ela- what's he to you?"

I looked at him and frowned. "Would it be wrong if I said I think I love him?"

"You're too young to know what love is," he said quietly, looking up the road.

"You sound like Tata Bebo," I told him with a small smile. "But I think I do know what it is."

"Tell me," he said.

I tilted my head and we continued along the avenue.

"It's when you totally feel the person- like not just so your heart beats faster, but your whole being aches to be with them."

I glanced at him and saw him looking fixedly ahead.

"Go on," he said.

"It's when you will do anything they ask... when you want to make them happy..."

"Hmm."

"Have you ever loved someone like that?" I asked him.

He glanced at me and smiled. "Yes."

"Tell me about her."

He hesitated, then shook his head, almost to himself. "I was engaged to a girl in the village," he said after a moment.

"But you were 17!" I exclaimed.

He shrugged. "It was our custom. She was young, though, just 14. Her parents approached mine. I was quite the catch, you know." He grinned and I laughed.

"I can appreciate that. So, what happened?"

"I died," he said shortly.

"I'm sorry," I said, feeling for the life he'd never been able to have.

We passed under the covered columned entrance of the theatre and I read the stars as we passed over them. They were recent- no Hollywood legends here, but valued nonetheless. I realised Ilia was as old or older than some of them. Toma, too, in fact, or rather, the demon inside him was.

"You know, the one thing that drives me crazy about Toma is that I never know what he's thinking. But I like it, too," I told Ilia with a smile, blushing.

"Still, however you like him, he's not the only demon on the scene."

"His sisters?"

"His entire coven. He might be looking out for you now, but I wouldn't trust any of them."

"They go for the bad guys," I said. "As far as I know, I'm not one. And if I really killed Susan..."

"You didn't, so stop thinking it!" Ilia admonished.

We passed the entrance to the old Marriott Hotel where I knew dad was at a business dinner in Parnas. I deliberately kept my eyes off the windows in case I saw him sitting there. But Ilia looked in. And stopped, frowning.

"What?" I asked, following his eye-line.

My dad was sitting in the window alcove at a white marble table with just one man. He looked familiar- I guess I'd seen him on TV somewhere: tall, well-built, black hair, smooth pale skin, expensive suit, gold watch... not your typical Georgian businessman.

"Speak of the devil and he shall appear," Ilia said under his breath.

"You know the guy with my dad?" I asked.

"Yes," Ilia answered. "It's the triplets' father."

I looked again, and saw him looking straight back at me.

My whole body went cold. His eyes were so black. Knowing what he was only made it worse.

His eyes flicked between me and Ilia and, seeing his dinner guest's changing expression, my dad turned to look, too.

When he saw me, he smiled and, with a few words to Tomas' dad, beckoned me in.

I groaned and shook my head.

Dad frowned, his lips pursed in displeasure and beckoned me again.

"Ok!" I mouthed and turned back towards the rotating doors.

"Should I be worried?" I asked Ilia out of the corner of my mouth as he walked through the grandiose foyer and into the restaurant with me.

"I won't let anything happen to you," he promised.

"Here's my girl," dad said with bright enthusiasm. I tried not to cringe.

"Eliso, this is Mr. Eristavi," he told me.

"Eliso! What a pleasure to finally meet you!" Toma's father said, holding out his hand and shaking mine. His skin was warm and smooth, his nails clean and manicured. At his touch, my stomach twinged. *Nerves*, I thought. *Not surprising.*

"Yeah, same," I said unenthusiastically.

"Sit," he said, flicking a look at Ilia, who went to stand by the bar some metres away, not taking his eyes off us.

I sat beside my dad, opposite the demon who, I noticed, looked nothing at all like the triplets save that penetrating gaze.

"How was the excursion?" Eristavi asked with a smile. "Did the triplets behave themselves?"

"You had an excursion?" my dad asked.

"Yeah- you signed the permission slip last week," I reminded him in an embarrassed undertone, then, answering Toma's dad: "It was good." I decided not to tell him about the priest incident.

"So, I understand you're in my son's class at school."

"The class below him, actually," I said.

"I tried pushing them to move her up- she's bright enough for it!" my dad said, giving me a side hug.

I sat, stiff and uncomfortable, until he took his arm away.

"Which universities will you apply to?" Toma's dad asked.

I shrugged.

"I haven't decided yet," I said.

"Haven't...? Ela, honey, we talked about this," dad said, his turn to sound embarrassed. He turned to the demon and smiled. "She'll be going to London. My sister lives there, so she'll be well cared for."

"I want to stay in Georgia!" I told dad through gritted teeth. Like he said, we'd had this argument before.

"What do you want to study?" Mr Eristavi asked politely.

"Psychology," I said.

"Interesting career choice," Mr Eristavi observed.

"I like to try and understand who people really are," I said, looking at him meaningfully. "And to find out why they do what they do."

"Don't mess with him, El," Ilia warned quietly.

The demon glanced towards the bar and back at me with a smile.

"I wish you every success in your...endeavours," he told me.

"Thank you," I replied- looking him straight in the eye, though my heart was suddenly beating hard. "So, what were you guys talking about before I came along?" I asked, wanting to change the subject.

"Just business," the demon said.

"What business are you in Mr. Eristavi?" I asked.

He smiled, the corners of his eyes wrinkling.

"Law," he said.

"Not judging?" I said before I could think.

He narrowed his eyes, though the friendly smile remained.

"We've called him in to consult on some new deals we've got going," dad put in. "Are you off home now?"

I nodded.

"Well, I'll be back late tonight. Keep an eye on your brother for me," he said.

I realised he was dismissing me and got to my feet, as did Toma's dad.

"It was nice meeting you," he said, shaking my hand with an iron grip that almost hurt.

"Sure," I replied, squeezing back as hard as I could.

My abdomen twinged again and I touched a hand to my side, wincing.

"Are you ok?" my dad asked.

"Yeah, fine," I said, feeling better as soon as Eristavi let my hand go.

He sat, watching me with those spooky dark eyes.

"Bye, dad," I said.

He waved and I left, Ilia right beside me.

"You ok?" he asked.

I realised I was shaking.

"Yeah. Strange guy," I said.

"That he is," my angel agreed. "What happened with your stomach?"

"Nothing. It's fine now. Just a muscle spasm or something. What do you know about him?"

We turned left and crossed over into the park, walking round the edges, past the trees labelled in memory of each person who'd been shot by the Russians on April 9th, 1989. It was a gloomy place and we didn't loiter long, heading down into Alexandrouli instead- with its statue of Zichy, famous illustrator of Rustaveli's Knight in the Panther's Skin- an epic poem hundreds of pages long which I'd learned maybe one quarter of by heart.

"Not much. I stay out of demon business."

"So?"

"He's the top dog here. Controls the demons, keeps them in line, oversees the training. His focus is on the triplets. When he's not doing that, he's a legal consultant for some of the top minds in the country."

"Judging?"

"No doubt. No act of corruption would go unpunished with him around- so I suppose there are positives in it all..."

"Do you think he knows I know?" I wondered.

"Well, you were dropping some pretty big hints."

I cringed, wishing I'd kept my mouth shut.

"You like playing with fire, don't you?" my angel observed.

We passed the mosaic river and the children's park- one mother was pushing her toddler on the swing- then turned towards the flower market. I stopped outside a minimarket.

"I'm just going to get a water," I said, digging in my pocket for some change and pushing through the door.

"I'll wait," Ilia said.

When I came out a few minutes later, he was standing there in the flesh, holding a white rose.

I smiled and blushed, taking it and sniffing. It was sweet, fresh, clean.

"Thank you," I said, kissing him on the cheek. He pulled me into a hug.

"What a sweet young couple," I heard an old woman say as she hobbled past with her shopping.

CHAPTER 49

Monday. I'd barely heard from Toma since our goodbye on Saturday. I'd texted him when I got home from meeting his father.

ME: Good hunting?

TOMA: Judgement complete.

ME: Did he survive?

TOMA: Of course.

ME: I met ur dad.

TOMA: Where?

ME: Parnas. Business dinner w my dad.

TOMA: What did he say?

ME: Just asked me about school & uni & stuff

TOMA: Ok

ME: I...may have let slip I know what he is. And he saw Ilia.

TOMA: He already knows about ur ghost- Ari told him in the summer. That's why we changed schools.

"Why do you think he made them change schools just for me?" I'd asked Ilia.

"To get to the bottom of why I'm with you, I guess," he'd replied with a shrug.

"And *do* you know why you're here?"

"I just need to protect you. I feel it with every fibre of my being."

Nina and Mariam were set against Toma for messing me around and even more for setting a priest on fire, even after I pointed out the sins the priest had committed.

"It's not their place to judge. Only God can do that!" Mariam told me on Skype on Sunday night.

ME: Maybe he's outsourcing?

MARIAM: Not funny.

ME: What's your dad say about them?

MARIAM: He calls them the 'Stolen Ones'- normal kids taken and brought up as demons. His group are seriously looking into it.

ME: They want to stop it?

MARIAM: Yes. It's evil. They want to save the kids more than anything.

ME: Save them how?

MARIAM: Exorcism. Putting their souls back in. There are a couple of priests here that say they can. But it's dangerous. Dad telling Toma like that was risky.

ME: Yeah, I told u how pissed off he was. So, u believe in angels and demons now?

MARIAM: I'm converted. Have you seen their powers?

ME: I've seen T light fires with his hands, play water and air...and break a boy's arm without even touching him.

MARIAM: You're playing with fire.

ME: Yeah, Ilia told me the same.

MARIAM: Have you thought of trying to contact the real Toma? Ilia used to be alive, right? So maybe Toma's out there somewhere...

ME: How would I even find him? Ilia told me he can't see others like him...

MARIAM: I've got an idea. When I come home at Christmas.

ME: Ur coming back?!

MARIAM: Yes!

After an excited few minutes planning what we'd do when she came home, her mum turned up asking her to go to bed and we signed off. As I brushed my teeth, I tried to imagine meeting the real Toma, an angel like Ilia. What would I say to him? That I was in love with the one controlling his body? I felt cold despair at the thought of Mr Walker's group getting hold of Lilu, of forcing him out and putting Toma back. Would Lilu die? Maybe it was Toma's right to have his own body, but Lilu had been in it for 17 years already. I didn't know the boy, but I knew I loved the demon. And I couldn't shake the need to be with him.

With such conflict in my heart, after school I got Nina to cover for me and, when Levan dropped me at her building and drove off, I jumped straight in a taxi to Kargareteli Street and got out in front of the beautifully ornate Art Palace museum. Feeling nervous, I'd decided to walk the last few minutes to the address I'd snuck from the receptionist's file while no-one was looking.

It seemed the Morgan's owned a whole three-floor house: a tall 19th century building with restored wooden windows and detailed plasterwork. I looked up to the roof and was unsurprised to see small stone gargoyles leering down at me.

"Please tell me you're not seriously going in there," Ilia said.

"I am, if they let me," I said.

"Well, I'm not."

"Some Guardian Angel you are," I joked, though I was secretly pleased I'd be able to have Toma to myself.

"I'll come if you need me," he said dryly. "Be careful." Then he disappeared.

My hand shook as I reached up to press the doorbell. The sound reverberated deep into the house and I started humming the theme tune to Addam's Family. I half expected Lurch to answer, and was also partly terrified the triplets' father would be the one to welcome me in, staring at me with those too-black eyes. But it was Arabella who came to the door, dressed in tight black jeans and a crop-top that showed off her belly-piercing, which was purple today.

"What are you doing here?" she asked, looking at me with a cool expression, leaning on the doorframe, her arms crossed.

"I..." I swallowed, annoyed my nerves had shown through. "I came to see Toma."

"You should call first," she said, not moving. "He's busy..."

The door opened wider and Toma filled the space.

"Hey," he said, smiling. Arabella scowled and disappeared back inside.

I hitched up my heavy schoolbag. "I came to get some help with my History homework," I said, grinning and blushing despite myself.

He glanced behind him, hesitating, then opened the door. "Come in."

I followed him up some steps into the wide, bright, open-plan living area. The floor was tiled in black slate with traditional Georgian rugs laid out across the space. The furniture was richly carved dark wood, the walls painted white with framed paintings- originals- of various scenes and figures from history. In front of a champagne-coloured sofa set was a tall marble fireplace, logs burning inside, and on the mantelpiece a crystal vase of blood-red roses. To my right was a kitchen-diner: dark wood with white marble worktops and polished stainless details. All the appliances were the latest models.

Arabella watched us from the bar, leaning her elbows on it and picking grapes off a bunch in a wooden bowl beside her.

"Come up to the den," Toma invited, taking my bag.

I took off my coat and scarf and hung them on the old iron coat stand by the door, then followed him up the carpeted wooden stairs into another open area with three sets of tall painted double-doors leading off. The floor here was oak laminate with rugs. Three walls were white; the third indigo-blue. There was a large TV screen hung on the indigo wall with a sofa and armchair in front of it. Underneath the screen was a shelf with videogames and DVDs. On another wall was a vast floor-to-ceiling bookshelf, weighed down with an assortment of titles in various languages- I saw Russian, Arabic, Italian...

"Do you know all these languages?" I wondered, walking along the shelf, touching a light finger to the spines.

"My father does. And I did at various times in my previous lives," he confessed.

I went to one of the two large windows overlooking their rear garden and saw a variety of fruit trees- now bare and dormant- a stone fountain and a summerhouse at the end. Everything normal. As un-demonic as it could be.

"Are you evil?" I wondered suddenly, too embarrassed to look over at him.

He came and stood beside me, hands in pockets, his eyes also on the garden. He frowned.

"How can we be evil? The definition of evil is 'wrong, ungodly and immoral,' but we're fighting exactly that- fighting for humans to do right and take moral responsibility."

"Even if your methods are questionable," I pointed out, remembering the church.

"You can't make an omelette..." he said with a shrug.

"So, I was thinking about those Ten Commandments" I said.

"I thought you wanted help with your History homework," he said with a smile and flick of the eyebrows.

"Religious History?" I suggested. His smile widened.

"What's it like? To be a demon?"

"How can I tell you that?" he asked. "I don't remember anything but."

"Tell me what you know."

"I've been in this cycle of hosting for centuries; never free, never at peace. I spent many of those years angry...angry at God, then at humanity. I took my revenge in horrible ways. We were all like that. That's how the myths started about us being evil."

I thought of Mariam and her father and swallowed.

"But then Ariman came up with the idea to train us to co-exist with our hosts and make better use of them. Each time we're reborn, we're retrained and re-taught to live with our fate, to do as we are expected to do. In a way, the act of judging and exacting punishment is satisfying in itself. Calming. Fulfilling God's Will."

"God's Will?" I asked.

"Yes. We're all part of the Great Scheme. We prod and poke and push humans to awareness of their fragile state, to become better. It's our job to help perfect humanity."

"Your poke means pain and death," I said, thinking of Lazare and my near-miss at Narikala.

"We don't aim to kill. Not at first, anyway. But it's the ultimate punishment when they refuse to learn. They may not see it until they're Beyond, but their time does come. That is and always was God's plan."

"But if you've never met God, then how do you know he's real? How do you know that what you're doing is what he wants?"

He stopped and thought about it, turning his phone round and round between his fingers. Then he held out one hand and a flame appeared, dancing across his palm. He shut his fist and extinguished it.

"I just feel it. How could I have the powers I have, if not?"

"What about..." I swallowed. "Satan?"

He smiled and looked out over the garden.

"A myth. I've only felt my own kind. And Nature. There is no head demon. Our lord is God," he glanced at me and smiled, "or at least the idea of him."

"And your dad?" I asked, remembering his hellish black eyes and false politeness.

Now Toma laughed. "Just another demon, like me."

"But he controls you?"

He gave a nod. "He tries. But he's just a teacher. When demons are bound, it's the job of the teacher to train them to adulthood."

"Then?"

"Then we get Fixed to our fates until our hosts die."

"And what happens when your host dies?"

"I'm nowhere, until I'm brought here again."

"You said you get fixed to your fate. What does that mean?"

A door opened across from us and Emily emerged wearing a pink sweatsuit, a lollipop in her mouth. She frowned when she saw us and went over to the coffee table to get something out of her school bag.

Toma let out a breath and turned away, tucking his phone in the back pocket of his jeans.

"How about we save that one for another time?"

"Telling her our secrets?" Emily asked him, sounding disapproving.

He shrugged. "She has a right to know."

I thought she'd argue that but instead she looked away, pulling out first one, then two of our classbooks.

"How many people have you taken over?" I wondered.

How many baby souls lost? How many families broken, people punished or killed...?

"Is this the Spanish Inquisition?" he asked with another smile.

"Been there, done that," Emily said grumpily, breezing past, textbooks in hand. Toma caught her free hand and kissed it, breaking her out of her negative thoughts and making her smile. I felt an unwelcome flash of hot jealousy and tried to push it down. Toma held his sister's gaze for a moment and then let her go. She went downstairs, glancing back at us.

"How come she's in my class and not yours?" I asked. There'd been rumours that they weren't actually triplets, or that she'd had a brain trauma as a child which slowed her development.

"That would certainly explain the 'crazy'," Mariam had said in a conference call with me and Nina.

"Do you want a drink?" Toma asked, going over to a minibar tucked in the corner and opening the fridge there.

"Just water, thanks," I said.

He took out a bottle and went over to the sofa, inviting me to sit.

"Emily was kidnapped when she was 13," Toma told me, taking my hand now and looking down at our joined fingers.

"Oh my God! By whom?"

"A group of people who don't like us," he said, vaguely. "Like your friend's father. It took us a while to get her back. And then she needed...therapy...to help her get over it."

"Therapy, I can relate to," I said quietly. "My parents put me in rehab when I was little because they thought I was imagining Ilia."

"That must've been hard," Toma said.

I nodded.

A shout came from downstairs: "Toma, the casserole's burning!" Arabella said.

"No, it's not!" he called back, then grinned at me. "It needs at least another 20 minutes. They're just trying to distract us," he told me, squeezing my fingers and leaning in to kiss me.

"You cook?" I asked after a moment.

"Of course. Don't you?"

"No- I mean, I can...but we have a woman come and cook for us. Since mum left, it's been kinda...disjointed at our house."

"Your dad's not a good dad?" he asked softly, reading between the lines.

I looked away, blushing. "He's ok. He closed up after mum left-threw himself into the business. It doesn't leave much time for me and Mikey...What's your dad like? I can't imagine him changing three sets of nappies and taking you out for walks in the park." I was remembering the crisp suit and gold, not a hair out of place: the picture of control and perfection.

Toma smiled, but there was nothing warm or affectionate in it.

"We're demon children," he reminded me. "Our life since birth has been about training and learning to live in symbiosis with our human bodies and human emotions."

"Tell me about the training," I said, taking a sip of water.

He stood up and walked to the book case, touched one or two books, thoughtful. I wasn't sure he was going to reply, but then he turned around and put his hands in his pockets.

"By nature, we were angry kids. Cruel, even. Because the demon was stronger than the body and the voices drove us to the point of insanity. We had to be home schooled until we were stable enough to go out. We started judging four years ago- just small stuff at first."

"Like what?"

"A kid steals some sweets and his bike chain breaks- that kind of thing."

"And you didn't do anything...cruel...anymore?" I wondered, thinking of 'Demon' and the violent videos.

"No. Because Father taught us to control the anger and focus our energy." He looked at the bottle of water and I saw three drops floating out of the top of it, catching the light as they spun in place.

"It's beautiful," I whispered.

I tried to touch them and they zoomed out of my reach and flew over to Toma to come to a stop a centimetre above his open hand. He beckoned me over with his free hand and I stood and joined him by the bookcase.

"Open your mouth," he said quietly.

Smiling, I did, and, keeping his hand still between us, he made the drops float between my open lips. When they hit the heat of my tongue, they dissolved. A tiny shock of electricity set me alight, then faded.

We looked at each other, studying each other's eyes. My stomach flared in need. He must have felt it, too, because suddenly we were all over each other.

He rained kisses down my neck and, going onto his knees, lifted my top up and ran his lips over my stomach. He traced my appendix scar with his tongue and I flinched at a sudden pain there. He didn't seem to notice and moved back up to my chest, then, lips back on mine, he made to undo my jeans. I stopped him, my hands on his; my whole body shaking and hot, remembering the tent... the feel of him...

"Your sisters?" I panted.

"Forget them," he said.

I laughed. "Your casserole?"

"Mmm...Don't care."

"Toma!" He pulled back slightly, his eyes burning into mine. I smiled. "Where's your bedroom?"

"Stay for dinner?" he asked, kissing my bare shoulder.

I hesitated. "If your family doesn't mind."

"Father's away on business."

"What if Emily makes me stab myself with my fork?" I wondered.

He turned me to face him and leaned forwards to kiss me, his look dark. "She wouldn't dare."

Downstairs, Emily was sitting with Arabella on the sofa, her homework books open on the table in front of her, leaning her head on her sister's shoulder as she flicked through the latest OK! Magazine. They both looked up as we came down, neither of them looking happy.

"Help me set the table," he said, tugging me over to the kitchen, seeing my discomfort in the face of their animosity.

He directed me to the crockery and cutlery and I got places laid for the four of us.

Arabella got out glasses and cherry juice, but Emily stayed put until Toma got the casserole out of the oven and put it on the table with a salad.

It was all very homely and surreal as we sat and tucked in.

"Not bad!" I said with a smile.

"I have many hidden talents," Toma said.

Emily rolled her eyes and picked up her plate. "I'm eating upstairs," she said.

Toma shrugged and she stalked off.

We talked about everyday things- from school to the next school holidays. I asked about their studies. Arabella gave short answers.

It seemed their being demons made no difference to their life plans- Toma was planning on following his father into law.

"Why law?"

"Behind every powerful man is an even more powerful lawyer," Arabella quoted monotonously. I glanced at Toma and saw him smiling.

"Father's favourite quote," he explained.

"I thought it was 'behind every powerful man is an even more powerful woman," I said.

"Ahh, but Arabella here is shunning that calling in order to become an Interior Designer," Toma told me with a smile.

"And Emily?"

"Fashion," they both said at the same time.

"And you'll keep judging?" I wondered.

"All our lives," Arabella said. "Though when we get to 18, we'll be able to kill, too. If we pass the test."

Toma coughed and I caught him shaking his head at his sister. She smiled and shut her mouth and I couldn't get another word out of them about it.

"You said your mum died, right? What happened?" I asked.

Arabella's look darkened and I swallowed, glancing at Toma uncertainly.

"She was an initiate of the Azruzai," Toma told me quietly. "Our biological father got her into it- she was only 18. Having three children was seen as an Omen. So, they encouraged her to give us up."

"And she did that...easily?" I asked, horrified, although my own mum had more or less dumped me and my brother without a second thought.

"No idea. Maybe. She died during the caesarean so we'll never know for sure."

"Tell us about *your* mum," Arabella said.

I took a sip of juice before replying. "She left when I was seven. She was," I swallowed, blushing. "She was a little messed up in the head."

"How so?"

"Like, the total opposite of my dad. Apparently, she wasn't always like that. She would have these dreams...and see things. Mostly about her sister, Victoria."

"Victoria?" Arabella shot a look at Toma.

"Hmm-hmm. Victoria was mum's twin. She committed suicide when they were 20."

"Suicide?" Toma asked, paling, with a glance at his sister.

I frowned. "Yeah. Why?"

"No reason," Arabella said, though her voice was heavy.

"Well, it was a big scandal with the Church here. Our family had to ship her body home to England to be cremated because they refused to bury her here."

Toma's look was intense, concentrated.

"What?" I asked, confused at his reaction.

"Nothing. That must have been tragic for your family," he said hollowly.

"I'd just been born- so I never met her, but yeah, it was. Mum was never the same. She always said Victoria was haunting her. One thing I remember mum saying over and over was 'She wants me to keep her promise.'"

"What did that mean?" Arabella asked, shooting another look Toma's way.

I shrugged. "Never found out. One day she just upped and left- we've no idea where. She just disappeared."

"Why?" Toma asked.

"I guess she had...issues. Couldn't deal with being a mum."

As I said it, I knew it was a lie- she'd loved Mikey like crazy, had craved him and revelled in motherhood when he was born in a way that it seemed she'd never felt with me. We'd never been close and I'd often caught her looking at me with a small frown creasing her brow, as if she didn't quite recognise me. I guessed it was because of the Ilia thing.

"But she's still alive, right?"

I shrugged again. "The police never found anything and she left a note saying she was going, so... they think she left the country."

Toma looked out the window, thoughtful.

"I'm amazed you're so calm about it," he said, turning back to me.

"I've done all the tears and anger," I said with a sigh. "Though you've heard I have an issue with the occasional 'sinful thought,' as you call it."

He frowned. "True."

"Do you have other brothers or sisters? Cousins?" Arabella asked.

"Just Mikey," I said.

"So, Victoria died childless?" Arabella asked.

"Yes," I said.

"Are you sure?"

"100%," I answered, frowning at her focus on my dead aunt.

"Could she have lost a baby before she died?"

"Arabella!" Toma said sharply.

I looked from one to the other. Arabella was glaring at her brother. He won and she dropped her eyes.

"Sorry," she told me reluctantly. "My curiosity got the better of me."

We ate a few bites in silence as I built up courage to ask my next question.

"Listen...I'm going to ask something that I've been dying to ask since...well since hearing what you are...and because of something I saw in Lucifer..."

Toma laughed and Arabella waited with a cold, unamused look.

"Yeah, I'm either going to be very embarrassed or scared by this but..."

"Just ask," Arabella sighed.

"What do you really look like? Inside, I mean."

The two triplets shared a look.

"Horns and tails?" I ventured.

Toma shook his head. "I've never seen myself in a mirror," he admitted. "But I've seen others. When we're pulled from the OtherWorld we're like wisps of black smoke."

"But with claws and glowing red eyes..." Arabella added with a menacing grin.

"We didn't look at your homework," Toma pointed out, opening the door to see me out and handing me my bag.

"We did something more interesting," I said, blushing and catching hold of his hand. "Oh- it's snowing!"

Soft flakes were floating gently down from the sky, and the temperature had dropped enough that they were already starting to settle.

"Is Levan coming?"

I shook my head. "He thinks I'm at Nina's. Wait- lying to your driver isn't a sin, is it?"

Toma grinned. "Just a little one." He grabbed my waist and pulled me tight against him and spoke against my lips: "I think I can let you escape punishment this time."

We kissed.

"Want me to call a taxi?" he asked.

"I'll get one on the way. But thanks."

"Thanks for coming," he said.

"See you at school?"

He nodded, then held me a moment longer, his eyes searching mine. Something in his expression was sad.

I leaned forward and kissed him. "Bye."

"Bye."

I walked away grinning. Ilia didn't make an appearance, though I was sure he was there.

CHAPTER 50

Toma stayed in the doorway, his eyes on Eliso as she walked up the street, a bounce in her step.

Arabella came into the living-room doorway and stood watching him, a crisp red apple in hand.

"Father pulled the birth certificates," she said.

"And?" he asked, not looking at her.

"It's confirmed."

Toma shut the door and leaned back against the wall beside it, lightly banged his head once against the plaster, then pressed his hands to his eyes in frustration and growled despairingly up at the ceiling.

He looked at his sister and shook his head, then slid down the wall until he was sat crouched on the floor.

"Should we bring her back?" Arabella asked, biting into the fruit- a hollow crunch followed by a munching and soft juiciness sounding in the silence as she waited for her brother's answer.

"No." He looked up at her; something pleading and pathetic in his eyes. "Is Father sure?" he asked her.

"Don't be foolish," Arabella said impatiently, having no sympathy for his feelings for the girl. "Everything fits. The timing, the vegetarianism, the anger, the attack on Susan…"

"What is it?" Emily asked, coming down the stairs and looking from one to another in consternation.

"We finally found Victoria's long-lost daughter," Arabella told her.

"And so, the sin is revealed…" Emily said with a grin.

CHAPTER 51

The snow came hard and fast over the next few days and my friends started planning for the ski season.

"Why so down?" Nina asked, flicking through photos of the latest ski suits on her phone while our nails dried.

I lifted my arm, healed but still delicate, according to the doctor. "Because I'm out," I told her.

I loved skiing. I'd been doing it since I was six- first spending every winter at the Bakuriani winter school, then, later, hitting the runs at Gudauri. And now my stupid arm would mean I was stuck in Tbilisi.

"Come with us anyway," my friend suggested.

"And watch you out the window?" I grumbled. "No thanks."

"Ilia can keep you company," she said. I scowled at her. "Maybe your doc will give you the all-clear before the snow melts; Gudauri's only two hours away," she reminded me. "We can go any time."

"I know," I sighed.

"Do you think the Morgans can ski?" she asked.

"I bet they can do everything," I said, thinking of their training. "And where better to break some sinning arms and legs than the ski slopes?"

"You weren't a sinner, though, were you?" Nina asked, nodding at my arm.

I shrugged. "In Em's eyes, loving her brother is as much a sin as any, I guess."

"You and Mikey want to come over to mine for Christmas?"

"Me yes- not sure if Mikey has plans. He might ask dad to send him to Aunty Lela in England."

My phone rang.

"It's Toma!" I said with a grin.

Nina smiled, though I could see the concern in her eyes. *Like a second Ilia!* I thought.

"Hey! Wassup?" I asked.

"Are you busy?"

"No, I'm not busy." I looked at Nina and shrugged apologetically.

My friend stuck her tongue out at me.

"I might be late to the party tonight. You can go with Nina, right?" he asked.

"How late?" I asked, my happiness being swallowed.

"Maybe an hour," he said. "Arabella and Emily will be there on time. I have a meeting with my father."

"He's back?"

"Just."

"Ok. See you."

"Bye"

"What is it?"

"My ride cancelled on me."

She growled. "Men! But you can come with me, no worries."

She applied a last coat of varnish to my nails and looked at the clock. "Once those are dry, we'd better head to the hairdresser's or we won't have time to get Saba a present."

"I'll go get dressed."

"Don't ruin your nails!" she called after me.

"Help me choose what to wear?" I asked my angel once we were behind the closed door of my room.

"For a date with Toma? Wouldn't Nina be better at that?" Ilia asked me grumpily, appearing in the seat in the corner, his fingers steepled, elbows on knees.

"Please?" I begged.

He sighed and came to stand beside me in front of the open wardrobe.

"Something funereal, perhaps?" he asked, pulling out my long black velvet dress with a zip from top to bottom and a slit up the side all the way to up to my thigh.

"Don't be morbid," I said, taking it from him. "But actually...it might work..." I held it against me in the mirror. It had a high neck and close-fitting sleeves. With the right tights and my ankle boots, it would be sexy but controlled...

"You're a genius," I said with a grin.

He gave a mock salute. "Glad to be of service."

"I'll be ok, won't I?"

"I hope so!" He hesitated, looking at me.

"What?" I asked, smiling.

He took my free hand and squeezed. "I love to see you happy," he said. "I just wish it were with someone better."

"Ilia!"

"I know, I know."

"But you'll always be here for me, right?"

"BFFs," he said in a girly voice, sticking up his pinky.

I laughed and linked my little finger with his, then hugged him. He stroked my hair and I felt the usual peace and safety being with him afforded me.

"Thank you," I whispered.

"For what?" he asked, looking down at me.

I shrugged. "For being you."

The look he gave me was almost one of longing, but he stepped back and hid it quickly.

With a smile, I twirled my finger in the air for him to turn around.

"No peeking," I said, starting to pull off my jeans. He gave a smile and faded away.

CHAPTER 52

"Here it is," Mr. Eristavi said, passing his son an A4 piece of yellowed paper- Eliso's birth certificate. Toma studied it with a frown.

"She thinks she's the daughter of Victoria's sister..."

"That's what she was brought up to believe. And when did she say the ghost first appeared to her?"

"When she was four. She's blocking the memory of what happened to trigger his coming."

Toma's father stood up and walked away. He pressed his palms to the stone alter in the fire-warmed underground chamber and closed his eyes.

Toma guessed he was flicking through the memories of hundreds of demon souls brought over, passed from the OtherWorld to host body in this very chamber. Toma waited for the verdict, dreading it. His sisters had forced him to talk to his father. He hadn't wanted to, but he'd known that he of all of them was best positioned for it- Emily and Arabella's hatred for Eliso might affect their father's ultimate decision.

Please let it not be true, he thought, and not for the first time since the Night Office incident. *Please. Not Ela...*

"Yes. She's the one," his father said quietly after a moment, his eyes still closed.

Toma let out a breath he wasn't aware he'd been holding. It was a breath of despair and Eristavi heard it.

He looked at his adopted son with narrowed eyes.

"You've become attached to her," he stated, disapproval lacing his words.

"Which one is she?" Toma asked, ignoring the question.

His father hesitated.

"Which one?" he demanded angrily.

"Lilitu. But you already knew that, didn't you? I guess that might explain the way you feel about her..."

Toma's shoulders slumped. "I thought she was lost."

"She might as well be while she exists like this."

"Why didn't you find out sooner?" he asked Eristavi. "You see her father almost every week!"

Eristavi's jaw clenched and he passed his hand over the flame in the bowl beside him, closing his eyes against the pain, using it to focus and calm him.

"All the evidence pointed to Victoria's child having died when Victoria did. I knew Machabeli had a daughter born around that time. It didn't occur to me that he and his wife were actually bringing up Victoria's child."

"What happened to *their* daughter?"

"I found the death certificate well buried. She had a heart defect. Machabeli paid a fortune to keep it hidden."

"And when Elizabeth brought Eliso here when she was four? Didn't you recognize her then?"

"I was on the island with you and your sisters."

"So, Uncle David was the Grand Master?"

"Yes. I never saw Eliso or Elizabeth. Lilitu was to be trained by Lali, Eliso's kindergarten teacher."

"Wasn't she one of the ones shot?"

"Sadly, yes. Right alongside your uncle. And in the cover-up, with the police sniffing around, Elizabeth and Eliso got away."

"That's why we stayed on the island so long!" Toma said, suddenly understanding.

"Yes. We had to keep a low profile. And because the papers we had on the family were destroyed, I had nothing to go on. I thought Lilitu was lost, unhosted, dead...Until Arabella told me you'd found her."

"I don't want Eliso hurt," Toma said decisively, standing and raising his chin, looking his father right in the eye- something only he of the three siblings dared to do.

But Eristavi shook his head. "Like this, she's dangerous, out of control."

"I can train her."

"You're too young for that and in any case, it's too late and you know it." He stepped forward and placed a hand on his son's shoulder. It was a hand of stone, of command, and Toma received no comfort from it. "You have a choice to make. Between a love you've had for centuries and a love you started in this short life."

"It should be *her* choice!" Toma said. "Not mine."

"It's not really a choice though, is it?" Eristavi said quietly as Toma turned his back and made to leave. "I'll give you until the summer solstice," his father said.

Toma stopped in the doorway, though he didn't look back. "Thank you," he said at last, and walked away.

CHAPTER 53

The *sakhinkle* restaurant smelled of roasting meat, beer and cigarettes. It turned my stomach but within ten minutes I was used to it.

I sat next to Mate and Megan on the tall-backed bench and Mate poured us some bright green tarragon lemonade. The table was already laid with salads, aubergine, pickled vegetables, bread, cold fried chicken, cheese and cold boiled fish. As soon as we sat, they started bringing out the hot dishes- piling them up unashamedly on top of each other; squeezing them in where they could- cheesebread, hot beef soup, roasted pork, fries- until the tablecloth was all but hidden. We tucked in and it wasn't long before Toma arrived and squeezed in next to me.

He kissed me lightly, under the watchful gaze of his sisters.

"How did it go?" Arabella asked him in Russian.

He glanced at me and nodded once at them, as if confirming something.

Emily shot me an evil grin.

"What's going on?" I asked Toma quietly.

"Nothing," he said.

"To the birthday boy!" Mate said, holding up his glass to Saba. "Another year older, another year wiser..."

"Another year with a hundred notches on the bedpost," Lasha said, making us all laugh and sounding more like his old self, perhaps coming out of his period of mourning for Susan which had left him a quiet and serious companion to our gatherings until now.

"*Sabas gaumarjos!*" we said, chinking our glasses and wishing him well.

Emily stood up and took out a vodka bottle and, checking none of the staff was looking, poured a generous glass for Saba, leaning over him so that he got an eyeful down her revealing dress.

"For the birthday boy," she whispered in his ear, moving to kiss him on the cheek. He turned his head and her kiss landed on his lips. But instead of pulling away, she leaned into him and kissed him back.

"Make that 101," Lasha said. Emily stuck her finger up at him, still kissing Saba.

I glanced at Arabella and saw her watching her sister hungrily.

"Won't you be bothered if both your sisters sleep with the same guy?" I asked Toma quietly.

He put his arm around my shoulder. "You know they're not really my sisters," he whispered in my ear.

"Yeah, but anyway," I said, feeling my stomach squirm uncomfortably at the thought of Saba messing with the Morgans.

"Emi," Toma called her. She broke away from Saba, leaving him with swollen lips and a goofy grin which made the boys tease him. "Ela wants to know if I'm going to be bothered when you fuck him," he said in Russian.

"Why would you be bothered?" she asked, moving to give the other boys a share of vodka, and though no-one else got one of her special kisses, you could see them wanting it, much to the annoyance of their girlfriends. Megan, Mate's girlfriend, gave him a sharp jab in the ribs after Emily had passed.

"What- she thinks you own me?" Emily asked her brother with a laugh.

I felt anger surge. "No, I don't think he owns you, but I think he would have a right to be bothered. Double standards and all that- considering how you act towards me," I said.

Everyone turned to look at me. Emily stopped. Arabella looked at me open-mouthed, a fry half way in. Toma was wide-eyed and Nina looked surprised.

"What?" I asked.

"You speak 'Triplet' now?" Nina asked.

"What are you talking about?" I looked at Toma. "I was speaking Russian."

He shook his head, a strange look in his eye.

"Then what...?"

"It's a language only we know," he told me quietly.

"I swear to you I just spoke Russian."

"When did you learn that gobbledegook?" Nina asked- then at Emily's sour look: "Sorry."

I shrugged. "I honestly thought it was just Russian."

Toma gave his sisters a look and the focus was quickly taken away from me.

"How can you do that?" Toma asked in a low voice as Arabella told them a joke about our Russian teacher.

I shrugged. "No idea. I'm good at picking up languages..."

"You don't 'pick up' our language," he said heavily. "It's ancient. No-one uses it but us."

"You three, or all dem- your kind?" I whispered, suddenly remembering the boys who'd chased me from Night Office and Ilia's conviction that they hadn't been speaking Russian.

"All our kind."

I shrugged again. "Is it such a big deal?" I asked, not liking the weight of his look or words.

"Maybe."

"So, how long have you been vegetarian?" Arabella asked from opposite me, with a pointed look at Toma, biting into a cucumber as the table conversation turned elsewhere, my strange linguistic moment forgotten by everyone but Nina, who was watching us carefully.

I shrugged and grabbed another slice of cheesebread.

"Since I was four," I said.

"Why?" she asked bluntly.

I frowned. "I don't remember. One day I could devour a chicken in minutes, the next even the smell of it made me ill."

"Ela, our animal-lover," Nina said. I stuck my tongue out at her. "But didn't your dad say it happened when your appendix got taken out?" she asked, reaching past me to take a pinch of salt from the small glass bowl.

I grinned. "Yeah- he said they cut the carnivore out of me."

Lasha offered a toast to the ladies and all the men stood.

I could see Toma was distracted when he chinked his glass against mine- though I seemed to be the source of the distraction this time- and as he sat, his eyes stayed on me, thoughtful.

I gave a small frown. "What?" I asked, smiling.

He shook his head and forced his look away, taking a couple of cigarettes from Saba and lighting one, blowing the smoke upwards. His jaw was tense.

"What is it?" I asked again.

He glanced at Arabella and she nodded.

"We need to talk," he said quietly, tapping the ash into the ashtray.

"I'm listening," I said.

"Let's go outside."

"And miss the party?" I asked as the waiter brought out my favourite cheese-filled button mushrooms.

"We won't be gone long," he said.

Then he stood and pulled me to my feet.

"Toma?" Emily called.

"Wait here," he told her, not even looking her way.

The look she gave me was full hatred.

I followed him out the swing doors and through the entrance, down the steps and into the street. I wrapped my arms around me against the chill.

"Where are we going?" I asked.

"The bridge," he said, nodding across the road. I glanced back and saw Ilia close behind, looking worried. But he didn't say anything and so I took Toma's hand and crossed the road, walking onto the bridge with him- the Metekhi church and Gorgasali statue looming over us against the backdrop of the heavy night sky. The previous snow had melted but more was forecast. On the other side of the bridge, we took the steps down to Saint Abo's chapel. Toma led me to the terrace hanging over the river and leaned his elbows on the edge of the railings, looking down into the water.

"It's time for you to start being honest with me," he said.

"There you go with the Russian again," I said, rolling my eyes.

"It's not Russian," he said, again in the language that to me sounded so familiar. "It's a demon language called Enochian. And yet you seem to understand it perfectly."

"Come on! Really?" I exclaimed, laughing nervously.

"What are you saying to each other?" Ilia asked, stepping forward, though remaining semi-transparent and so for my eyes only.

"You're saying I understand Demon?" I said in English for Ilia's benefit.

"It's impossible," they both said at the same time.

"Like I said, I *am* good at languages," I said with a shrug.

Toma shook his head. "Not that good. There's more to it than a good ear," he said in English. "So how come you suddenly start speaking it tonight?"

"I don't know," I said, then, to his sceptical look: "Really."

He shook another cigarette out of the pack in his pocket and lit it with the stub of the one he was just finishing and put the butt into his pocket.

He exhaled the smoke harshly before turning to me. "What do you remember about the appendix op?"

"Nothing. I told you, I was too small."

"I don't believe you."

"She's telling the truth," Ilia growled, materialising.

Toma turned and looked at him directly. "Stay out of it, ghost! I know what I'm talking about."

"Hey!" I interjected, shocked, "Stop calling him that!"

"I name it what it is," Toma said angrily. "You think he's something special? He's not. He's just the left-overs of a boy that once was. A boy who sinned and is paying for it through an afterlife serving you- protecting you against a curse laid on you by someone else."

"What do you mean?" I asked, glancing at my angel. He frowned and looked away down-river, his cheeks flushed. "What's he talking about, Ilia?" I asked.

"Think about it, El," Toma said. "Why would the "great" Lord God send an angel, a real angel, to come and protect a single human? What makes you special enough to deserve such attention?"

"I...nothing. I'm not special."

"But that's clearly not true, is it?" he asked, looking at us both. "We came after you because of him." Toma tilted his head towards Ilia. "Because he's a sign that there's something wrong in your past that called you to be protected. I'll bet she was an angry child, right?" he asked my angel with a dry smile.

Ilia slowly nodded. "She had...anger issues. But we worked through it together."

I frowned.

Toma nodded, unsurprised. "But you struggle to control it some-times, right?" he asked me now, and, before I could answer, "After what happened at the club..."

My insides went cold. "What happened?" I asked, my mouth suddenly dry, my heart beating too hard, my stomach clenched. "Is this about Susan? Because if it is, I already told you..."

He shook his head. "I don't know what happened to her. And until they find her, we won't know for sure. But we all felt it- those boys, me, Arabella," he hesitated, pulled on his cigarette, took a breath. "This, like, huge anger- like a rolling darkness. It was hate, jealousy, indignation- wild fury. It changed Susan. My friends- those boys you got arrested? – they were on the bridge when Susan passed them, took off her jacket and jumped. And when we followed that energy back to its source, we found you, unconscious on the ground."

I felt the blood leave my face and leaned against the railings. The river flowed past, a huge brown giant, cold and fast; indifferent to the city and its people. I imagined Susan jumping into it, the smack of her body against the water; the current pulling her down and along. She would have floated past this very point...

"Susan jumped?" I echoed dully.

"More like was pushed," he answered. "By the dark energy surrounding her."

"The police couldn't see who pushed her on the video."

"They wouldn't," he said. "It wasn't exactly a 'who'."

I tried to imagine it- the energy that gave Toma the gift to make beautiful gentle patterns out of water and fire; a force capable of breaking bones and killing...

"Those boys said *I* killed Susan," I said quietly. "That force came from *me*?"

Then it would only be a matter of time until the police came for me...

Toma hesitated, then softened his voice, seeing my shocked expression. "No-one saw that and nobody's found a body. It could be your angry energy influenced her to *do* something...but no-one saw *you* kill her. That said, your anger was involved..."

"What are you driving at?" Ilia asked him.

Toma looked at me. "When you get angry-"

"My 'sinful thoughts'?"

He nodded. "Where do you feel it most?"

"Her heart, of course," Ilia said, speaking for me. "Like everyone does..."

"No," I argued. "I feel it here," I said, touching a hand to my abdomen. Ilia frowned.

"And does anything ever happen? When you're angry?" Toma asked.

"Like what?"

"Like the things you imagine happening."

I thought about it, hugging myself against the cold.

"You know, there have been times I get so angry it's almost like I make things happen," I said. "A boy was teasing me at school once and I wanted him to fall and he did. Cracked his skull, actually. And Nina broke her phone the other day after that call with Mariam's dad. Just the way I'd imagined...and Susan...I imagined bad things for her for betraying Lasha... But it's just weird coincidence, right?" I looked from him to my angel, pleading.

Toma said nothing.

"Ela – why didn't you tell me?" Ilia asked.

I shrugged. "It doesn't happen often. What's all this adding up to?" I demanded of Toma. "I want to know!"

"There've been signs...hints...but nothing concrete. Then, when you told me your mother's name I realised who it was...but even then, I wasn't sure till I spoke to Father tonight, and then just now in the restaurant..." He huffed out smoke and looked at me with a small, sad smile. "I didn't want it to be, I suppose..."

"What?" I asked, my stomach now burning in fearful anticipation.

"You were supposed to be one of us."

Everything froze- my thoughts, my feelings, time. I shook my head.

Toma looked away, his jaw tense in agitation.

"Tell her," Ilia said.

Toma looked at him, eyes narrowed in dislike, and then glanced at me, away; thinking. Then he sighed.

"What does it mean?" I asked quietly.

"When your mother was pregnant with you, she promised you to the Azruzai. Your soul was supposed to be torn out of your body and replaced by a demon. And it seems the ritual was started but never finished..." he nodded down to my stomach and I touched a hand to my appendix scar.

"But this is me," I argued. "I'm 100% Eliso. No-one else. This is me."

"Yes. But I think there's also a demon inside you; usually dormant but every now and then breaking free and attacking people, especially when you get angry. Anger feeds it and as it's not bound to you, you can't control it."

I tilted my head, my mouth open to question, but the thoughts wouldn't form. Instead, images- fuzzy, confused -flooded my brain: underground, flames, my mother's face, that pain in my side, the feeling of cold fingers creeping under my skin, moving up...then my father's angry shouts, asking over and over: "How could you?!" and my mother replying, "Victoria made me...I have to keep the promise she made them, she said they'd take Michael if I didn't..."

My balance tilted and I would have fallen if Ilia hadn't caught me. He helped me to sit, my back against the cold wrought iron, the icon of Mary and baby Jesus frowning down at me. The cars and pedestrians passed on the bridge above us, oblivious. If anyone had seen me, they probably would've thought I was drunk. I closed my eyes, fingers pressed to temples.

"Do you remember something?" Toma asked.

"Leave her alone!" Ilia growled.

"No, it's ok," I told him, holding my hand up against his anger. I looked up at Toma.

"I remember."

CHAPTER 54

I saw myself as a four-year-old, sitting in my mum's room at her white dressing table, a cream lace doily in one corner with a selection of small perfume bottles on it, some nearly empty, some half-full. I could recognise all of them as the smell of my mum, though I was too young to be able to read their exotic names.

Mum stood behind me, brushing my waist-length hair, her pregnant belly a huge mound between us. A red ribbon was laid out on the desk in front of me.

I sat straight and tense, feeling nervous and excited but not knowing why. I kept deliberately still as she worked- not at all my usual fidgety self, terrified to bring out my mum's fury if I wrinkled my new red dress. I remembered it was made of silk, with black netting under the skirt. The belt was black, as were the long sleeves and lace details on the bodice. When I first put it, on I'd danced round the room, spinning and giggling like a princess. But then I'd caught sight of myself in the mirror and stopped, frowning. Something about the dress was...wrong. It was too dark, too gothic, though at the time I didn't know either of those words to put a name to the strange uncomfortable feeling the dress gave me- the black lace setting off my hair and pale skin. I'd stayed that way, staring at myself and frowning, until my mum had called me into her room.

I asked her if we were going to a party.

"Yes," she said. "A very special party."

"Is it my birthday?" I asked.

She'd hesitated, then smiled at me in the mirror, her eyes wrinkling at the corners in a way that showed me how happy she felt. I smiled back.

"Yes, it is," she said.

"Will I get presents?"

"You'll get the best gift you could ever be given."

My child's mind filled with thoughts of candy, dolls, dressing-up clothes and all the other miniscule and unimportant things that little girls love.

"I hope I get a mermaid tail," I said excitedly, sitting on my hands to keep still in my excitement.

"Oh, you'll get something better than that!" she promised.

The black car with black windows drove us through the dark streets of Mtatsminda and Sololaki.

"Where's daddy?" I'd asked.

"He'll come later," she promised.

The car stopped us in Puris Square in the Old Town and we'd had to walk uphill ourselves, up the stone steps, past the Betlemi churches; the wind whipping our clothes every which way. My hood kept my hair in place, but mum's was a wild curly bush, her face sombre and pasty beneath.

I started to get a feeling of foreboding as she pulled me up some brick steps and knocked on a wooden door with a peep-hole cut into it. After a moment, it opened.

"You're late," a gruff voice scolded us.

"The traffic," my mum stammered.

"They're waiting. Move," another voice said.

I got a sense of men but saw no faces as it was already dark. I was hustled quickly through the courtyard and down through a narrow stone entrance.

At the bottom of the steps, the space opened and burning torches lit and warmed the way. I held tight to mum's hand as we followed a man dressed in a red cloak.

For a moment, I wondered if this was a fancy-dress party. But when I heard the chanting up ahead, I stopped expecting balloons and clowns, or for my kindergarten friends to jump out and surprise me. There was nothing friendly or fun here. My feet froze in fear.

"Can we go home?" I whispered.

Mum glanced behind her at the two men following us and then shook her head.

"You are home, little one," the tall man in front of us said, turning to look at me. He had a short grey beard and smoky grey eyes, then he turned back and mum pulled me along behind him.

"What does he mean, mummy?" I whispered.

"Shh!" she said.

I frowned, feeling myself beginning to tremble.

I didn't want this party anymore. Or the promised present.

"She's here," I heard greybeard say as he entered the room. The chanting stopped and the eyes of five grown-ups fell on me.

"She's older than usual. Why did you not inform me?" a man's voice spoke out from the circle of grown-ups as mum carefully helped me out of my coat.

I glanced at my mum, confused, and saw her blush and look to the ground.

"My husband...doesn't believe. I wanted to bring her sooner but..."

"A promise is a promise, Grand Master," greybeard pointed out. "She has brought her."

"The extraction will be difficult. The soul will be more greatly attached..."

"But not impossible," was the eager reply from another person. It was a voice I recognised.

"Miss Lali?!" I questioned.

My kindergarten teacher pursed her lips as she peered out from under her red hood.

"Be quiet now, Eliso," she said. "Do as you're told."

"Yes, Miss Lali," I replied automatically, quietly, shyly.

Mum let go of my hand and nudged me forward.

"Go and lie down," she told me.

I looked around for a bed but saw only a stone slab too high for me to climb onto.

It looked cold, hard, and definitely not the kind of place I wanted to lie down on in front of all these strangers.

"Help her," a voice said, and greybeard took me under the arms and sat me on the edge of the stone.

The chill of it hit me through my tights and brought my skin out in goosebumps. I shivered, the heat of the flames burning in bowls around the low-ceiling stone room – *cave*, my mind whispered – not reaching me.

I looked over at my mum and saw her putting on a red cloak which had hung on a rusty nail banged into the wall by the door.

I wanted to ask her why but my voice had stopped working.

"Lay down, Eliso," Miss Lali told me.

I put my feet up and straightened my skirt before laying down. I noticed my feet were slightly lower than my head. I looked around and saw the people move closer, looking eagerly down at me.

"What do I do?" I whispered.

"Shh!" someone insisted harshly.

I shut my mouth.

Then they put a cloth over my eyes and my world went black.

CHAPTER 55

"I don't remember anything else," I said.

"You must," Toma insisted.

"I don't- sounds, feelings," I said, remembering pain and rubbing my appendix scar unconsciously. "Nothing specific."

"That's the day God sent me to you," Ilia said.

Toma rolled his eyes.

"You know something?" I asked my angel, surprised. "Why didn't you tell me?"

"My job is to bring you peace and comfort. The past is the past."

"She deserves to know," Toma said.

"Then you tell it, demon," Ilia said.

Toma lit up another cigarette and sat on the cold stone beside me, looking up at the rock face and night sky above us. "They'll have drained enough blood to weaken you and force you to black out," he told me. "They don't use anaesthesia, so as not to hurt the demon. Then they would've opened you up."

I felt bile rise up my throat and swallowed it down.

"Opened me...?" I couldn't even finish the question.

Toma ran a finger over his abdomen, left to right, just where our mutual scars were.

"*Not* appendix," he said.

"So, what?"

"They were going to take out your soul."

"My soul's a physical thing?" I asked, surprised and sickened. I could feel my hands trembling.

"No- but some black magick helps to separate it from the body. Then they would have put a demon in."

Another memory came to me: a demon boy asking me, *'So, who are you supposed to be? Empusa? Hantu?'*

"Like they did with you."

"Yes."

"But it didn't happen. I'm still me."

I tried to remember what happened after the pain and cold but it was hazy.

"Ela- you understand our language, you became vegetarian after the ceremony, your anger is an entirely separate sensation within you..."

"Coincidence," I argued.

"I know what I'm talking about," he said firmly. He wedged the cigarette into the corner of his mouth and began undoing the buttons on the cuffs of his jacket. "Lie down."

I felt that pull of our blood link and fought it.

"People will see," I told him.

"No-one can see us," he said softly and, as I looked around, I saw a bubble around us like I'd seen in Timotesubani. A couple walked past on the bridge across from us, moving at an impossibly slow speed, arm-in-arm, not even glancing our way.

I reluctantly laid down, and Ilia moved to rest my head on his knees.

"What are you going to do?" he asked Toma.

"Prove a point," Toma replied and stubbed his cigarette out and rolled back the sleeves of his shirt.

"Unzip your dress," he said. "I need to see the scar."

Nervous, I did as he said, pulling the zip all the way down to the top of my knickers and pulling it wide to show my belly, glad I was wearing my silk vest against the cold.

I looked up at Ilia and he gave me a small reassuring smile.

Sudden ice-cold pain slammed into my midriff and I doubled over.

"What the-?" I swore, falling back against Ilia, panting.

"Watch," Toma instructed.

I looked down, apprehensively watching as he once again moved his right hand towards my appendix scar, mouthing silent words. As he did, a shadow formed under my skin and I felt pain building. When Toma's skin contacted with mine, I felt the same electric volt charge through me, ten times what I'd felt in his house when he'd licked me there. He pulled back as I doubled over and curled to my side, tears squeezing out of my eyes.

"Enough," Ilia said, comforting me.

After a moment, I sat up and looked at Toma.

"Was that... the demon?" I asked.

He nodded, looking pale. "She's awake."

CHAPTER 56

"Got your Lilitu back, have you?" a sharp voice asked. We looked up to see Emily emerging from the shadow of Abo's smallest chapel where she'd clearly been standing, watching us.

"Emily," Toma said gently, getting up and walking over to her. Ilia helped me to my feet and I leaned against him, a hand to my stomach but deliberately not touching the real pain which throbbed just behind my scar. I felt dirty, out of control, weak. I wiped my wet cheeks with my sleeve, noticing how the air practically thrummed with Emily's anger.

"What did Daddy say?" she asked her brother.

"Don't worry about it," he soothed quietly. "Let's go." He started to lead her away but she resisted, glaring at me.

"I know what you're up to," she said, looking at me. "I know your tricks." Her voice rose and Toma held her back as she stepped towards me. "Well, don't think it's going to work! You weren't around when he needed you and we were. He's ours!" she practically screamed the last, her eyes blazing, her fists clenched. Then she shot a look at her brother. "Right, Toma?" she asked, anger replaced by a little girl's uncertainty in a heartbeat.

"That's right," he confirmed. "Come on."

But she refused to budge. "You know we have to kill her, right?" she whispered, her hands cupping his face, her lips centimetres from his, her eyes pleading with him.

Ilia stepped in front of me, though he didn't materialise.

"Emily..." Toma warned.

"She's a Yazatai. She has to die!"

"But not yet," Toma said.

"Why wait?" Emily whispered with a glance at me. It was almost as if she thought I couldn't hear them. Toma didn't even look my way. "We know how to do it. We've been to enough Solstice ceremonies...one slice and it'll be done."

"Father wants us to wait until June," Toma told her.

"Why? Let's just do it!" She brought out a steak knife, taken from the restaurant, and looked at me, then back at her brother. "Don't you want Lilitu back? You do, right? No reason to protect stupid Victoria's spawn..." She pawed at Toma's shirt as he looked down at her expressionlessly. "We'll kill her, end the ghost and then everything will be alright again...like it was before..."

Instead of fear, I felt anger flare in my gut. *How dare she insult my aunt? And threaten Ilia.*

I straightened, suddenly furious with both of them. I wanted to... my fingers clenched and released. I didn't know what I wanted to do but I felt the need pulsing through me and now Ilia did materialise- to stop me getting closer.

Emily turned to me and growled low in her throat, like an animal sensing threat, and Toma looked at me, surprised. I glared at them over Ilia's shoulder.

Then my phone rang, cutting the atmosphere with the bright sounds of "Happy."

Scowling at Emily, I took the call.

"Hi, dad."

I watched Toma speaking in a low, indecipherable voice to his sister, holding her close to him, his voice insistent while, in my ear, dad reminded me to ask Levan to pick me up and not use a taxi.

"Ok, got it." I said.

He must have heard something in my voice. "Are you ok, sweetheart?" he asked.

"Yeah, dad, all good."

I looked up from ending the call to see Toma leading Emily away.

He didn't look back at me, but Emily did and for a split second her eyes glowed red.

"Ela, let's go," Toma called. It was a blood command. Reluctant, I followed them back across the bridge, with Ilia's fingers linked tight with mine; his strength holding me up.

"I want my simple life back," I grumbled quietly, making Ilia smile.

"Your life was never simple."

"Compared to this," I said, waving a hand down at my stomach.

"True," he allowed.

"I'm scared," I told him.

"I'm here for you," he promised. "As long as you need me."

I rested my head against his shoulder, watching Toma and Emily ahead of us, walking in almost the same lover-esque position.

"She's going to kill me," I predicted.

"No, she won't. I'll kill her before she even gets close," Ilia growled with uncustomary vehemence.

I looked up at him. "Why are they convinced you're a sinner?" I asked.

He shook his head. "Another time."

I couldn't push it because we were back at the restaurant and he had to disappear.

"I'm taking Ela home," Toma told our friends, who were laughing uproariously about something while a small group of polyphonic singers belted out a deep-throated folk song from the mini-stage in the corner.

Nina gave me a once-over, saw me standing clutching my stomach, pale-faced, and got to her feet.

"What happened?" she asked. Then, coming closer and speaking more quietly, "Did he hurt you?"

She glanced at Toma who stood having a serious conversation with both his sisters, Emily looking miserable but passive; Arabella cold.

"No, no," I lied. "Just a stomach ache. I'll be fine."

"I'll come with you," she said, turning to go and fetch her coat. I put a hand on her arm to stop her.

"You stay, Ni. I'm just going to get in a taxi and go home and sleep it off."

"Your timing sucks," she said, sounding disappointed.

I smiled sadly. "I know."

I went to Saba and kissed his cheek. I could see he was half-drunk already.

"Have a good night," I told him.

Emily and Arabella came and stood either side of him, sliding their hands over his shoulders. I looked up to see Toma and Ilia by the door waiting for me, Toma on the phone talking to someone. Emily slipped onto Saba's lap and Arabella turned his face to kiss him- at which point I might have well as been invisible. Succubae at work...

"Bye, then," I said, waving to the others.

"Bye, El."

"Feel better."

Nina gave me a hug. "Call me tomorrow when you wake up," she said.

I nodded.

"Let's go," I told my angel and demon.

Outside, I doubled over as the pain surged up.

"What have you done to her?!" Ilia demanded of Toma angrily.

"I need to take you to Father," Toma said as I straightened up, wincing.

"Now?!" I asked, shocked.

"Yes. He'll be at the Ateshga. It's not far. He'll know what to do."

I glanced at Ilia and saw him looking helpless: this internal demon was an enemy he couldn't defend me from. My mind flashed back to a conversation we'd had around the time mum left.

"Are there any other people like me?" I'd asked.

He'd shrugged. "I can't see others of my kind."

"But you can see God."

He smiled. "Actually, no. But I feel him and feel what he would want me to do."

"And he wants you to protect me forever?" I'd asked with child-like wonder.

He nodded and bumped a fingertip to my nose. "That he does." We'd laid in silence a while, looking up at the clouds as they drifted across the blue sky.

"Ilia?" I asked, sitting up and pulling up a handful of grass, then sprinkling it over my angel's arm.

"Hmm?"

"Am I special?"

"You are to me," he'd said with a smile.

"I mean- why did you come to me?"

He frowned and hesitated, as if debating with himself whether or not to tell me.

"I think because of your mum," he said carefully.

"What about her? Is *she* special?"

"I... think she wanted you to be sad inside...I don't think she loved you the way she was supposed to," he said, again thinking out his words before speaking.

"So, God told you to come and love me instead?"

His golden smile broke through at the childlike simplicity of the concept.

"Yes, he did."

CHAPTER 57

"I know this place," I said. "This is where my mum brought me for the ritual." I stopped at the bottom of the stairs, the memories resurfacing, and with them, the fears. "I'm not going in there."

"Nothing will happen to you. There'll be no-one but me and Father."

"And that's supposed to be reassuring, is it?" Ilia asked dryly.

Toma slid his fingers between mine, linking us. "Yes," he told both of us.

We climbed the narrow brick steps to the double wooden doors at the top. Toma waved his hand over the left one and it opened of its own accord.

"No key?" I asked.

"Since my dad bought it and the house beside it, this door only opens to our kind at night," he said. "During the day, it's tourist central."

"Your dad bought it?!" I exclaimed. "The sign outside said it's on the Cultural Heritage list."

"His dad's an influential demon, remember!" Ilia said from behind me.

It was clearly answer enough because Toma said nothing, allowing me to go in before him.

I walked through into a small courtyard at the back of a simple Old Tbilisi house.

Ilia, a shadow behind me, tried to enter but hit an invisible wall. He held his hands out and pushed, but remained the other side of the entrance.

I looked from him to Toma, shocked.

"No 'angels' allowed," Toma told me.

"If you invite him in?" I asked, thinking vampires.

He shook his head and walked past us.

"If you go in there, I can't protect you," Ilia told me from the other side of the threshold.

"I need to know," I told him pleadingly. "I need to speak to his father."

"He can just as well tell you out here," he said.

"No, he can't," Toma said.

I looked at him and saw him holding his hand out to me.

I hesitated, weighing my options. A sharp, eager stab in my abdomen won me over.

"I'll be back," I told Ilia quietly.

He looked heartbroken and I broke my gaze from his, feeling awful.

"I'll wait here for you," he said. "Be careful."

I turned and took the demon's hand. And as I walked away, and through the low-beamed entrance into the temple proper, I felt a ripping sensation all down my spine, as if I was joined to Ilia and we were being pulled apart as I stepped through the doorway.

I cried out and stumbled. Toma helped me up. I looked back and saw only an empty space and the steps beyond: no Ilia.

"What've you done?" I asked Toma.

"You did it yourself," he reminded me. "It was your choice."

"Have I lost him?" I asked, feeling my throat tighten in panic at the thought, turning back.

"No," Toma told me, holding me in place. "He'll be there when we're done."

"Done? You're not going to cut me up are you?" I asked, digging my feet in again.

Toma shook his head, hurt showing in his eyes, and kissed me.

"We're just here to talk to Father," he promised in a whisper, his forehead to mine.

The temple was small and we entered on a modern wooden platform suspended over the rocks below. The walls were made of thin orange bricks, most weather or battle worn. All four walls had a pointed-arch recess with a smaller version of the same shape in the centre of each- shelves, on which burned oil lamps. The roof was a newly renovated arch of clear plastic and the air was heavy with the scent of sandalwood and frankincense.

"This is it?" I asked, part disappointed, part relieved.

Toma grinned and tilted his head downwards.

I followed is eye-line and saw a flat, rough, oval slab of rock below floor level.

"That's where the real temple is," he said. "Always has been."

"How do we...?"

He waved his hand again and the rock slowly, with a grinding sound, flipped over, its upper edge coming to rest near our toes. I saw its reverse side had time-worn steps carved into it. Beneath was darkness with a faint red glow to the edges.

Pit of Hell, my mind whispered, following the demon down into it.

We walked along a short corridor. I remembered the darkness, the smell of torches and incense- but this time there was no chanting as we entered the cave on the left. Inside was the sacrificial plinth and, to the side of the doorway, the rusty hook from which my mum had taken her red cloak- with every intention to see the demons kill me. The difference was a low table with three terracotta cups on and three bamboo chairs, soft with red cushions, placed beside the plinth. *Clearly not a work day, today,* I thought with a wry smile even as my nerves made me tremble.

"Eliso, welcome," Toma's father said, coming in from a small side-chapel, a terracotta jug in hand.

He was wearing a red cloak, the hood down, but in that instant, I knew where I'd seen him before. I stopped cold in the doorway, resistant to Toma encouraging me forward.

"You were there the day they tried to kill me," I said. "You're the Grand Master."

Mr Eristavi smiled. "I am *a* Grand Master...but the one *you* dealt with was my brother. My twin. Come and sit," he said, offering me a chair.

I backed up a step, shaking my head, and he threw a look of annoyance at his son.

"Ela, come in and sit down," Toma commanded me.

I scowled at him as my body obeyed. He sat opposite me, at a right angle to his father's chair.

"My brother was the one," Eristavi said quietly, sitting and pouring thick red Saperavi wine into a cup and placing it in front of me, ignoring my head-shake. Toma took the next offered cup and sipped from it. "He fed the demon into you to keep it alive. His hand was forced and then we lost you without a trace- everything destroyed to keep the police and Church away. And now here you are, back where you belong- the demon alive and well..."

"But Ela's still dominant," Toma said. "How's that possible with the demon inside her?"

"You know, I've participated in the binding of hundreds of my kind, but I've never heard of a case like hers," his father admitted, then looked at me watching him in stony silence. "My brother had no choice. Your uncle and his police friends disrupted the ceremony. People were being killed. The demon was vulnerable. We had to put her into you or lose her."

"He put her in *before* taking Ela's spirit out?"

"Unprecedented but possible," Eristavi said with a nod. "The door to the OtherWorld was already closed. And then the girl was removed before we could recall order."

"I want it out," I told him, and they both looked at me. "It's my body, my right."

"Is it?" he asked, seeming amused. "But your mother promised you to us before you were born. You were snatched away from us by her family once, twice. But promises cannot be broken."

Promise...keeping Victoria's promise... I pushed the thought away.

"But that wasn't *my* promise," I argued. "I'm my own person now and you're not going to take that away from me."

He stood up, flicking his cloak back so it fell smoothly down, and circled the stone chamber, pausing at the fire pit to throw on more kindling. I recognised the smell- the same as that Toma had used in the beach house. My nose twitched.

I looked at Toma and he looked steadily back, then drank from the wine cup again.

"I was told how your uncle ran in with his friends and attacked my clan. Quite horrific. They killed some of our number, my brother, your kindergarten teacher..." Eristavi said, one hand on the plinth, watching me.

"Miss Lali?" I asked, wide-eyed, hearing echoes of memory: bangs, screams, moans of pain. "But you said my uncle did that? I don't have an uncle."

Eristavi smiled. "Admittedly, it's hard to imagine that soft, passive, pudgy man you call dad rescuing you from the midst of a Binding ritual, but he wasn't alone and there it is. They say he came in shooting wildly, then grabbed you and ran out, your aunt chasing behind as we tended to our wounded."

I remembered running, an argument, hot blood running down my legs...then Ilia and peace.

"My dad is my dad," I said stubbornly, glancing at Toma, seeing sympathy in his eyes.

"No, your real father was one of us- and one of the ones your uncle shot in revenge for having persuaded your mother to make the solstice promise when she found herself pregnant with you."

My stomach bottomed out and I felt my world teeter on the edge of a yawning black hole.

"You were adopted, El," Toma said, putting his cup down and leaning forwards. "When your family stopped your mother, Victoria, from keeping her promise, she killed herself."

"You survived, somehow, and your aunt and uncle took you into their care, setting up all the documents to make it look like you were theirs," Eristavi said. "Your aunt – the one you called mum – tried to bring you home to us when you were four but your uncle foiled her attempt, not realising that when he took you, you weren't alone."

It made sense. The way my mum, my aunt, had never seemed to love me like she did Mikey, the way she'd gone crazy about Victoria's death and talked about fulfilling a promise... But, still, every instinct fought against the version of my life Toma and his father had just hit me with.

"How long have you known?!" I asked Toma, feeling hurt; wanting Ilia by my side.

"I recognised the name Victoria. I've heard the Elders talking about her- 'the one who got away.' She promised her child to us at the Winter Solstice, but then her family found out something of what she was into and hid her away. We thought her baby died with her. Her husband tried to find her but by then she'd already killed herself."

My head was spinning.

Eristavi returned to his chair and settled back, smiling.

"I'm sure it's very difficult for you to take in. Have some wine."

"No shit," I swore. "You've just rewritten my entire identity..."

"Ela," Toma warned, his tone suggesting I should watch my language around his father.

I frowned at him and shook my head sharply. "Everything I thought I knew, Toma! And it's all a lie...if I believe you," I said, looking at his father.

"Ask your uncle if you don't believe me," he said, holding out his phone, my dad's number ready to be dialled.

I frowned at it, then shook my head.

"This is the kind of conversation we need to have face-to-face," I said.

Eristavi smiled. "Good idea." He leaned forward, elbows on knees and the fingertips of both hands pressed together. "Now, about that other little detail of your heritage."

"What?"

"That's not an appendix scar, Ela," Toma said softly. "All the aggression you feel- these little accidents, you being averse to eating meat, speaking our language...it all adds up."

"The demon?" I didn't even want to touch the place my scar was hidden- feeling repulsed that something else was living in me. I felt like if I thought about it too much, I'd go insane. Insane like my mum.

"Her name is Lilitu," Mr Eristavi said. Toma flinched, picked up his cup and took a big swig of the alcohol as his father went on speaking. "You've lived in symbiosis with her for 16 years. She's a part of you."

"Who made barely an appearance until now," Toma pointed out.

"I think you and your sisters are to thank for that. You overcame the power of the ghost who was supressing her," Eristavi told his son.

"But Ilia said he didn't know," I argued.

"He probably didn't," Toma told me. "But his presence kept Lilitu mostly dormant. Our- my -presence began the awakening."

"What does that mean?"

"When your uncle took you from us, the ritual was left incomplete. The demon was in you but not bound to you," Eristavi explained.

"That's why, whenever you're really angry, things happen- the demon flies out of you. She's wild, uncontrolled and, because she was never bound to you, she remains infantile, untrained," Toma added.

"I have a *baby* demon living in me?" This was getting crazier by the second.

Eristavi nodded. "More like a toddler."

"But if she can come out, why doesn't she stay out?" I wondered.

"Because she recognises you as her host and she cannot survive in this world without a host. May I?" he asked, reaching a hand towards my abdomen.

I shifted back, shaking my head, the pain Toma had caused still at the forefront of my mind.

"I won't touch you," he promised.

Tense, I stopped moving, watching him warily.

Eristavi closed his eyes, reaching out with his energy, whispering silent words I couldn't catch.

I groaned as an ache, much like a period ache, pulsed in my lower abdomen.

Eristavi smiled. "It seems Lilitu knows I'm here."

"Get it out of me!" I begged them.

"But you were promised as her host."

"Let someone else host her!"

Eristavi shook his head and sat back.

"Why not?" Toma asked him, sounding hopeful. "You always say the Tearing is harder the older the host is. And she hasn't grown in maturity with Ela: she's almost as fresh as the day David put her in. If we found a baby..."

I felt nausea roll around my insides at the thought of subjecting another human to Tearing; another baby sacrificed and lost.

His father shot him a look of impatience, which changed into a thoughtful musing and then, with a sly smile, he looked at me.

"Ok, then," he agreed. "We'll take it out of you. You can be free to live your life and forget any of this ever happened."

I sat forwards eagerly, though I noticed Toma didn't move. "Thank you!" I told him gratefully.

He held up a hand against my gratitude. "We will remove the demon from inside you IF, and only if, YOU choose the next host."

My knee-jerk reaction was to laugh.

"You're kidding me, right?"

I looked at Toma and back again. Neither of them was smiling.

"*Au contraire*, I kid you not," Eristavi told me. "The only way you can break the promise your mother made is for you to promise another in your stead."

The nausea and ache came together.

"I can't sacrifice a baby to you monsters," I said.

"*We* monsters," he corrected. "At the moment, you are one of us," he said, unperturbed by the insult. "As you will remain unless you bring us another by sunrise on the Summer Solstice."

"June 21st?"

He nodded once.

My stomach churned again.

"I need to go," I said, getting to my feet, bumping the table in my haste. Wine sloshed over the edge of my cup and spread in a blood-like circle on the wood.

The men stood with me.

"I'll come with you," Toma said, glancing at his father- perhaps for permission.

His father nodded.

"It was nice to see you again, Eliso," he said as I reached the doorway. "Come back any time."

I looked back at him, seeing his black eyes watching me; the light of the flames dancing in his pupils as his silhouette painted darkness on the wall behind him.

CHAPTER 58

I retched dryly into the gutter.

"What happened in there?" Ilia asked, one hand on my back, the other holding my hair up out of the way.

Toma didn't reply; just blew out his cigarette smoke and looked up the street.

I straightened, tested my balance, took a breath, pulled my hood up and then began walking downhill away from them.

"Ela?" Ilia asked.

"I need to be alone," I said, not looking back.

Toma let me go, but Ilia returned to invisibility and followed me anyway. It was a comfort that he was there but didn't speak.

I walked through the old streets, through Gudiashvili Square and along to Apkhazi Street, then left heading up to Freedom Square. The street was bustling with life- tourists, locals and shop-owners standing and chatting. Music, voices and car horns merged into a background noise that I was deaf to. The smells were varied: the tang of wine in wooden barrels, the grease of kebabs, the hot cheesy scent of cheesebread, the heady church incense drifting out of the icon shops. I hadn't eaten for hours and my stomach might have rumbled if not for that incense- it put me straight back in the chamber with the demons.

My dad isn't my dad.

I tried the idea on for size but still couldn't make it fit. Nor could I get my head around the other revelations about my family. And Mikey! If the demons had told me the truth, then he wasn't my baby brother... I felt tears sting my eyes and bit my lip hard till they went away.

I tucked my chin into my collar, shoving my clenched fists deeper into my pockets. I felt cold inside. Or maybe it was the demon that was cold. Where I began and she ended, I had no idea.

My phone beeped.

It was a message from Toma: *'I'm sorry.'*

This time I couldn't bite back the tears, nor did I fight when Ilia materialised and pulled me into a hug.

ME: You said your dad was into exorcism.

MARIAM: Yeah. So?

ME: I need his help.

MARIAM: What's going on?

ME: I need to tell you something.

MARIAM: Shoot.

ME: It's about this Morgan-Demon thing.

MARIAM: I'm listening.

I typed what I knew then hesitated, re-reading, my finger over the Enter button.

"Sure you want to do this?" Ilia asked, his hands on my shoulders.

I nodded. "I have you but you're a part of this whole supernatural...thing. I need a human friend, a girlfriend to confide in."

"I understand. But why not Nina? She's here, she already knows about me and the demons."

"Exactly. She sees the Morgans as often as I do- which puts her in danger. I can talk to Mariam without getting her in trouble."

"Good point," my angel said.

"She's a problem solver," I said, still with my finger over the key.

"Stay away from them. Problem solved," Ilia replied.

"I don't think it's that easy anymore," I said. "I have one of them inside me."

"You think Mari's dad can help?"

"No idea. But I'll be damned if I'm sacrificing someone's baby in my stead," I told him.

I pressed Enter and waited for her reply.

TO BE CONTINUED IN DARK WINGS 2: DEMON

COMING SOON!

SNEAK PREVIEW OF DARK WINGS 2: DEMON

Flames all around us. Some people were on fire, the smell of burning flesh and cloth filling my nose and throat. I could hear screams and shots being fired.

"Keep your mask on, Eliso," my daddy whispered as he scooped me up off the cold stone. "Don't look."

My stomach clenched angrily and I moaned at the pain.

"The police are on the way. If you try and follow us, I'll shoot!" daddy shouted.

"Get her out of here," a gruff authoritative voice told my dad. "These child-killers don't deserve to live." Then I heard a click and a bang. I heard Miss Lali cry out and the crack of bone contacting with the stone floor. Then the flickering lights were replaced by cool darkness as daddy carried me quickly along the corridor and out onto the street.

"It's ok, sweetie. It's ok," my daddy told me as he ran with me held tight against his chest. I heard mummy running behind, calling to him wildly, demanding he stop and take me back.

"I don't want to go back," I whimpered.

As he ran down the cobbled street, he reached up and pulled off my mask. Over his shoulder, I saw mummy close behind, her red cloak slipping off her bare shoulders and whipping out behind. Suddenly, she stopped and doubled over, crying out and pressing her hands to her big belly.

Daddy immediately stopped, put me down and went back to her. I followed.

"Elizabeth?" he asked.

But Mummy's focus was on me and as soon as I was close enough, she grabbed my wrist and started pulling me back up the way we'd come.

"Victoria's waiting for you Ela," she said. "You have to go to her…"

I screamed and fought her. She jerked my arm roughly and bent down, her face in mine. "Eliso, listen to mummy," she said, sternly. "We need to go back and fix you, ok?"

"I'm scared," I whimpered. Then daddy grabbed my other arm, trying to pull me away, but mummy held tight. I thought I'd split into two.

"Elizabeth, stop!" My father's voice, deep in his fury.

"I have to," my mother said. "She was promised to them. Victoria won't stop haunting me."

"You're pregnant with our child- do you think they'll spare *him*? Think of our baby, Elizabeth! Think of Victoria's daughter!"

I had no idea who Victoria was.

"We have no choice! If they could find us here, they can find us anywhere. There's no escape- not from them, not from my sister."

She turned away and dragged me after her and out of daddy's grasp.

"Elizabeth, don't...!"

Daddy grabbed her arm and spun her to face him. She let go of me and I stumbled back, falling and hitting my head on the edge of the road. Black spots danced across my vision and when I touched gentle fingers to the back of my head, I felt the bulge of a bruise and started to cry again. My parents didn't even notice me lying on the cobbles at their feet, so intense was their argument.

"It's ok," a calm voice said. "Up you get."

I looked up through tear-blurred eyes and saw an older boy crouched down in front of me with his hand out.

I took it and he helped me to stand and then took a tissue and gently wiped my cheeks.

"What's your name?" he asked.

His accent was strange- Georgian, but different, somehow, and rougher than I was used to hearing.

"I'm not supposed to talk to strangers," I told him quietly through a curtain of hair. Then I remembered he'd given me a tissue. He seemed nice. "Eliso," I said shyly.

He held out his hand like the grown-ups did and smiled.

I reached out and took it and he shook twice, making me feel like a big girl.

"Nice to meet you, Eliso," he said. "I'm Ilia."

Follow the Author at
www.facebook.com/KatieRuthDaviesAuthor

And the Blood Omen Saga at
www.fb.com/bloodomensaga

Also check out the author's blog:
katieruthdavies.blogspot.com

Please take time to write a REVIEW on Amazon and
Goodreads and tell your friends about this book and encourage
them to buy their own copy.

Thanks for your support!

About the Author

Born in the UK, I've spent the past 17 years living and teaching in Spain, New Zealand and The Republic of Georgia. I've got two beautiful young daughters and a handsome little boy and I work as an English Language Specialist and as Copy-Editor for several cultural and business journals in Tbilisi. I'm also the Editor-in-Chief of Georgia's leading English language newspaper, 'Georgia Today'.

I've lived in Georgia since 2007- I was brought here by love and, since then, the love has only grown. Georgia is a country full of treasures and ancient tales- the birthplace of wine, one of the first 'European' countries to take on Christianity and boasting its own unique alphabet. The nature is wild and diverse- from snow-capped mountains, waterfalls and caves to black sandy beaches, raging rivers and lakes full of fish. The people are friendly and hospitable- most willing to give a guest their last piece of bread and cheese, because all guests are 'God-sent'.

I was inspired to write the Dark Wings story in the summer of 2016- sitting on Ureki beach near sunset, that quiet time of day when the air is cooling, the sea is still and the crowds are thinner. I was watching the people around me and one boy caught my eye. Dark-skinned, dark-haired, standing with his arms wrapped protectively around a girl. He was my demon, Toma. My angel, Ilia, came from a trip to Mestia and a story I heard about the belief that every child is born with a guardian angel. The demon joined the angel in my mind and the Dark Wings tale began to weave itself...